The Blue Orchid

Luona Blankenship

Peridot Light Publishing

Luona Blankenship / Peridot Light Publishing

Publisher's Note: This is a work of fiction. Names, characters, places, and incidents are a product of the author's imagination. Locales and public names are sometimes used for atmospheric purposes. Any resemblance to actual people, living or dead, or to businesses, companies, events, institutions, or locales is completely coincidental.

The Blue Orchid / Luona Blankenship. -- 1st ed.
Print Edition ISBN 978-0-9992519-0-4

Dedicated to my mom, Iris, who is always the first person to read my stories.

Thank you.

Contents

Rosemary Part I..1

Cassandra Part I..18

Danielle Part I..35

Alicia Part I..52

Cynthia Part I..70

Rosemary Part II...86

Cassandra Part II...105

Danielle Part II..124

Alicia Part II...146

Cynthia Part II...165

Part III...184

Chapter One

Rosemary Part I

The man in the suit wouldn't look her in the eye. That's when Rosemary knew he had cheated. He shifted from one foot to the other, restless, wary of being caught.

"I'll take a dozen of the tangerine roses," he said. "That should do it."

That should do it. How many countless times had Rosemary heard those words uttered? As she backed out of the flower cooler a few minutes later the glass door slammed shut and Rosemary caught a glimpse of her reflection. She noticed her hair was strewn about so she rested the dozen roses cradled in her arms on the table beside her. It was time for a haircut thought Rosemary ruefully. She brushed her bangs to the side with her fingers and the soft white hair with gleams of silver and ash complied. She had a bob cut but now it was several inches too long. She wasn't even sure this length of hair had a formal name. Rosemary pushed the rest of her hair behind her ears then fluffed the back. That would have to do for now.

She gathered up the blazing orange roses once more and hurried back out to the front of her shop. Rosemary owned The Blue Orchid, a flower shop that specialized in rare orchids. She had opened the shop when she was thirty, after her first divorce. She had been the proprietor for the past thirty-seven years. When she would look back on her life it was hard to believe it had all slipped by so fast. Where had the time gone? And lately she wondered, where was it going?

For the past year Rosemary had wrestled with the idea of retiring. She was at *that* age. Whatever *that* meant. She was very conflicted about the idea of handing her shop, the business she had nurtured, grown and cared for, to a complete stranger. That's why Rosemary liked the busy times of the workday, especially mid-morning and late afternoon. During these peak hours she couldn't do anything but focus on the task at hand. Presently she was focused on arranging the dozen roses she had just pulled from the storage room cooler into an arrangement in a cut-glass vase. It was going to be lovely, Rosemary could tell. She could always tell. She just had the knack as her mother would have said.

During the slower times of the day, when she and the two ladies who worked for her had nothing to do but clean and rearrange items on the store shelves, those were the moments Rosemary considered the possibility of retirement. Secretly she had always hoped her daughter would want The Blue Orchid. But alas, that wasn't to be. Finola, her only child, had married Matt Harris right out of college. Soon after they had two boys: Harrison who was eight and Vincent who had just turned six. Rosemary always shook her head in disbelief at the names Finola had bestowed upon those innocent children. They were such old-fashioned names, not at all in vogue. Rosemary could only hope they would eventually grow into the adult sounding names. She didn't even want to contemplate what the other kids at school called them. Children could be so cruel.

Finola had declared years ago that she didn't want the flower shop. She begrudgingly worked at all. To keep the Harris family afloat Finola worked part time as an office manager for a small promotional merchandising company. Matt's salary as a construction foreman just wasn't enough to cover all their living expenses. What Finola really wanted was to be a stay at home mom. This was something Rosemary had never wanted herself. Finola had practically grown up at The Blue Orchid, playing in the small back room she had made into a makeshift daycare for her daughter.

Rosemary had married a boy named Stephen when she was twenty-six. Back in her day twenty-six was ancient, practically an old maid. The union had been brought about by her family and his. Looking back, they had hardly known each other. But they had both come from wealthy, privileged families and it was the *right* thing to do. At least it was according to her mother. It wasn't a surprise to Rosemary when the marriage had ended three years later. When it was all said and done it seemed to have been a good bit of time wasted and much ado about nothing in her view. That was when she took her divorce settlement and opened the flower shop. It felt like the first time Rosemary had ever been in control of her own destiny. It was a marvelous feeling.

As a matter of fact, it was Finola who had planted the idea of Rosemary retiring four years ago while they were having dinner when the grandchildren were still just babies. Rosemary had treated her daughter to dinner as she was having a meltdown with the boys under her tired feet all day and night. But when she had asked Finola about taking over The Blue Orchid her daughter had brushed away the idea as if she were swatting away an annoying fly on a hot summer day. This was why Rosemary thought of turning to the two ladies who helped her run the day to day operations. She was hoping one of them might want to buy The Blue Orchid. At least then the shop wouldn't end up in the hands of a stranger. It was a time consuming but profitable business to be sure. When clients were charged a hundred or more for one orchid due to their rare nature it was bound to add up. Rosemary's business was an interesting sleight of hand. There were definitive reasons as to why someone purchased an orchid.

The orchid was an exotic, mysterious flower. Roses were romantic, lilies beautiful and daisies sweet. These were always kept in stock. But customers sought out The Blue Orchid for one reason: the cultivated, delicate, expensive orchids. Rosemary had over three decades of experience to tell her why men and women sought out her wares. Hardly anyone bought an orchid for a birthday or anniversary. No, the reasons behind purchasing an orchid were much more dramatic. *Betrayal...Forgiveness...Jealousy...Lies...Apology...Infidelity...Political Maneuvering.*

3

To remind *her* that *he* exists. Rosemary had heard it all. Like she was some type of flower bartender or horticultural shrink. The customers expected her to hold all their secrets, possibly keep them chilled in the back-room storage cooler.

The one thing Rosemary had never seen the orchid utilized for, at least in Southern Florida, was death. She was glad of this. Rosemary had refused to even stock the mournful peace lily. When customers requested the sad, condoling flower she sent them around the corner to the generic flower shop. Let them deal in death. Rosemary had seen enough death in her lifetime to not wish it upon her shop. She had plenty of jealousy, infidelity and betrayal on her hands as it was.

"Rosemary, delivery."

Rosemary looked up and realized Julia was addressing her. She glanced at the clock and saw it was nearly noon. She thanked Julia, patted her on the shoulder as she moved past her and went to the storage room to open the door that led to the alley. Most of the deliveries came in through here.

"Afternoon Mrs. Melton!"

"Hello Kenneth. Please come in."

Kenneth bustled by her with his cart full of fresh flowers and began filling up a cooler. As he worked he talked to Rosemary about his little boy's most recent t-ball game. He often smiled at her kindly. It had taken her several years to get used to this treatment. The grandmother treatment. At some point younger men had stopped treating Rosemary like a woman and more like a grandmother. She hardly noticed it anymore, but when she did she attributed it to the color of her hair. Her good friend Clarice still dyed her hair buttery blonde and as a result still got hit on every now and then. They were the same age. When Kenneth was finished Rosemary thanked him then shut the alley door firmly behind him.

"Julia dear, I'll be back in a bit. Just running out for a moment."

"Sure thing Rosemary! We'll hold down the fort."

Rosemary smiled, tossed her raspberry hued knit scarf over her shoulder and breezed out the front door. It was still much too hot to be wearing such an accessory, but she loved how it looked on her. Plus, it was a light fabric and breathed well. C'est la vie.

She knew exactly where she was going. To the local independent book store three blocks down. It was her favorite place to escape for a break during the day. All the crisp volumes calling to her, willing her to read them and crack their spines. It was a form of intoxication. Forget the finest champagne or the most luxurious silk. Nothing could be more *wantable* than books in Rosemary's mind.

Of course, she didn't buy all her books here. Although she would never tell the owner that! Rosemary certainly supported local business after all. No one could ever accuse her of such a thing. But, during the evenings or over a long weekend, Rosemary had the guilty pleasure of purchasing half her books online from a discount retailer. Not only did she usually get a better price, and often free shipping, but she also adored their message boards. Almost every night after work she would go home, slip into a comfortable dressing gown, brew a pot of tea, log on as Rosie and spend some time chatting online.

Now, Rosemary belonged to a "real-life" book club, which was all good and wonderful. It was quite delightful to spend one night a month discussing the plots and nuances of the latest author du jour or even the latest political biography. They even reread several classics each year such as the latest, Wuthering Heights, to try and understand or reason out for the twentieth time why Catherine and Heathcliff just didn't run off together. At Rosemary's age she disliked the dysfunctional emotional games they played and was quite tired of those two characters acting so damned foolish. The problem with the real-life book club was just this: The people in the club *actually knew who you were.* Ergo you had to be more guarded, more politic. Plus, everyone was around the same age.

Rosemary was pretty sure almost no one was her age in the online forums. Or if they were, they were lying and not revealing it. Statistically speaking it was bound to happen. But she didn't care about that. She enjoyed the more stripped-down discussions she got there. She was amused by the flare-ups and dust-ups that sometimes occurred online. Passions could run high online. She often envisioned the acronym www as Wild Wild West. And as it stood Rosemary couldn't see her real-life book club discussing some of the books she had purchased online. Rosemary reasoned there was nothing wrong with a little chick lit or a bodice ripper. The soul needs a romance or two per year as a salve for the daily grind.

"Mrs. Melton! Mrs. Melton!"

Annie came hurrying up the aisle, her arms full of books that were trying to escape her grasp and tumble away at any moment. Annie was a college student who worked part time at the bookstore. Rosemary was convinced she was the most discombobulated young lady she had ever met.

"Mrs. Melton, I'm so glad I saw you!" she said breathlessly, as her black, chunky glasses slipped down her nose.

"How are you Annie? Do you need any help?"

"Oh! No Mrs. Melton," – a book crashed to the floor – "I just wanted to let you know that your order still hasn't come in yet. It was supposed to be here last week but the publisher pushed the date back. A printing glitch I think."

Annie smiled kindly at her. As if Rosemary was her grandmother. Rosemary sighed inwardly and resolved to get her hair cut the very next day. Maybe it was time to get a buttery blond dye job too.

"Thank you, Annie. That is perfectly fine."

"Ok. Well, let me know if you need any assistance today Mrs. Melton."

And with that Annie bounded down the aisle, books falling and tumbling in her wake. As Rosemary roamed the aisles her mind wandered back to her present dilemma. To retire or not to retire? That certainly was the question. Even Shakespeare, her all-time favorite author in all his wit and wisdom, couldn't help her. Just what would she do with all the free time? Travel? Rosemary tried to envision a fruity umbrella drink in her hand. Maybe she should move? But where? She already lived in Florida.

Wasn't that where most folks her age retired to? Why, she was already here! She was one step ahead of the game as her mother would have said. Maybe she would spend more time with the grandkids. See if there were children hiding behind those dreadful adult names.

Rosemary stopped in front of a large book display. The theme was do-it-yourself weddings. Each book promised an easy, yet fantastic wedding experience. *Don't waste money! Anyone can pull together a fabulous wedding! On the cheap! Super easy!* Rosemary let out a loud cackle which startled Annie, who was behind her stocking shelves, causing books to scatter everywhere.

~ ~ ~

Rosemary stood off to the side, almost hidden beneath the giant sycamore tree. It was dusk and all the party lights had just flickered on. The country club lawn had been transformed into a fairy tale vision. Sleeping Beauty, Cinderella, Snow White and all those other princesses would have been green with envy. And it was all for her. Or so she had been told by her mother. Her mother had planned the whole soiree and had spared no expense. Rosemary had a sinking suspicion this event was being staged to finally lock into place her family's return to "good" society. She knew she would have to rejoin the posh party-goers soon, but wanted a few more minutes of solitude just to breathe. She was tired of being gawked at like a caged animal at the zoo.

"Rosemary Margaret Pope!"

Oh no. Her mother's voice and she was mad. She only used her daughter's full name when she was in a riled-up state.

"What are you doing hiding behind this tree? Do you know how many people are here to see you?"

"It's Rosie Banks," said Rosemary quietly.

Her mother stared at her like she had just sprouted wings.

"It's Rosie Banks," she repeated. "My new name."

"Well of course it is dear," said her mother with an exasperated sigh. "Really Rosie, you must get back out there and mingle. It is expected of you! Stephen is out there entertaining all the important guests by himself."

Rosemary scratched her neck for the hundredth time that day. The lace made her throat itch. She couldn't wait to escape the wedding dress. Her mother had picked it out and it was a monstrosity of lace and ruffles, bows and train. It was perhaps the most uncomfortable thing she had ever worn. Mrs. Pope swatted Rosemary's hand away from her neck.

"Do you see what you are doing? Your neck has turned completely red!"

"This dress itches mother!"

"Well it will be off soon enough. And anyways, you have more important things to worry about. You are now Mrs. Banks. The Carters are dying to know when you two are going to start a family."

Rosemary wrinkled her nose.

"None of that young lady! You will now have adult responsibilities. Your job will be to raise the children."

"But I thought…maybe I could open my own business. Like daddy did. I know I could do it. Maybe…maybe a little flower shop along Main Street -"

"Don't be absurd!" her mother interrupted. "You won't have time for that now. This from the girl who wanted orchids as her wedding flowers! Whoever heard of such a thing? It's time to get your head out of those books and – *what is that in your hand*?"

Mrs. Pope glanced at the champagne flute in Rosemary's hand filled half-way with mimosa.

"Is that a *straw* in your drink?" she asked incredulously.

Rosemary looked down sheepishly.

"Your father and I import the finest champagne and you put a *straw* in your glass? I've seen it all now! Really Rosie! What will the guests think?"

"I don't care what they think!" Rosemary hissed.

"I'm going to give you five minutes' young lady to pull yourself together and get out there and mingle. And you are not to bring that glass with you unless you remove the straw."

Rosemary watched her mother stalk off into the crowd. She took a long sip of the mimosa through her straw not caring about all the snobby guests.

There was only one person whose society she longed for. Rosemary wished with all her might that her sister Susan had been here. Without Susan this was just another fancy party, not a life altering event. But Susan had been gone for a long time. It made Rosemary's heart ache to think about her sister.

~ ~ ~

"How does this look Rosemary?"

"It looks perfect Julia. Just place it over there."

A last-minute wedding order had come in while Rosemary had been browsing at the bookstore. The quick turnaround time had all three of the flower shop ladies hustling. Rosemary was very glad to have Julia's assistance as they made multiple arrangements. Julia had an artistic eye and a flair for dramatic arrangements. Rosemary remembered the day she had hired her two years ago. At the time she had hired her out of sympathy. Julia had several purple streaks running through her light brown hair and a pierced nose. Rosemary had worried that no other business would want a young lady with such shocking fashion accessories. It was a pity hire.

"I love these arrangements with orchids whimsically tossed in," Julia sighed.

"I do too dear. I wanted orchids at my wedding but my mother had a very different notion."

"I thought you eloped?"

Rosemary laughed. "That was my second marriage. That's when I became a Melton."

"I didn't know you were married twice."

"Oh yes. My second husband and I were madly in love. I hadn't married anyone I was in love with until he came along. But Anton was a nobody according to my mother. Once I found out I was several months along with Finola we just took the plunge. It was one of the best decisions of my life."

"Why is that?" asked Julia out of curiosity. "I mean, you guys still got divorced."

Rosemary completed a white rose boutonniere, smiled and said, "Because it was *my* decision."

Peals of laughter rang out across the room and Rosemary looked up to see two young children racing through the shop. Their poor haggard looking mother was chasing after them. It was going to be a busy afternoon. The thought made Rosemary happy.

~ ~ ~

When Rosemary was a child a shadow followed her wherever she went. The shadow's name was Susan. Her sister had been born a mere sixteen months after her and so Mrs. Pope had made the decision to hold Rosemary back so the two girls could go through school and life together. You could do that back then. Mrs. Pope had thought it would be absolutely adorable. Rosemary found it more often than not absolutely annoying.

Though the two girls were forced to live in some faux fraternal twin universe they weren't anything alike. Rosemary was of a serious bent, a studious nature, a calm exterior. Susan was a lively girl, had a hyper heart and a rambunctious imagination. And though the two girls often clashed there was a bond that held them together. The two opposites were very fond of one another growing up. And so the Rosie and Susie show began. The Pope girls on parade.

The girls had grown up in a privileged world. Their summers were spent in Key West and during the school year they attended a private all girls' academy. This irritated Susan to no end. She was a flirtatious creature. The only boy she ever found to flirt with at the academy was actually a man. He was a student teacher during their senior year and his dalliance with Susan Pope had gotten him fired. That was the same year Rosemary had joined the debate team and enjoyed an activity without her shadow. Susan had said she had better things to do. *Apparently*.

All the other activities the girls had tackled throughout their childhood had been shared. Piano, ballet, swimming, ice skating, tennis, any type of supposedly "fun" lesson. Rosemary often felt overlooked, unseen or underappreciated. She felt like the pepper half of a salt and pepper shaker set. Everybody liked salt, but pepper, that was an acquired taste. Rosemary's father was the person she turned to during these peppered times. She was a daddy's girl while Susan was mother's favorite.

"Patience and fortitude conquer all things Rosie Posie," he would say to comfort her.

Rosemary's father loved books as much as she did. She and her father were both independent thinkers. He especially loved Emerson. Once she heard her father tell Susan, "All life is an experiment. The more experiments you make the better." Rosemary thought this was a mistake. Susan would never grasp what Emerson had really meant.

Sometimes Rosemary wondered what her father had seen in such a silly person as her mother. He had even married her no less! It was all a mystery to her, much like a Sherlock Holmes or Agatha Christie novel. At times Rosemary felt sorry for her father. He was trapped in a house with three women plus their housekeeper Kay. Most days though he seemed contented and happy with his lot in life. Rosemary had often wished Susan had been a boy. That would have balanced out the house perhaps. No boy would have been her shadow and followed her to ballet lessons.

Many times throughout their adolescence Rosemary had to cover for her sister's indiscretions. To an outsider this wouldn't be perceived as fair. But Susan had so many troublesome episodes that to add more to the heap would have been unthinkable to Rosemary. If Susan got into more than her usual trouble their after-school activities were suspended. Rosemary figured that if she was going to suffer the consequences she might as well take some of the blame. For some reason if the trouble was spread out between them nothing had to change; after-school activities continued as usual. At times Rosemary's reputation was just as blemished as her sisters though her conscience was a clean slate.

Their mother had never let Rosemary forget the time she let two dozen goldfinch birds loose during Sunday service. In the sanctuary. During prayer. The church had almost excommunicated the Pope family although several parishioners swore it was a divine miracle. Divine miracle of what no one was quite sure. The only problem was, Rosemary had not committed the flight of fancy. Susan had of course. But Susan was already grounded that week for shop lifting lip gloss from the drug store. If Susan had gotten in trouble again next Saturday's out of town tennis tournament would have been forbidden. Susan had merely wanted to impress the new boy in town who kept birds as pets. Rosemary had never been fond of birds since the Great Goldfinch Escapade of 1959.

Yet no matter how many times Rosemary had to concede to cover for Susan's outrageous antics, she still loved her sister. When no drama was ensuing the two mismatched girls enjoyed each other's company. Salt and Pepper; Birds and Books. To thine own self be true – regardless of shadows.

~ ~ ~

Rosemary stopped off at a favorite quaint diner before she headed home. After her second divorce she had plucked up her courage and gave solo dining a try. Years ago she would have found the whole experience daunting and embarrassing. But Rosemary had learned to throw caution out the window, into the wind and pretty much anywhere else you could toss caution. Plus, at her age she just didn't care anymore. Rosemary did things that made her happy. She liked eating out. It saved her from having to cook for one – too much leftover food that went to waste! – and besides, food prepared by others tasted better anyways.

"Ah! Miss Rosemary! What can I get for you tonight beautiful orchid lady?"

Ramon, Rosemary's favorite waiter. Prompt, courteous, never shy with beverage refills and always a little bit tipsy by this time in the evening. She always tipped him well and he made sure to give her a generous slice of to-go cake when she ordered it. This was a good relationship. Why couldn't either of her ex-husbands have been this accommodating?

"Oh, Ramon, be sure and put a straw in that mimosa please. And while you're at it throw an umbrella in there too!"

Ramon raised one perfectly sculpted black eyebrow but then went merrily on his way to the bar. Rosemary chuckled to herself. This would give her an opportunity to practice sipping those alcohol filled retirement cock-tails with the colorful umbrellas. Maybe Ramon would throw a wedge of pineapple in there too. The straw was merely for nostalgia. Rosemary rarely indulged in alcohol without a specific reason. She firmly believed drinking and driving were not a good mix. As she had told Finola, when she caught her daughter sneaking a beer with her friends at sixteen, that combination can produce grave consequences.

~ ~ ~

Susan was going to be late for curfew yet again. Even though the uni-versity was co-ed, the men and women lived in separate dorms and there were strict curfews in place. Violating curfew lead to warnings, then de-merits with suspension of privileges, and if enough violations piled up then to expulsion. Rosemary feared that if Susan was expelled her mother would force her to follow suit. They would then have to enroll in another university but Rosemary loved *this* school. The English Lit program was phenomenal and she even worked part time at the university library de-spite her mother's dismay that one of her daughters wanted a job.

Rosemary hurried across campus towards Kathy Heyner's room. She was almost sure that was the place Susan was hiding out. The effect Kitty (Kathy's preferred nickname) was having on Susan was palpable. Kitty was a party girl whose family owned mines in West Virginia. Several times a week she had co-ed parties in her decidedly non-co-ed dorm room. This was strictly forbidden and if the dorm wardens found out it would mean expulsion for all involved. Students liked Kitty's parties because usually large amounts of alcohol were involved. Susan always returned from Kitty's dorm drunk.

As soon as Rosemary reached the third-floor stairwell landing she could hear music echoing down the hall. How had Kitty managed to keep these parties secret? Rosemary started to wonder about the competence of the dorm warden staff. Maybe they had seen one too many parties and were too jaded to care anymore. Before Rosemary reached Kitty's door it swung open and a fellow freshman stumbled out into the hall. She was clearly inebriated. Laughter spilled over as Rosemary peeked inside to look for Susan.

Rosemary spied her sister in the corner of the room sitting on Eric Reynolds's lap. He was Susan's latest crush. Eric was on the boys' tennis team and that was how they had met. He had watched the girls team practice one afternoon and had flirted with Susan afterwards. Eric had a shock of bright red hair and a pale face plastered with freckles. He was a cute boy if the freckles didn't distract you. Rosemary frowned at the couple as she strode across the room pushing drunken co-eds out of her way. When Susan spied her older sister, she broke into a huge grin.

"Rosie!" she shouted.

"Susie! What are you doing here? Curfew is in fifteen minutes. Let's go!"

Susan jumped off Eric's lap, stumbled and grabbed Rosemary's arm for support.

"No! Let's staaa-y a little bit looon-ger."

Susan was singing that damn doo-wop song. She reeked of something that smelled like peaches and spirits. Rosemary would have to make sure her sister took a shower when they returned to their dorm so no one would smell it on her.

"We are going, now!"

Rosemary grabbed Susan's arm and began to pull her to the door. But when they reached it Eric was blocking the way.

"Not so fast! Susan promised to look at my new car."

Eric reeked of the funny peach smell too. Rosemary pushed past him and dragged Susan down the stairwell. Once outside the cold air hit both girls in the face. Winter was waning but spring had yet to blow in for good. It had rained for most of the day and misty fog was rolling onto campus as dusk fell like a stage curtain. The path back to their dorm room was slick so Rosemary was careful to support Susan so she wouldn't fall. If Susan broke a leg or twisted her ankle she would have to wait hand and foot on her. Rosemary had way too much studying to do and wouldn't have time to play nurse.

Rosemary hadn't noticed that Eric had followed them until he grabbed Susan's other arm and pulled her away. They almost fell and the two drunken party pals burst out laughing. Rosemary looked around nervously in case any school officials were nearby. Getting caught plastered wouldn't be good news for any of them. Eric started to pull Susan down the wrong path and Rosemary ran after them.

"You're going the wrong way!"

"No, I'm not," Eric snickered. "My cars this way."

Eric stopped as Susan clung to him and looked around. He seemed confused. He probably had no clue where they were or if they were even going in the right direction.

"We don't have time for that," demanded Rosemary.

"Please Rosie!" begged Susan. "C'mon, let's just have a quick peek!"

Rosemary sighed and gave in. She didn't want to hear Susan cry and whine all night about not seeing Eric's stupid car. She followed the staggering twosome towards the school's car lot. It was a steep path and all three of them almost fell several times. The grass beneath their feet was slippery and Rosemary worried about Susan not only twisting an ankle but also getting a grass stain on her light pink skirt. Once they made it to the parking lot Eric led them over to a shiny cherry red Chevrolet Impala. Even Rosemary could admire that it was a beautiful car. Until Susan just had to sit in it.

Eric thought this was a capital idea so he opened the passenger door. Susan plopped down on the seat and made a fuss over the interior. Eric was drunkenly proud. He strutted to the drivers' side and climbed in. Rosemary looked at her watch nervously. They only had five more minutes until curfew. But it wasn't until she heard the engine of the car roar to life that she grew scared. Susan hopped out of the car and told her sister excitedly that Eric was going to take her for a ride.

"You can't do that Susie! If you are late for curfew just one more time -"

"I won't be! Eric said we'll just go around campus and then he'll drop us off in front of our dorm. It'll only take a few minutes. Please Rosie!"

Rosemary's shoulders slumped in defeat as she gave in for the second time that night. Susan climbed back in the car and Rosemary followed. The three passengers were now squished into the front. Eric pulled out of his parking space and started cruising around the campus. Whenever they passed anyone they knew Susan would lean over Rosemary's lap and yell out the open window. Rosemary was mortified and tried to slump down in her seat. She was glad their dorm was up ahead.

But when they reached the dorm Eric hit the gas and blew right past it. Susan shrieked with laughter and Rosemary yelled out a profane word. Rosemary never cursed and it caught Susan off guard. After staring at her older sister in shock for a brief moment Susan stared giggling uncontrollably. By the time Rosemary noticed they were headed off campus it was too late. The tires of the Impala spun and skidded on the wet pavement as they raced down the highway. The frigid air blasting in through the open windows chilled Rosemary but she left it down in the hopes that it would sober up her companions.

Eric ventured off the main highway and they ended up on a twisty side road. The fog was now so thick Rosemary could barely see where they were going. She wasn't sure how Eric knew where he was going but he was so blitzed she didn't think he even noticed the rolling waves of fog. Suddenly Eric pulled over to the shoulder of the road and darted from the car. In the distance Rosemary could hear him vomiting. Just the sound of it made her want to vomit too. And she hadn't even been drinking! By the time Eric crawled back to the idling car he looked even more pale than usual.

"I can't...I can't drive. Can you drive Susie bug?"

Susan perked up and a smile crept across her face.

"You may *not* drive Susan Pope!" Rosemary cried.

"Why not? Eric just said I could! It's his car!"

"I will drive! I'm the better driver anyways."

Eric climbed over the drivers' seat and lay sprawled out in the back. Rosemary sincerely hoped he wouldn't vomit in the car. She didn't want to think about the chain reaction that would occur. Suddenly Susan slid over into the drivers' seat, crossed her arms over her chest, and resolutely refused to move. The two sisters argued for a few minutes until Rosemary recalled they were now late for curfew. Someone on their hall was bound to notice they weren't in their shared dorm room. Desperate to make it back Rosemary let Susan drive.

The car revved to life and off they sped once again into the dark night. The fog was so dense it was hard to see anything along the road. After a few minutes, the Impala rounded a curve and Susan was going so fast she quickly passed the stop sign posted near the entrance of the double lane highway that lead to the college. The cherry red car shot across the road and was instantly struck by another vehicle. The collision sent them into a spin. Rosemary could hear her sister screaming. The Impala plunged into the recessed grassy median and smashed into a large tree. Glass shattered and tires popped before the remains of the car groaned and settled to its last stop.

Smoke snaked in plumes off the smashed-in hood of the Impala. Rosemary's head throbbed and she put her hand up to her forehead to make it stop. When she pulled her hand away a sticky red substance coated it. A wave of nausea rolled over her as she breathed in the smell of burning rubber and smoke. Rosemary felt sleepy as exhaustion fell over her. But she pried her eyes open and rolled her head to the side to look for her sister. Susan was slumped over like a limp rag doll. Her eyes were closed and blood poured down her face. A shard of glass was sticking out of her neck. Rosemary let out a soft, pained moan and tried to reach for Susan but a black veil she couldn't fight took her under.

Chapter Two

Cassandra Part I

The cars lined up in a row lurched forward, moved a few spaces and then abruptly stopped. The stop and go pace always frustrated Cassie. Surely there was a better way to drop off and pick up children besides this archaic system.

"Mom, my shoe come undoned."

"Untied, Sylvia. Joe, help your sister tie her shoe."

Cassie's youngest, Noah, had already been dropped off at pre-school. She peered into the rearview mirror and watched her oldest, Joseph, help with the malfunctioning shoe. Joseph had a streak of strawberry jam smeared across his cheek. Breakfast had been so hectic this morning Cassie hadn't even noticed. She and her husband Marc had been discussing their credit card payments. Cassie rummaged through the glove compartment for a tissue and handed it to Joseph with instructions to wipe his face clean.

Finally the van pulled up to the official drop-off curb and Joseph's second grade teacher Mrs. Rodriguez approached the door. Cassie was so happy to finally have two of her children in elementary school. It gave her more free time during the day to get errands, chores and the like accomplished. In two more years Noah would enter elementary school freeing up even more of her time. Cassie couldn't wait.

"Mrs. Rodriguez, I just tied Sil's shoe!"

"That's wonderful Joseph. Hello Cassandra. Sylvia."

Joe jumped out of the van and then helped Sylvia negotiate the step down to the curb.

"Cassandra, don't forget the parent teacher conference coming up next week. We need to talk about Joseph's class participation."

Cassie nodded, waved goodbye to the kids, then pulled out of the stop and go lane. She was not looking forward to the upcoming parent teacher conference. Sylvia was only in kindergarten so that meeting would be easy. Unless there was some wayward finger painting exercise Cassie wasn't expecting much. But Joseph's meeting would be difficult. Her son often had bouts of extreme shyness unless he knew you well and sometimes suffered panic attacks when he became stressed. He was uncomfortable in large groups. Cassie was hoping he would eventually grow out of this and felt that Mrs. Rodriguez constantly harping on it did not help. She and Marc would be in for a fight with the teacher come conference day. They would need to present a unified front. Marc would need to back her up for once instead of just automatically agreeing with Mrs. Rodriquez.

Cassie pulled into Bell Cleaners parking lot and began collecting the pile of dirty clothes in the front passenger seat. She visited this business once or twice a week because of her husband. Marc worked in pharmaceutical sales and needed a multitude of dress shirts. On the way out Cassie caught a glimpse of herself in the reflective windows. She looked like an absolute mess. Her thick, layered auburn hair was up in a messy twist and she had dark circles under her light blue eyes. Sylvia had been sick last night so she had stayed up with her. Cassie pulled her long amber hued wrap sweater tighter to her body in an effort to cover her hips. Once upon a time she had been a very pretty girl, but now she was carrying fifteen extra pounds of weight from her last pregnancy. For some reason she hadn't been able to shed those last few pounds. They had clung to her for dear life. She was only five feet, five inches tall so all the extra weight had settled on her hips and thighs.

Once her errand was complete, and Cassie was back in the van, she let out a long sigh. As Cassie put her seat belt on she realized for the first time that she had her own jam mishap as well. The light grey t-shirt underneath her wrap sweater had a sticky pink stain.

"Just great," she muttered.

Cassie's clothes used to be so stylish back in college. But now, only thirty-one and married with three kids, she was lucky if the items she wore were merely color coordinated. In the back of her mind Cassie sometimes wondered how her life had ended up like this. It certainly wasn't the life she had planned. She loved her children dearly, but she sometimes wondered how she had strayed so far from the goals she had back in high school and college. Back then she had been very active in theatre. She had always wanted a career in the arts. So how had she ended up a housewife in upstate New York with blotches of strawberry jam smeared on her clothing? How had she become so isolated?

Beyond the ladies at her children's school and at church she didn't really know anyone else in Marc's hometown. The truth was, Cassie was often lonely. When she was younger Cassie had thought the *lonely housewife* was such a cliché. How could anyone with a husband and children to love and care for, and so many activities to race to, feel a true sense of loneliness? It had sounded so absurd. But only a decade later Cassie understood. The loneliness wasn't something one could see on the surface. It was a loneliness that went deep, to the core. It couldn't be seen, only felt.

Cassie turned right on Ward Avenue and looked down at the strawberry stain once more. How in the world would she get that out? Cassie raised her head with a defeated sigh, looked once again out her front window and let out a piercing scream. She slammed on her brakes, but not in enough time to avoid a bicyclist who had swerved in front of her van unexpectedly. The vehicle and the bicyclist collided with a horrible shattering sound. She couldn't tell if the sound had been her headlight or the bicyclist! The van skidded to a stop and the bicyclist disappeared from Cassie's view. She fumbled with her seat belt with trembling hands, stumbled out the door and went to the front of the van to find the bicyclist.

~ ~ ~

Cassie stomped into room 133S, slammed her books down onto a desk near the windows, and then threw herself onto the wooden seat. She crossed her arms and scowled at the blackboard. How she had ended up in detention was beyond her. It had been Marla who had copied off her Humanities test, not the other way around! But that is not what Marla had convinced Mr. Sullivan to believe. Marla was quite the little liar. Cassie wondered how one developed skills like that. She certainly wasn't a very good liar. Her mother had taught her lying was wrong. The thought comforted her slightly. She wasn't dishonest, that horrible Marla was! Cassie raised her chin up and then looked out the window. All the other kids from her middle school were racing towards home or the new baseball diamond over on Westlake Field. It was a beautiful, crisp September afternoon. And she was stuck in detention. Cassie sighed in defeat.

"Looking out the window and wishing you were out there won't make it happen. Might as well take your punishment like the rest of us Red."

Cassie froze in her seat. The rest of us? And just who was calling her *red*? She had thought she was the only student in detention today. Cassie slowly swiveled in her seat so she could see who the quiet voice had belonged to. Sitting two chairs behind her was a sullen looking boy with messy black hair and deep, dark brown eyes. He was skinny, pale and sort of alien looking. Cassie flinched at the sight of him.

"Who are you?" she asked without hesitation.

The boy let out a chuckle and shook his head.

"I've been in your Humanities class for almost a month now. But I bet you've never noticed. You're too busy brown nosing to Mr. Sullivan."

Cassie gasped at the nerve of this boy! Yes, she was a good student. She didn't need to cheat unlike Marla. And she didn't need this strange boy telling her what she did or didn't notice.

"Oh, look at the shocked face" - the boy rolled his eyes - "I'm Eli by the way. Since you have no clue."

"I do too! I have lots of clues!"

Eli chuckled again and Cassie noticed he had two dimples in his cheeks. He sort of looked *beautiful* when he smiled, which wasn't a state normally assigned to a boy. His smile seemed to transform his whole face. But as soon as the smile broke over his face it vanished just as quickly. Eli was staring at her in a way that seemed like he was trying to size her up. Cassie did not appreciate being sized up.

"Why'd you let Marla dupe you like that anyways? She's a stuck up princess."

"I didn't! I tried to explain to Mr. Sullivan -"

"Yeah, yeah, yeah. He ain't gonna believe you over princess. She's got half this school snowed."

In a sudden jolt Cassie suddenly recalled who the strange boy was. He was the new kid in the eighth grade – her grade. His family had moved here from New York City. In dusty New Jersey that was always sort of awe inducing. Her family was strictly bridge-and-tunnel, or at least that's what her mean cousin Albert always said. He lived in Manhattan. Cassie had been to New York City once with her father. They had gone there to visit her uncle who was in the hospital for lung cancer. Afterwards her father was quiet and they had spent hours walking around the city. It was such a big and wondrous place. They had gotten large salty pretzels from a street vendor and her father let her ride the colorful carousel in the park. Afterwards he had taken her to see Strawberry Fields. Cassie's father was a John Lennon fan. She had laid down on the Imagine mosaic and stared up at the blue sky. The visit had been magical in her mind.

"I've seen you in class you know Red. You don't need to suck up to Sullivan. You're too smart for that."

Cassie sat up a little straighter.

"I am?"

"Sure you are. You just don't believe you are. That's why princess conned you today."

Cassie frowned. Eli was right. How did this boy know so much?

"Shit! Turn around! Pretend to read!"

Cassie wasn't sure why, but she followed Eli's instructions and quickly turned to face the front of the class. She flipped the book on top of her pile open and pretended to read. The door to the detention room squeaked opened but Cassie kept her eyes on the pages in her book.

"Elijah Epstein. Back again I see."

"Present," said Eli in a monotone voice.

"And Cassandra Mueller. This is a surprise."

Cassie looked up and saw Mr. Hicks scowling at her. He was one of the most unpleasant teachers in this school. Mr. Hicks taught shop so thankfully she'd never have him. He reeked of pipe tobacco. It made Cassie gag.

"I'll be right across the hall," Mr. Hicks warned. "If I hear one word out of either of you, you'll get another day in here. Got that?"

Cassie nodded slowly as Mr. Hicks exited the detention room. The door closed softly behind him.

"That guy is such an asshole! It's ok, you can turn around again."

"But we'll get more detention!" Cassie hissed.

"Nah. He's gone down to the lunch room to flirt with that blonde cafeteria worker."

Cassie spun around in her chair once more.

"What! The lady who never smiles and barely speaks?"

"Yeah her."

Eli laughed at Cassie's innocent shock and she smiled back. For the next forty-five minutes he told her so much gossip about the teachers and students at their school she couldn't believe he was the new kid. Cassie found herself laughing quite a bit. She never really made friends all that easily so this came as a surprise to her.

Later that week, during Humanities class, Cassie saw Eli dump a container full of what looked like mulch and worms into Marla's bright pink bookbag. She stifled a giggle as he winked at her. Take that princess!

~ ~ ~

The automatic doors to the emergency room swung open and Cassie looked up anxiously. She had been waiting for the injured bicyclist to come out, but so far there was no sign of him. Cassie checked her watch once more; two hours had passed. The police officer who had arrived at the scene of the accident hadn't charged her with anything since it had been just that. He had been concerned about her health until she had informed him that the stain on her shirt was not blood but merely breakfast. Apparently, a dog had lunged at the bicyclist pushing him into Cassie's van. It had all been an unfortunate chain of events.

An ambulance had escorted the bicyclist to the hospital and Cassie had decided to follow it. She was worried about the man her van had collided with. Even though nothing she could have done would have prevented the incident she still felt guilty. Cassie knew her feelings were irrational but she had to make sure he was alright.

The automatic doors swung open once more and finally the bicyclist emerged. He was still clothed in his now dirty and ripped blue and yellow bike uniform. His left arm was in a sling. Cassie bolted from her seat and approached the man.

"Excuse me, I'm Cassandra Smyth. I was driving the van."

Comprehension dawned on the man's rugged face. He had longish brown hair and sharp green eyes. He was tall and very fit. Probably from all the bicycling.

"I'm sorry about your van. I promise to pay for any repairs it may need."

"I, what? Oh no! I have insurance, please don't worry about that. I just...I needed to make sure you were ok. That was so horrible back there..."

Cassie trailed off, unsure what to say next. The man stared at her for a moment and Cassie self-consciously pulled her sweater tighter around her body. Now that she could get a good look at him, he seemed to be her age.

"Well, again, I'm sorry about your van."

"Do you need a ride?"

"A ride?"

"Yes, your bike got mangled."

"Don't trouble yourself. I'll just catch a cab."

"Oh, please don't do that. I can drive you home. Please…"

The man took a long look at Cassie then nodded his acceptance.

"Thanks."

"No problem. I'm out this way."

The two strangers set off for the parking garage.

~ ~ ~

Cassie peeked around the corner. The hallway was empty. She huddled by the girls' bathroom entrance and waited for Eli's signal. Another minute passed and then she heard a low whistle. Cassie took another peek around the wall and saw Eli grinning at her. She stayed low and hurried down the hall.

"Did you see anyone?" he asked.

"Nope. You?"

Eli shook his head and his hair swayed.

"Ok, let's take the North hall. Less chance of being spied."

Cassie stifled a giggle. They were about to make another break from Thornton High School. Cassie had skipped out of Home Economics – when would she seriously need that knowledge? – and Eli had skipped Geometry. He was so brilliant he could've attended once a week and still have an A average at the end of the semester. As they made their way down the hall they kept their eyes peeled for teachers. Or worse, Principal Lane.

At last they reached a door that lead to the back athletic fields. Eli slowly and quietly pushed the door open and let Cassie escape. He followed closely behind. As soon as they were past the door the two truants made a brisk run for it. They ran down the sloping green grassy hill until they reached the first dug out on the baseball field. Here they could stay hidden until the next bell and then return to the school and blend in with the other students on the way to their next class.

"Do you have your monologue ready?" Eli asked.

"Yes, but…"

"But what?"

"I'm just nervous Eli. Last year the lead role went to Whitney Larson. *Whitney Larson!* I'm sure she'll get it again this year. She's a way better actress than me."

"Says who? Not me."

"I wish you'd reconsider and try out for a part too. You could be the Romeo to my Juliet."

"I thought I already was."

Eli grinned, then reached out, and gently twisted one of Cassie's cascading ginger curls around his finger. Cassie blushed and looked down. They had recently begun dating. It was new after being best friends for almost two years, She absolutely adored Eli. In the last year he had grown taller and was no longer the skinny boy she had met in the eighth grade. His black hair was long, wavy and glossy. He was still pale but his porcelain skin made him look mysterious and quite handsome.

"I'm no actor Red. I want to be a director one day. And I will be. And you will be my muse and together we'll make films. We'll live in a loft in the city and drink overpriced coffee every morning from the local bodega."

Cassie giggled.

"Eli -"

"Shhh."

Eli leaned in after letting go of her hair and kissed her lightly on the lips. Cassie's whole body tingled. No one had ever kissed her until Eli had the night of the Fall Fling dance. That's when they had known. He kissed her with more pressure and Cassie responded in kind. At the moment she couldn't remember anything, not where she was or the day, heck even her name. All she knew was this kiss.

Eli pulled back and said, "You will be the loveliest Juliet ever."

And she was.

~ ~ ~

"I'm Cassandra Smyth by the way."

"Yeah, you said that back at the hospital."

"Oh…that's right. Sorry. You can call me Cassie. Most everyone does."

Cassie turned left towards Ivey Gardens as the bicyclist requested.

"I'm Ethan Carson."

"It's umm, nice to meet you Ethan. I'm sorry it's under such unfortunate circumstances. Believe me, I've never ran into anyone on the road before."

"I believe it was me who ran into you and threw you off course."

"Does it matter?"

"It always matters."

Cassie peeked over at the man sitting in her passenger seat. He was staring straight ahead.

"Turn here," he instructed.

Cassie turned her attention back to the road and focused on where she was going. She didn't need another accident today.

"Will your job be affected by your arm?"

"I'll need to rearrange some things until it heals. It won't be too bad. Plus, I can still drive since I have my right arm."

"What do you do? If you don't mind me asking."

"I'm a scenic and lighting designer for the Weatherwood Playhouse."

"The theatre downtown?"

"Yes, that's the one. Do you go there often?"

"No, not much unfortunately. I love the theatre though. I've heard good things about Weatherwood's productions."

"It's a professionally accredited theatre so the quality is high. I also teach public speaking courses part time at the community college."

"How do you find time to do all that?"

"Well, not having a social life whatsoever does wonders for your professional life."

Ethan laughed and Cassie found herself laughing with him.

"So, what's coming up at Weatherwood?"

"Ah, *Three Sisters*!"

"Chekhov!"

"That's right. Are you a big Chekhov fan?"

"Well, sort of. I...I knew someone once who thought very highly of his work. That was a long time ago though."

"You should come down and see it. It'll open in November. Rehearsals have just started and I'm playing around with some ideas for the scenic elements."

"I'd love to. I used to be really involved in the theatre back in high school and college. But lately -"

"So, what's stopping you?"

Cassie let out a high-pitched laugh.

"Lots of things," she finally said.

"That's a shame. We always need volunteers."

"You do?"

Ethan nodded yes as Cassie pulled up in front of Ivey Gardens. It was a modern apartment complex. Cassie admired it while Ethan unfastened his seat belt.

"Well, thank you for the ride Cassie. Maybe we'll run into each other down the road."

"Yes, maybe. I hope you feel better soon."

Ethan smiled, nodded and then exited the van. He gave Cassie a wave and then entered the complex. Cassie pulled away from the curb and hurried off to pick up Noah. She was already late and was sure a teary scene would await her.

~ ~ ~

The street was dark and cold but Cassie waited patiently outside the temple. She sat huddled in her warm coat on a low wall while waiting for Eli. Since they had decided to attend college in New York City, and most of his extended family still lived here, it was pretty much a requirement that he attend services a few times a month. A yellow taxi rushed past and the wind whipped down the narrow street. Ten minutes later people began streaming out of the front double doors.

Cassie spotted Eli with his Aunt Dalia. She was a very stylish woman. Cassie always admired her elegant dresses, high heels and long coats. She thought this was the way grown-ups should dress. Aunt Dalia waved to Cassie. Eli kissed his aunt on the cheek, then took off running down the temple steps. Eli darted across the street and barely missed a taxi which prompted the cabbie to lay on his horn. Eli just laughed.

When he reached Cassie he grabbed her around the waist, lifted her off the ground and spun her around. Cold air swirled around her face and she began to laugh too. Eli set her down, grabbed her face between his hands, and gave her a long kiss. His kiss heated her face and lips.

"Are you ready for your surprise?" asked Eli.

"My surprise? What surprise? What is it?"

"It won't be a surprise if I tell you!" he laughed.

Eli hailed the next taxi that came down the street and off they went. Cassie's stomach was full of butterflies. She didn't know where they were going and she didn't care. Anywhere she went with Eli was bound to be good. Last night Eli had snuck into her dorm room and spent the night there. Her dorm was supposed to be women only but her roommate had been out for the weekend. When Sarah was gone Eli always stayed with her. Cassie loved waking up to Eli's peaceful face inches from her, his black hair covering his eyes as he slept. The taxi finally came to a stop in front of the opera house. Eli paid the driver and soon they were standing in front of the impressive building.

"What are we doing here Eli?"

"You'll see. C'mon!"

But instead of heading towards the front doors Eli lead her around to the side of the building. He knocked quietly on an almost hidden door and a moment later it swung open. Cassie recognized the guy in the open doorway. He lived in Eli's dorm.

"Thanks Craig!"

"No problem man."

"What are we doing in here?" asked Cassie again.

Eli gave Cassie a quick kiss than grabbed her hand and led her up through a maze of stairs. After several flights they came to a door. Eli turned to face Cassie and gave her a sly grin. He had recently cut his hair shorter in the back but left the front slightly longer and the style really suited his slender face. Eli pulled a piece of red glossy fabric from his pocket, unraveled it, and then held it up for Cassie to see.

"What is *that*?" she giggled.

"The blindfold you are about to wear love."

While quietly laughing Cassie shook her head no, while Eli grinned and nodded yes. He circled Cassie until he was standing behind her. He reached out with his hand, his fingertips lightly brushing her neck before pulling her long red curls back. Cassie shivered in delight. Eli leaned in, gently kissed the back of her neck and whispered, "I love you". Then he placed the red fabric over her eyes.

Cassie heard the door click open then Eli took her arm and led her through it. The floor beneath her feet seemed to vibrate. Cassie could hear the faint whispers of faraway voices and for the first time since this scheme began felt nervous. Why would Eli parade her before strangers? They came to a stop…and waited. Cassie couldn't tell how quickly or slowly time was passing. Her pulse has quickened and her heart raced.

Finally, Cassie heard the opening notes of a beautiful piece of music and the blindfold was whisked off her face. Cassie blinked, focused her eyes and gasped. She realized they were standing on an elevated service platform, the central catwalk high above the opera's latest production. The view from high above was breathtaking. Cassie turned to look at Eli.

"La Cenerentola. Limited engagement."

"Cinderella?" asked Cassie in amazement.

"Yes," he said as he lifted her hand and kissed it.

He then guided her to an unfolded blanket and a cooler that held two plastic glasses and a cheap bottle of champagne. Eli filled a flute and handed it to Cassie.

"Happy anniversary Cassiopeia."

"Anniversary?"

"Yeah, this is the date of the Fall Fling dance."

Cassie let out a laugh, heard the echo of it and clamped her hand over her mouth. Eli's dark eyes twinkled.

"How did you remember that?" whispered Cassie.

"I remember lots of things."

"Wait. What did you call me?"

"Cassiopeia. Or Cassiepeia as classical authors called her. She was a beautiful queen with the loveliest locks of hair. Of course, I doubt her hair was as lovely as your hair. She now lives in the stars."

Cassie mulled that over while she took a sip of champagne and Eli lifted a lock of her hair and twirled it around his finger. She had asked Eli weeks ago to find a suitable lovers nickname for her. She was tired of him calling her 'red'. That was cute when they were kids. Not so much now. Cassiopeia…Cassiopeia….

"I like it," she whispered.

Eli winked at her. "Me too."

Cassie scooted over next to Eli and rested in his arms as the opera floated up from below.

"Craig helped me set this up. I'm sorry I couldn't afford seats for us. But one day…one day…"

"I know Eli. One day we'll do it all. This is lovely by the way."

Eli kissed the top of Cassie's head.

"Brady told me his walk-up will be available next fall. He said if we want it…"

Cassie looked up at Eli when he trailed off.

"We can have it?" she finished.

Eli nodded yes. Cassie reached up and kissed his chin. She knew her father would go ballistic at the thought of her living with a boy during their senior year of college. Since her mother and uncle had passed he had become very protective of his only child. But she wanted this more than anything. Her whole future was Eli. She would deal with her father and any other obstacles that came along later. For tonight the future could wait.

~ ~ ~

"I'm just glad you're ok Cass."

Marc leaned over and kissed his wife on the forehead.

"Was it scary mom?" asked Joseph.

"It was baby, but I'm ok, and the man on the bicycle is ok. So you don't have to worry one little bit."

Cassie ruffled Joseph's dark brown hair as he winced at the nickname she always called him. He was outgrowing it. Joseph had his father's hair. Somehow only Noah had inherited her red locks.

"Sil, don't play with your food," admonished Cassie.

Sylvia stopped touching her mashed potatoes. Marc sat down at the kitchen table and flipped open the folded newspaper. He was scanning the sports section as usual. Marc was a big baseball fan. He had just started taking Joseph and Sylvia to games and would take Noah when he got older. Joseph liked the whole spectacle of the games but Sylvia did not. Sylvia had complained about the lack of ballerinas at the ball park. Cassie's daughter was completely infatuated with ballerinas. Whenever Sylvia saw one she'd let out an excited squeal. Her bedroom and closet was currently devoid of any color but pink. Cassie hoped this was a phase that Sylvia would soon grow out of. Surely her little girl would like another color besides pink one day.

"Marc, did you call the bank today?"

"Hmm…"

Marc was reading the newspaper intently and had barely registered Cassie's question.

"Marc!"

"Huh? Oh, sorry. What Cass?"

"Did you call the bank about the credit cards?"

"Yes, it's all taken care of dear."

Dear.

Cassie sighed at the generic term of endearment and got up to start washing dishes. She stared out the window over the kitchen sink and looked up at the stars in the sky. Suddenly she remembered back to a time when she was one of them. Usually she didn't think about such things much anymore, but tonight it made her feel sad. It was probably because of today's distressing events. She tried to shake the melancholy off by scrubbing pots and pans vigorously.

"Cass, I'll help the kids brush their teeth and change them into their pajamas. Ok?"

"Thanks Marc."

An hour later Noah was fast asleep in his bedroom. Sylvia sat on Joseph's bed while he snuggled under his covers. The siblings took turns each night. One night the bedtime story was in Joseph's room, the next Sylvia's. Whoever got to snuggle deep in their bed did not get to choose the story. Cassie's children liked a variety of stories, but Sylvia especially loved fairy tales.

"Ok Sil, what have you chosen tonight?"

Sylvia produced a light blue hard cover book from behind her back and handed it to her mom. Cassie flipped it over and looked at the title. Her heart gave a little squeeze.

"Cinderella."

"It's one of my favorites," whispered Sylvia.

"Mine too," Cassie whispered back.

A little while later Joseph and Sylvia were fast asleep. Marc had carried Sylvia to her own bed in her bubble gum pink bedroom. Marc then retired to the den to watch ESPN. Cassie quietly slipped outside and sat in a chair on the back deck. She pulled her sweater tight to her body to ward off the cold. She had never gotten a chance to change out of her stained clothes. The strawberry jam on her t-shirt had probably set for good by now.

Cassie stared up at the stars once more. They seemed to be extra shiny and twinkly tonight. She rarely came out to look at them anymore. It made her sad to stare up at their beauty. Most of all they made her remember. The truth was life wasn't a fairy tale. Those stories always worked out for the girl and the boy in the end. They didn't end in a late-night phone call from your boyfriend's Aunt Dalia, who is crying so hard on the other end of the line you can barely understand what she is saying. And when you finally do comprehend what she's trying to tell you somehow you wished you hadn't understood.

Elijah Epstein had stopped off at the Quik-N-Go late one night to grab a few snacks. When he entered the convenience store he had walked in on a robbery in progress. The police had told Aunt Dalia he was probably dead shortly after his body hit the floor from being shot in the chest. Cassie hadn't wanted to go back to college her senior year but her father had insisted. Sometimes she thought she had gone back just to get away from his constant hovering after Eli's death. She had hated the stupid counselor he had made her see twice a week. It was the same person he had seen after her mother's death. At the time she had wanted to curl up and die herself.

One beautiful fall day during finals Marc Smyth had come to her assistance. She had been cramming in front of the Science and Mathematics building before a final unaware that her loose-leaf notes had slipped out of her notebook and were now being carried by the wind over the lawn. Marc had come to her aid to help reclaim the sheets. Cassie had married Marc a little over a year later when they had discovered Joseph was on the way. Ten years later her life seemed unrecognizable.

Later that night, after Cassie had crawled into bed exhausted, she thought about Ethan Carson. She hoped he was going to be alright. For a long time she stared up at the dark ceiling while Marc snored lightly beside her. She thought about Ethan's suggestion that she volunteer at the Weatherwood Playhouse theatre. Finally, she drifted off to sleep and dreamed of Cinderella, except this time no one came to claim her with a glass slipper. Instead she was trapped in an upside-down throne floating in the sky with no prince charming in sight.

Chapter Three

Danielle Part I

When things fit together perfectly it always pleased Danielle. Ever since she was a young child puzzles of all kind had fascinated her. Puzzle boards, block puzzles, jigsaws, crosswords, Jenga, Sudoku, Tetris, Word Roundup, even the silly simplicity of hang-man and tic-tac-toe. Dani loved working to make it all fit together so that when the final moment came, when the last piece was inserted and the puzzle was complete, it was perfection. There was something very satisfying about working towards the goal of making something whole and then seeing it come to fruition.

Unfortunately, over the years, Dani had come to realize that real life wasn't like a puzzle that you could piece together in a few hours. She often thought life was more like those jigsaw puzzles you found at garage sales or in thrift stores. Sometimes puzzle pieces were missing from the box, or there were pieces that belonged to another jigsaw entirely. This is how Dani felt about her life. She was a jigsaw puzzle missing some pieces. And not superfluous pieces either, but heart of the puzzle pieces. Without these pieces the picture trying to form would never make sense and you wouldn't know what the puzzle was all about.

"Danielle! Dinner will be ready in a half hour! Wash up!"

Dani waved to let her know she had heard, then watched her mom slip back into the shade of the house. She had wiled away another long, boring summer day sitting out in the back yard trying to get a tan. Dani could swear each day was longer than the one before. She slowly got to her feet, gathered up her towel, beach chair and crossword puzzle book and headed for the back door. Dani could hear Mr. Campbell and his wife next door discussing their tomato plants. She waved when she was parallel to them in her own yard. A fence separated them so Dani could only see their heads and shoulders. Mrs. Campbell looked aghast at the terror wrought by the local rabbit and deer population. She thought Mrs. Campbell would eliminate the pesky creatures if she could. Dani assumed Mrs. Campbell wasn't a fan of the cartoon movie *Bambi*.

Once inside Dani went upstairs to the bathroom she shared with her younger sister Chelsea and took a cool shower. She had another month until she would be able to escape to college. Dani had a terrific grade point average and could have attended any college she wanted. But she had chosen a small, private liberal arts school in Georgia. Her parents had not been pleased, especially when she had been accepted into Virginia Tech and the University of Virginia. They couldn't understand why Dani didn't want to go to a university in her home state. But Dani had her own reasons for wanting to go to the little college town in Georgia. She just couldn't share these reasons with her family.

Dani crept downstairs once she was clean and heard her sister in the kitchen with her mom. They were both listening to country music which Dani hated. Chelsea was gossiping about her middle school friends and some dance that was coming up. Dani sighed and popped her iPod ear buds in. She had to set the table each night but she didn't have to be subjected to the soundtrack of trucks, dogs and beer. Jeff Buckley filled her head as she set about her task of placing plates and utensils.

Dani had been reminded many times throughout her life that she was the piece that did not fit with her family's puzzle. The first time she had really noticed this was during a visit to the library when she was eight years old. Chelsea had become rowdy as usual so their mom had taken her outside to play while Dani checked out the books she wanted. Chelsea was four and books did not hold her attention. Dani had exited the library, her arms piled full of books, when she found her mom and sister sitting on a bench out front. A tall, pretty lady with dark skin was talking to her mom and as Dani got closer she could hear them.

"She looks just like you Elizabeth! She has your eyes and nose and even your chin."

Dani's mom let out a pleased laugh.

"She has Peter's hair and cheeks."

"Well, she's just perfect Elizabeth."

Dani had come to a quiet stop beside the bench. The tall lady had looked down at her and then said, "Can we help you sweetie? Are you lost?" To which Dani had replied indignantly, "I'm not lost. That's my mom."

"Sarah, this is my other daughter Danielle."

The dark lady had stared at Dani with such a suspicious, funny look that it had made her feel uncomfortable. That was the day Dani had realized she didn't look anything like the rest of her family. Maybe it just hadn't occurred to her to care before that day. The uncomfortable scenario at the library had been repeated often enough throughout her life: At school, church, the grocery store and even during summer vacations at the beach. It was always depressing to be pointed out as an anomaly in your own family during an otherwise perfect day at the beach. The day wasn't so perfect after that and all the sandcastles and ice cream cones in the world couldn't make up for it.

Even without numerous people pointing it out to her, Dani knew she looked different from her parents and sister. They all had dark brown hair, blue eyes and olive skin. They were short to boot. Dani was tall. By the tenth grade she was her dad's height. She was also a blonde – a true blonde! – with milky pale skin and a smattering of freckles sprinkled over her nose. Her eyes were hazel and without mascara she looked like she had no eyelashes. Currently Chelsea was only fourteen but she was already curvy. Dani, at eighteen, still had a boyish figure.

Not only were the sisters physically different, but their personalities and proclivities also diverged. Dani had a puzzle table set up in the basement that no one was allowed to touch. She loved to read in a quiet spot away from everyone and everything. Dani loved a good mystery novel. That had started with Nancy Drew. She probably loved mystery novels for the same reason she loved puzzles. They were so much fun to figure out. Chelsea on the other hand thought she would die if a spotlight wasn't focused on her twenty-four-seven. She had just returned from cheer camp and was getting ready to start a three-week summer improv class for teenagers at the community theatre.

When Dani was in ninth grade she and her best friend Becca had started their own book club. Granted they were the only two members, but the girls could spend hours dissecting the latest book they had just read so it didn't matter anyway. Unfortunately the book club never quite got off the ground because Chelsea's baton practices kept interrupting. Each time Dani and Becca would set a book club meeting date it would inevitably have to be cancelled to pick Chelsea up from practice or take her to a competition. Dani's parents just couldn't grasp the importance of the two-person book club. No ribbons or trophies would be given out after all. Apparently unless a cheap tin trophy or a flashy ribbon was awarded it was all for nothing.

Then came that fateful day in the seventh grade when that horrible Marionn had made conjecture collide with reality. That was the day Dani had finally and truly known she was an outsider in her own family.

~ ~ ~

"Seriously, do you know how many states have banned this stupid game?"

"How many?"

"Lots. That's how many," Becca sighed. She rolled her eyes as they sat on the indoor gym bleachers and said, "You know, except for us. So lame."

"It's a brutal game," Dani replied. "I'll have this bruise on my leg for a week now."

Dani had taken a painful hit from a dodge ball. The impact had sent her out of the game to join Becca, who had pretended to get hit at the start of the game so she wouldn't have to play.

"A fifth grader in Portland had his arm ripped right off his body playing this game."

"What? That sounds like an urban legend Becca."

"Nuh-uh. I'm tellin' ya."

Becca brushed her short brown hair off her round face with her hand then blew a large bubble with the wad of gum in her mouth. She let it snap at the same moment Coach Hill blew her whistle. This sound sent fifty seventh graders scurrying to the locker rooms to change. Twenty-six girls crammed themselves into a tiny room at the same time. Sometimes tempers and Rave Hairspray flew.

Dani had just finished braiding her long blonde hair when Marionn cut in front of her at the mirror wall. This was the place all the girls would go to check out their clothes and hair before rushing back out into the halls of Jackson Middle School. Marionn was an obnoxious girl with broad shoulders, a bad frizzy perm and a mouthful of metal braces. She was your typical bully.

"Move over skyscraper!"

"Shut it brillo!"

Marionn snapped around and glared at Dani.

"What did you call me?"

"You heard me, *brillo.*"

Being taller than most of your classmates gave Dani some advantages even if it didn't exactly put her on the A list with the cool kids. That was reserved for jocks and cheerleaders after all. Dani couldn't ever figure out why anyone would want to show off their butt in a short-pleated skirt while yelling such ditties as, 'C'mon guys, you can do it! Just put your strength into it!' All the cheers seemed to be brainless and in need of syntax restructuring. They didn't even really rhyme!

"Well, at least my family wanted me skyscraper."

A small crowd had now gathered at the backed-up mirror wall. They were watching the spat between Dani and Marionn. Becca pushed her way through the crowd so she could stand beside Dani.

"My family wants me!"

"No, I mean your real family," Marionn sneered. "The ones who gave you up for adoption."

"What did you say?" hissed Becca.

She may have been small, but as Dani had always known, her best friend was a scrapper. Becca was the kind of person you wanted on your side in a dog fight. Or in this case a Hello Kitty fight.

"Everyone knows it's true! My mom told me you were adopted skyscraper."

Dani froze into place. It's not like she hadn't considered that possibility given her physical differences, but this was someone coming out and just saying it. The way Marionn had sneered the word *adoption*, well, she made it sound so dirty. Maybe it was. Dani's family had certainly never discussed it before. Maybe it *was* a bad thing you weren't ever supposed to talk about, which is why they never had.

Becca scooted by Dani, yelled "You ass!", then stomped on Marionn's foot. Marionn screamed out in pain and a brawl broke out in the cramped locker room. By the time Coach Hill broke the melee up much hair had been pulled and many training bras snapped. The fight even made the yearbook in the spring. Later in high school the 'Girls Locker Room Debacle of the Seventh Grade' would go down in infamy. Many girls would claim to have been there that day, but only a few had.

By the time Dani's mom had bailed her out of the principal's office, the truth had been out for over an hour. Later that night Elizabeth and Peter James had explained to Dani just how she had come into their lives. Elizabeth had tried for many years to have a baby, but it just hadn't happened. Until one day, four years after Dani's adoption. Her parents claimed that both of their daughters had been wonderful miracles. But ever since that day Dani had a sinking suspicion that only one of them had been just that.

~ ~ ~

40

Dani sprinkled parmesan cheese liberally over her spaghetti. She was the only one in her family who liked the stinky cheese, as Chelsea called it, so it was all hers. Chelsea liked extra sauce and the red liquid was currently trying to escape the confines of her plate she had piled on so much.

"Chelsea, please be careful with your plate honey. That sauce is going to run everywhere."

Their mom was eyeing Chelsea's plate with trepidation. Dani kept sprinkling on the parmesan.

"Danielle, that's enough," her father admonished.

Dani didn't think so but she snapped the lid back into place and set the plastic jar down. She knew how and when to choose her battles. Stinky cheese would not be one of them.

"I ripped my hoodie at cheer camp mom. I need to get a new one."

"But we just bought you that Chelsea."

"I know mom. It wasn't on purpose! It was an accident."

Dani's sister was so careless with her clothing that she always ended up getting triple the clothing. Dani had never been careless with her clothing. She shook her head and continued to enjoy her parmesany noodles.

"Well, I am taking Danielle shopping for dorm supplies tomorrow. You can come along too and we'll get you a new jacket."

"Hoodie mom," Chelsea smiled.

Dani gave her mom a disappointed look, but her mother didn't even notice. She rarely got to go shopping alone with just her mom and Dani had been looking forward to it. Her extra parmesany spaghetti became less appealing after that blow.

Dani had realized a while after the seventh-grade locker room revelation that the problem with her parents' explanation of her adoption was how little information they could actually provide about her birth parents. The only information they could tell Dani was her birth mother's name, the adoption agency's name, and the fact that the James' had not had any further contact with Shelby Perry since the adoption. According to her parents they thought Shelby had left the state shortly after the adoption had taken place. They knew nothing about her birth father.

For a couple of years Dani had let this information percolate in the back of her mind. At first it was all just a game of imagining. Dani would daydream about an older woman who looked just like her. She wondered what it would be like to look into the face of another person who looked similar; a person who had all her same physical characteristics. What must that be like? While most people took that for granted, Dani couldn't. She had no clue what it would be like to be tied to another person in such a tangible way.

Dani also wondered if her likes and dislikes were similar to her birth mother and father. No one else in Dani's family liked to read and be alone the way she did. Were her birth parents off somewhere right now enjoying a good book? Did one of them – or both of them – chew their lips the way she did when she was nervous or bored? Did her phantom parents like stinky parmesan cheese? These thoughts would spin around in her mind like a continuous mobius strip. Dani couldn't quite put her finger on the exact day, but somewhere in all the imaginings, she had become obsessed with two questions: *Who am I?* and *Who were they?*

It wasn't until Dani was in high school that she realized she had to do something about her obsession. And so, like the characters in the mystery novels she loved so much, Dani began to sleuth out her unknown origins. She began to put together the puzzle of who she was and where she had come from piece by piece. The only other person who knew what she was doing was her best friend Becca. Dani never told her parents or sister what she was up to. She didn't know if they would support her or if they would try to stop her. She couldn't take that chance. They were complete in themselves after all. How could they possibly understand?

Dani's search was kicked up a notch once both girls got their driver's licenses. Becca had even helped Dani get her own post office box for the secret mission. This came in handy for receiving records and documents she had requested from the hospital and adoption agency. Slowly, over the years, Dani had collected a pile of information about her birth mother. Shelby Perry had led a nomad's life for a while moving from state to state. But Dani had eventually traced her to a little college town in Georgia.

From all that Dani could gather Shelby was still there. *This* was the reason she had chosen to attend college so far away from home.

Dani had compiled all her findings in a bright yellow binder. That object held all her future dreams of a family that belonged to her. Not just a family on loan to her, which is sometimes how she had felt growing up. Yes, her adoptive family had always loved her and cared for her. But had they understood her? Could there be two people out there who would? It was an exciting and sometimes scary thought. Often Dani would lie awake in bed at night and try to imagine what she would say to her ghost family. Or what they might say to her. Sometimes she could imagine a thousand words flowing from her and other times no words at all. Dani could only be comforted in the thought that she had another month before school began to figure it all out. Like a puzzle.

Later that night Dani shut herself away in her bedroom. Chelsea was having some friends over for a Friday night horror movie 'fest. The way Dani saw it she was the only person her age who disliked horror movies. Slasher flicks and torture porn freaked her out and gave her nightmares. All her friends, even Becca, liked those gory movies. They would all go to the dollar movie theatre in town on the weekends and spend several hours watching body parts and blood fly as the people on the screen were decapitated by chain saws and tortured by the ever-present psychopaths. Horror movies were supposed to be her generations' movie du jour, but Dani just wasn't simpatico.

One time Chelsea had told Dani to chill out as the movies were obviously fake. She had said it was all props, smoke and mirrors. But this explanation had freaked Dani out even more. She didn't like the idea that something that looked so real was fake. What if real life was like that? What if her life turned out to be nothing but props, smoke and mirrors? When Dani had proposed this Orwellian theory out loud Chelsea had just laughed, called her a nerd and looked at her like she had a screw loose. Maybe this idea didn't bother you if you were a natural born son or daughter. Maybe then you didn't have to worry about smoke and mirrors. But when you were adopted a piece of you was always worried about the truth. Your life already had enough smoke and mirrors; you certainly didn't need it in your entertainment options too. Besides, how could anyone enjoy a cherry slushie with blood being splattered everywhere? Chelsea had said that the blood on the screen probably was cherry slushie.

As the evening wore on Dani could hear the reverberations of faint screams echo up the stairs. Sometimes the screams came from the movie and other times from Chelsea and her friends. Dani eventually shut her bedroom door to get some peace and quiet. She was clicking her way through her favorite social networking sites whenever Becca wasn't chiming in with messaging chatter. Besides reading and working on her puzzles Dani had found this was the perfect way to kill the slow-moving summer nights. Mostly Dani was fascinated by how much people online discussed sex.

Dani's high school friends rarely talked about sex. Probably because hardly any of them had ever had sex. There wasn't much to talk about. Dani herself had certainly never had sex. The biggest sex scandal at her high school had occurred at the end of their senior year. Becca had sworn up and down to Dani that she had heard Melissa Rhea, a sophomore cheerleader, had lost her v-card to George Nelson, a senior football player. Apparently there was even a limerick about the event in the boy's bathroom on the third floor near the science classes. Becca had declared if that bit of witty rhyme wasn't proof of the deed she didn't know what was. Dani was more skeptical of the gossip. Didn't Melissa come from a Catholic family? Didn't those people have strict rules about that sort of thing? You know, the no premarital sex and no sex for fun thing? Becca had said that Melissa was non-practicing, whatever that meant.

Dani had only had one boyfriend in her whole existence. She had dated Reed Roth, a boy she met in her youth group class at church. They dated only a few months at the beginning of her senior year. Reed was cute enough. He had beautiful grey eyes. But he had a buzz cut and Dani preferred guys with longer hair. Reed always wore plaid shirts, whether casual or dress, and it seemed a bit redundant. The shirt thing always distracted her. They went to different schools which left them few people in common to discuss. Reed was also more conservative than her; Dani considered her social viewpoints progressive. Soon enough the novelty of them being a couple had played itself out and they went their separate ways.

Once, last fall, they had attended the local fair on the outskirts of town. Reed had won her a stuffed dog with his dart balloon popping skills. After he had drove her home they sat in his truck in her driveway listening to the radio. Reed eventually worked up the nerve to French kiss her. Honestly, she had been less than impressed. It looked so much better on TV and in the movies. Reed's saliva had tasted like hot dogs and onions. That couldn't possibly be right. Dani hoped the men in her future tasted better. At the bare minimum shouldn't they taste like a fresh chewed mint or a stick of Juicy Fruit gum?

Reed had been nice enough to escort Dani to her senior prom as she didn't have a date. There just weren't any boys at her school Dani was taken with. She had a secret fear this trend would last her whole life. What if she never met anyone she was crazy about? She shuddered but then cheered up when she thought about Chelsea. She figured her sister would get married and divorced many times. It was inevitable the way she went through boys at school.

When Dani grew sleepy she got offline and crawled into bed. Every once in a while, she would hear a muffled scream rise from down stairs. After the fourth shriek woke her tentative slumber Dani reached over to her nightstand and grabbed her iPod. Jeff Buckley sang Dani to sleep. She bet his breath hadn't reeked of onions. He had probably tasted of raspberries or some other red ripe fruit.

~ ~ ~

Dani stared out the window and studied the sky. It was a mix of grey and white. So far this year they hadn't had one lousy snow day. But finally, late last night, the weatherman had called for a slight chance of snow today. Dani would have loved nothing more than to see snow flurries. She knew that's all it would take. The school district Dani lived in freaked out at the first sight of snow activity. Surely if a few flakes fell they would be let out of school for the rest of the day.

The door closed behind her and Dani turned away from the first-floor window. Ms. Espinosa took a seat behind her cluttered desk and opened the folder in her hand. After reviewing the papers inside, she looked up at Dani.

"Are you *sure* this is what you want to do Danielle?"

Ms. Espinosa adjusted her tortoise shell glasses and continued to stare at Dani.

"Yes. I've already told you."

"I know that, it's just -"

Ms. Espinosa broke off and stared at the papers in the folder once again. She was the toughest guidance counselor at her high school.

"You've already received early acceptance to both Virginia Tech and UVA. Do you know how many other high school students would like to be in your place?"

"Then they should have studied as hard as I did and got the grades I did. Spent time logging hundreds of hours at the food pantry and the ever exciting tutoring program down the hall."

Ms. Espinosa did not like sass-backs. She crossed her arms and peered at Dani over her glasses. Dani figured the counselor was in her thirties and would be very pretty if she ever loosened up and quit pulling her dark hair back into a tight face-pulling twist.

"Sorry Ms. Espinosa, but I know what I need to do now."

"I just don't understand your sudden interest in this college Danielle. It won't be able to offer you half the things these other universities can. Universities you've already been accepted into!"

"Look, haven't you always told us to pick a path and then stick to it. Well, that's what I'm doing. I have to go to this college Ms. Espinosa."

"Why?"

"That school holds my future. I need to go there. I have to do this. I don't know what else to say to convince you. I'm gonna get in there with or without your help. This is going to happen."

"You sure sound determined."

Ms. Espinosa looked at Dani skeptically. She knew the guidance counselor was trying to understand her. But this decision was one Dani couldn't fully explain. When she realized last summer she couldn't trace her birth mother out of the little college town in Georgia, she had a feeling that Shelby Perry was still there. Going to the nearby college would give Dani the time she needed to find and then reconnect with her birth mother. It was a long shot, but Dani was determined to take it. What did she have to lose?

~ ~ ~

Chelsea's replacement hoodie had now turned into a full-blown shopping spree. Dani checked her watch again. They had been looking at clothes for over two hours now. Dani slumped down in the dressing room chair and watched her sister try on outfit after outfit. Currently she was trying to decide between low cut, boot cut, straight leg, skinny or stretch jeans. After that Dani knew the decision would morph into blue washed, laundry white, indigo dark or classic fade. The styles, fit and colors were endless. Dani leaned her head back, closed her eyes and let out a long sigh.

"I know this isn't what we had planned Danielle."

Dani opened her eyes, twisted her head and looked at her mom who had sat down in the chair beside her.

"And yet here we are. As usual."

"I guess I should have told Chelsea we'd do this later. How about we go out shopping for your dorm items later this week? Just you and me."

"Whatever."

"C'mon Danielle, cut me some slack. I'm trying."

"Trying to appease Chelsea," Dani muttered.

"Honey, you know your sister is a force of nature. I promise to make this up to you."

Dani felt like she had heard the same excuses her whole life. She couldn't wait until she was the number one child. The only child. In one of her fantasies her birth mother had no other children and therefore gives Dani her undivided attention. Sure, it was a pipe dream, but dreams should be a little out there and fantastic, right?

"While we are here Danielle why don't you try on some new clothes too? Don't you want some new things to take to college?"

"I have plenty of clothes."

"I'm sure your new school will have dances and all kinds of socials. You need to be prepared."

Socials? What was this? The 1950's? But then a thought occurred to Dani. She did want a special outfit.

"You know what? I am gonna pick out some things mom."

"That sounds good sweetie. Pick out whatever you want."

For the next half hour Dani searched until she found a dark blue top and a fitted black skirt that looked nice on her. She decided this would be the outfit she would wear when she met her birth mother. The idea was almost overwhelming to her at this point. She had been working for years to make the idea a reality. Maybe she would go out to dinner with her birth mother in this outfit. Maybe not. It didn't really matter. Whatever they did would be just fine with her. At least she wouldn't have to share the moment with anyone else. On this day that sounded perfect to Dani.

Later that evening Dani was dealt another blow concerning her sister.

"Do I have to mom?"

"For the sixth time Danielle, yes. Chelsea needs a ride. We've already discussed this."

"But -"

"No 'buts' young lady! You know the rules. If you want to use the car, you must help out. Chelsea needs a ride to the movie theatre and you're already going out to meet Becca anyways."

"Fine!"

"And I expect you to pick your sister up on time Danielle!" said Elizabeth as Dani sulked down the hall.

Dani grabbed her jacket out of the foyer coat closet and yelled at Chelsea to hurry up. She had promised Becca she would meet her at the library around six and now she was going to be late thanks to her little sister.

"Chels! Let's go! *Now!*"

Chelsea came bounding down the stairs and the two girls bolted out the front door. Her sister was hyper as usual and Dani couldn't wait to drop her off.

"What time am I supposed to pick you up spazz?"

"Hey! Mom told you to stop calling me that!"

"Well, mom's not here is she?"

"I'm gonna tell her you're being mean to me and then you'll have your driving privileges suspended."

"Then who will drive you to the mall dork?"

"You just want to keep driving so you can go to the boring library with Becca. What are you doing there all the time anyways? You never come home with any books."

"That's none of your business," Dani snapped. "What time am I picking you up?"

"Nine. But don't worry if you're late. Jimmy is gonna be at the movies too! Carrie found out from Shelly who heard from Luke."

Jimmy was her sister's latest crush. Chelsea was practically bouncing in the passenger's seat. Her sister had unlimited energy. Dani could sit still in the same place for hours if she had a book or puzzle to entertain her.

"Doesn't Jimmy date Sophia?"

"For now," Chelsea sniffed.

So, her sister had a new conquest in mind. Dani rolled her eyes.

"You can stop judging me," snapped Chelsea.

Dani hadn't even realized her sister has seen her roll her eyes. She felt a little bad until Chelsea started talking again.

"Just because you never dated doesn't mean I shouldn't."

Her sister sounded resentful.

"I have too dated!" snapped Dani in defense.

"You mean that awkward loser from church? Puh-leeze! You guys didn't even do anything."

"We did too!"

"Oh yeah? Like what?"

"Like none of your business."

"I thought so" said Chelsea smugly.

Chelsea pulled out one of their mom's bright lipsticks from her mini back-pack and began applying it to her lips.

"Does mom know you have that?" asked Dani.

"Yes."

Chelsea was a brilliant liar. She could tell a fib without blinking an eye. In a strange way, Dani admired this talent of her sister's.

"Right," said Dani.

"Fine! I *borrowed* it. Don't tell her, ok?"

Dani shook he head and kept driving.

"I know what you think."

Dani glanced over at Chelsea.

"What do you mean?"

"You think I'm stupider than you. You know sometimes it's hard being your sister. Mom and Dad always want me to be more like you but I just can't. I can't be as boring as you Dani."

Dani was offended. She wasn't boring, just contained.

"What do you mean, Mom and Dad want you to be more like me?"

"They say it all the time to me. Why can't you be more like Dani? Like I want to sit for hours at the library with Becca doing who knows what."

Dani sat in dumbfounded silence for the next few blocks. She never knew her parents told Chelsea to behave more like her. If anything she always thought they wanted her to be more like Chelsea, more out-going and popular.

Irritated, probably by the silence, Chelsea continued.

"You never do anything fun and unexpected Dani. I don't know how you can be so boring. You'll probably go to college and just sit in your dorm room doin' nothing new."

The car finally approached the mall and Dani pulled up to the entrance to drop Chelsea off.

"Be waiting for me at nine Chels. Don't be late!"

"Yeah, yeah."

"Don't yeah-yeah me. Be here at nine."

"Have fun at the library dork."

"Later spazz."

Chelsea stuck her tongue out at her sister and hopped out of the car. She stuck her head back in the door and said, "You know, one day you're gonna miss me. One day you'll grow up, have a nerdy family of your own and realize you miss me."

"I highly doubt that. Go!"

Chelsea slammed the door hard and ran off into the movie theatre. Chelsea was wrong as usual thought Dani. She was about to do lots of new, exciting things her sister couldn't imagine. Wouldn't she be shocked when Dani called home one day with news about meeting her birth mother! Her little sister may have been clueless about many things, but she was right about one. Dani couldn't wait to have her own family. She just had to find them first.

Chapter Four

Alicia Part I

The alarm clock had beeped shrilly three different times in the past half hour. Each time long elegant fingers had reached out and hit the snooze button. Finally, the alarm accomplished its task on the fourth round as Alicia Williams sat up in bed and rubbed her eyes. She was so *tired*. Of course she had no one to blame but herself. She had spent all night watching old movies. She had started with *Roman Holiday* and ended with *Breakfast at Tiffany's*. It had been an Audrey night. Now she would be late for work.

A car alarm started blaring outside so Alicia shut the flimsy glass pane in her third-floor apartment bedroom and turned on the window unit air conditioner. It was only seven in the morning and already it was muggy. That was July in Washington DC though. She really wanted to climb into a cool shower, but since she was already running late she settled for splashing cold water on her face. As Alicia patted her face dry she appraised her reflection in the mirror. How was it possible for a black woman to have dark circles under her eyes? That just wasn't fair she thought.

Alicia tugged at her long braids trying to style them but finally gave up. She really needed someone to work on the mess that was her hair. Alicia fumbled with a bright red hair clip until she heard a snapping noise.

When she pulled the clip away from her head she saw that it had broken in two. That was just her luck. Although Alicia didn't believe in luck. She really should have though since she had so much *bad* luck.

"Screw it," she mumbled.

Alicia gathered everything into a twist and picked up a silver clip to hold the braids in place. She made a mental note that when her shift was over at work she would run next door to the new salon that opened a few months ago. Alicia always admired the hair of the women that left the salon. Whoever was running the place was good with ethnic hair. Even in a mostly black neighborhood such as this that could still be hard to find.

When she glanced at the clock she realized it was already seven forty-five. Where had the past forty-five minutes gone? Alicia grabbed her purse, house keys and made a dash for the door. The day had already started without her as her grandmother used to say. Alicia's grandmother had just about single handedly raised her. She could recall numerous mornings when her Gram had fussed about her getting up on time so she wouldn't be late for school. It always annoyed Alicia. She couldn't help she was a night owl. Morning people just didn't understand night owls. Alicia never had any desire to greet the dawn. What was the point?

She was grateful as she rushed out the door that her work was so close. Alicia was a teller for a bank. Her boss was a tough Hispanic lady. Anytime Alicia was even a smidge late for work she would get a lecture and she feared getting fired. Alicia couldn't afford to have that happen. She was trying to afford rent and utilities until a plan she had been working on paid out. Luckily the bank was only a few blocks away. Alicia flew down the street not bothering to stop at the coffee shop where she purchased croissants and coffee each morning. The caffeine hit would have to wait until lunch time.

A few minutes later Alicia arrived at the bank and began pulling her start up drawer together. She had made it with two minutes to spare but even this had earned her a raised eyebrow from the boss lady. The older woman just didn't like her thought Alicia ruefully. It was going to be a long day. Alicia's co-worker caught her eye and winked at her. Rico had been flirting with her casually for the past few months but Alicia just couldn't see them together. He was too pretty in his flashy suits and shiny gold-plated cuff links. Alicia preferred a manlier man. Maybe someone who worked with his hands.

The neighborhood that housed Alicia's new apartment and job existed on the fringe of DC. It wasn't kept up very well. Tax money from the capitol never seemed to find its way here. The roads had pot holes, street lights were cracked and there was one notorious housing tenement. It was a far cry from the tree lined street her Gram had raised her on. By the time Alicia was six she had been passed around from house to house. She had certainly never lived in a home. She lived with her parents until she was three. Her father had split that year. Alicia hadn't seen him since. Well, except for once when she thought she saw her father standing on a street corner, but really that could have been anybody. She had been on a tenth-grade school field trip to visit a local newspaper and it had been raining. The school bus window had been partially fogged. Still, he had looked like the man from her memories.

Five days after her fifth birthday her mother had been incarcerated for drugs and her Aunt Tuni had taken her in. "Aunt Tuni" wasn't really her aunt. She was one of her mother's friends. Alicia did not like living with Aunt Tuni. There were already way too many kids in her house. The older kids were mean and the house smelled funny. That was probably due to the many dogs Aunt Tuni owned. Alicia saw one dog, Buster, pee on the living room floor one day. No one bothered to clean it up.

Alicia's grandmother, Natasha Williams – Netty to all who knew her – had won a house from Save-A-Bunch Grocer. Netty always enjoyed shopping at the Save-A-Bunch Grocer. It was located in a nicer part of town than where she lived and Netty thought the produce section was much better and more abundant. The vegetables at the Save-A-Bunch Grocer were not covered in mold. There was some talk that the management at the Save-A-Bunch Grocer didn't want to award Netty the little blue house. This rumor made its way around Netty's church and all the folks who talked about it cried foul. There were whispers of racism. There were always whispers of racism. But Netty had kept her cool. Alicia's Gram always did. And sure enough the little blue house was awarded to Netty without so much as a fuss from the Save-A-Bunch Grocer big wigs. Those rumors had probably been all talk anyways. At least that's what Netty had told Alicia. Still, whenever her Gram told the story there was always a mischievous twinkle in her eye.

One day Netty came to Aunt Tuni's house and told Alicia to pack her bags. She would be moving into Netty's new house. Alicia was six. When she moved into the house Alicia noticed there were differences between this neighborhood and her old neighborhood. The new neighborhood had mostly white people living in it. Kids rode their bikes down the street and played in the road. Nobody hassled these children for playing in the streets.

These new streets also had a sense of calm instead of radiating an edgy energy. For a short while Alicia had fretted about this, felt as if she didn't fit in, and Netty had tried to reassure her granddaughter that this was normal. Alicia had remembered Aunt Tuni telling her that white folks didn't like their kind. Gram had waved away that kind of talk and asserted that there was no such thing as a white town or a black town – only towns. Alicia wasn't fooled. She had eyes and ears after all. But she soon settled in and came to love living on the sweet tree-lined street. Alicia even made a new friend, Vanessa. They lived just three streets apart so they could walk to each other's house.

The little blue house was now being rented out. Alicia didn't like the idea of living there without her grandmother. Netty had passed away a little over a year ago. Too many good memories and then the jumble of bad ones near the end clouded her mind there.

"Sister…Sister…can you help me with these checks?"

Alicia came out of her caffeine-free induced daze and realized Mrs. Murphy was standing in front of her. She was a petite, old black matron who called every other black woman 'Sister'. Once a month she would come in to the bank to deposit her retirement check and take a little cash out. Once Alicia felt sure she had a grey cat in her large purse. As if she had decided to take the pet on her errand run. Maybe they had stopped off at a café after and had lunch. The idea made Alicia smile. Besides, as her Gram used to say, you just never knew what someone else was going through. Alicia tried to carry this wisdom with her wherever she went. The world was so full of strange characters.

Alicia went through her day making deposits, dispensing change and troubleshooting account problems. Her days weren't exciting but after the drama of the past two years the monotonous day-to-day routine acted as a numbing agent that Alicia melted into, relied on. She needed the stability and the focus. If her plan was going to work she needed to make it through the next three years.

Alicia looked at the clock and realized only an hour had passed. She wished she was back in her tiny apartment watching classic movies or reading a book while the air conditioner kicked out cool waves of air. It was Alicia's Gram who had inadvertently sparked her love of reading years ago as a child. Netty was always collecting used books for the church literacy drive. One day Alicia was bored and she went through the book box and found a book with a pretty cover. It drew her in and a few hours later she had read all the pages inside. She was hooked. Each time Netty collected used books Alicia would see what she could pilfer from the stash. Yes, the books were for the needy, but Alicia had reasoned that she was just as needy.

As a teen she would take the bus to the large glossy book store in the rich part of town. Alicia loved that book store. You could order a cup of coffee and just walk around the store browsing and reading for hours. Once she figured out that local custom she quickly grew to adopt it. Who knew something called a Java Chip Frappuccino and brand-new books went together so well? It was like church with caffeine it was such a divine experience. She liked that the other book store patrons didn't judge her. They didn't call her "white girl" when they caught her with Shakespeare's *Sonnets* like some of her high school friends. No, these people didn't judge her choice of books or the color of her skin. Netty would have loved it. A color free town that was built of towering books.

When lunch time finally rolled around Alicia stepped out of the cool bank air onto the concrete sidewalk. Stale heat instantly washed over her body and Alicia found the first sandwich shop to duck into. At the counter while waiting for her food Alicia rubbed her neck. Not having her morning coffee had been a bad decision. A small TV above the serving window caught her attention and Alicia squinted up at it. Onscreen Tony and Maria from *West Side Story* were dancing and snapping their fingers. It's love at first sight for the movie characters and Alicia's chest constricted at the image.

~ ~ ~

Alicia pulled the bag of popcorn from the microwave and dropped it on the kitchen counter. The hot butter seeping from the top of the package burnt her finger so she sucked on it to get the throbbing to stop.

"What are you doing stupid?"

"I burned my damn finger!"

"Shhh! Don't let my pops hear you cussing. He'll ground us both!"

"Only my Gram can ground me," Alicia sniffed.

The two girls grabbed their popcorn, a two liter of Coke, a bag of Oreos and headed for Vanessa's bedroom. They had rented *West Side Story* for the sixth time in three months. Since Alicia had gotten up on time for school the past two weeks Netty had let her spend the night with Vanessa. They were supposed to go to the eighth-grade spring dance, but at the last minute they decided to ditch and rent *West Side Story* once again. Vanessa had gotten her love of classic movies from her mother who had made her watch them with her as a little girl. Alicia hadn't seen any of these movies and had grown fascinated by them. They were so romantic but Alicia doubted these things happened in real life.

Alicia had wanted to go to the spring dance, but Vanessa had broken up with Ryan and didn't want to see him. Why hadn't anyone told Alicia the eighth grade was much more drama filled than seventh grade?

"See Maria?" asked Vanessa. "I'm gonna look like her one day."

"Yeah, I could see that."

Vanessa had the same coloring as Natalie Wood. All dark hair, olive skin and big brown doe eyes. She was the perfect, petite Latina girl. Her parents had immigrated from Colombia when she was just a baby.

Vanessa playfully grabbed the bag of Oreo's away from Alicia and plopped down on the bed to watch the movie. They had been best friends ever since Alicia had moved into the blue house with her grandmother. One day Alicia had been reading a book on the front porch when Vanessa had ridden her bike onto Gram's lawn to find out who she was.

"Anyways, one day Ryan will regret I caught him sucking Debbie's ugly face off underneath the bleachers during P.E.!"

"Well, that is how she got her nickname, Suck Face Debs."

Vanessa reached over and pulled a thin pink book out from under her mattress.

"Whazz thwat?" asked Alicia, her mouth full of popcorn.

"I'll tell you if you stop hogging all the popcorn!"

Alicia shoved the bag of popcorn towards Vanessa and pouted.

"Oh please girl! That move only works on Kevin. He wants you, you know."

"He does not," said Alicia glumly. "Kevin took Melissa to the dance."

"Ali-Bee, Ali-Bee. So naïve to the ways of the world."

"Says the ho with the Barbie book."

"It's not a Barbie book! This is my new journal."

"A diary?" Alicia rolled over onto her back and laughed. "What are you, five?"

"No stupid! It is a *journal*. Not a diary! I'm going to record all my secret love affairs in here. You just wait and see."

"So you have what, half a page filled so far?"

"You little bitch!"

Both girls laughed then proceeded to imagine all the wonderful and glamorous adult things that could fill up the journal as Maria and Tony danced and snapped their fingers. As usual the girls snapped their fingers along to the musical.

~ ~ ~

After high school Netty had helped pay Alicia's way through community college so she could obtain an associate's degree. Once that was complete Alicia had dreamed of then being accepted into Howard University. But once Gram had become ill and needed all her extra money for doctor bills, medication and hospital stays, Alicia had put the associate's degree on hold. She took a part-time job at the Save-A-Bunch Grocer and helped care for Netty. Her social life had ceased to exist. That hadn't bothered Alicia too much as she wasn't dating anyone and she still had her best friend Vanessa. Plus, she wanted to take care of the woman who had taken her in as a little girl when no one had wanted her. Taking care of Netty was a way of paying her back for all the love and kindness she had always showed her.

Now all that had changed. Alicia was on her own and had to find a way to make ends meet. It had been tough at first. Netty didn't have much to leave her except the blue house, her old station wagon and a small checking account. Alicia quickly realized the part-time job at Save-A-Bunch Grocer wouldn't be enough to pay the bills. She needed to get a full-time job. That's when she had seen the advertisement for the teller job at the bank. It was thirty-minutes from her house so she would have to commute each day. Alicia hoped the old, worn down station wagon was up to the task.

Even though it was exciting to get the teller job Alicia knew this could be the decision that would keep her from going to Howard University and getting a degree. The thought made her sad. She never wanted to slide back into the life she had lived before Netty had rescued her. Alicia felt sure the way to do this was to get a degree and then get a nice paying job afterwards. But she couldn't afford to pay bills on the blue house and save for college. That would take forever.

On the day Alicia had went back for her second interview at the bank she got the job. When she was walking back to her car she saw a sign in a window a few streets over advertising a cheap apartment. Suddenly Alicia knew how she could pay the blue house bills, take the full-time teller job and save for college. She would rent the blue house until she could move back in and afford all the bills, probably sometime after she graduated. In the meantime, she would save up the rent money for her Howard University fees. The money she made at the bank would pay her living expenses at the small apartment and pay for her last few credits at the community college. She figured she could take evening classes at the community college after work to finish up her associate's degree.

In the space of three weeks Alicia had rented the house to the Phan family, packed up her life and moved into the cheap apartment near work. Most days Alicia missed the nice blue house. The apartment had no central air, only window units that were noisy. The bathroom had no tub but instead had a shower with only five minutes' worth of hot water per day. About once a month she would find a roach in her kitchenette which grossed her out. Her bedroom ceiling had water damage. Every night she went to sleep staring up at a big brown blob. Alicia longed for her light peach bedroom in Gram's house. But she couldn't return just yet. Alicia had to stick to her plan and everything would work out. At least, that's what she kept telling herself. Alicia told herself each day to hope for the best, that Gram was watching over her and everything would be alright.

~ ~ ~

The back door of the bank buzzed signaling a delivery. The boss lady told Alicia to go take care of it so she left her cash drawer for a moment. She didn't really like answering the back door for deliveries. Alicia thought the men who delivered to the bank were creepy, especially the guy who delivered their ink toner supplies. He always leered at her and talked to her chest, never to her face. As Alicia unlocked the door, ready to face the worst, she was pleasantly surprised when a tall man with smooth ebony skin entered. He was handsome and a bit exotic looking with sharp cheekbones and full lips.

"Good afternoon! Where would you like these?"

"These?" asked Alicia, staring at the stranger like a star struck teenager.

The man chuckled and it was a deep, pleasant sound.

"The boxes?"

"Oh, I'm sorry, yes the boxes. Just, just place them over there."

As the gentleman was setting the heavy boxes in place Alicia quickly adjusted her hair clip and tugged her top down to straighten it. As she did this Alicia noticed she had gotten a small mustard stain on her ivory blouse. A remnant from lunch she thought ruefully trying to hide the yellow stain with her arm. As he unloaded the last two boxes from his dolly she noticed his brown uniform fit him in all the right places. Why did she have to look so craptacular today of all days? Oh right, because she had stayed up late and then woken up late. Alicia mentally smacked her forehead with an imaginary palm. This was the most handsome man she had seen in a long time.

As he left the facility Alicia told the man to have a nice day then said the exact same thing not even ten seconds later. The man chuckled again and left in his delivery truck. Alicia rested her head on the closed back door completely embarrassed by her behavior. She had dreaded going to the door because of creepy men and in turn she had behaved like a creep. It was no wonder she hadn't had a date in two years. Acting like this she doubted she would have another date this century. Was this day never going to end?

After work Alicia stopped to get a pizza slice to go from the hole in the wall pizzeria a few streets over. All they had was a serving window and two cheap plastic tables with chairs out on the sidewalk if you wanted to stay and eat. No one ever stayed to eat. While waiting for her order to come up she suddenly remembered being here a year ago.

Right out of high school Vanessa had followed Alicia to the community college. Both girls had signed up for their first classes together. It had been a special and exciting day. The start of their adult lives. While Alicia had opted for general studies Vanessa had entered the dental hygienist program. Her friend really had a knack for it too. But shortly after Alicia had dropped out to take care of Gram, Vanessa dropped out also. At the time Vanessa was living with her boyfriend Dwayne on this side of town.

To this day Alicia still didn't understand why Vanessa had dropped out of the dental hygienist program. Her parents had agreed to pay the tuition while she lived with Dwayne. How many parents would do that? They loved Vanessa and just wanted what was best for her. Of course, they didn't like Dwayne too much. Alicia couldn't really blame them. Dwayne was sketchy. It was more him than Vanessa that had triggered her memory.

Alicia had been taking a rare break from caring for Gram and had decided to get pizza. As she had stood outside in the line for the to-go window she saw Vanessa and Dwayne exit the bar across the street. Alicia had noticed that Vanessa had been drinking a lot lately. She had been meaning to talk to Vanessa about all the binge drinking but Alicia hadn't had any free time so far. She had so much to do between caring for Gram and working her cashier job.

When Alicia had looked back over at the bar again she saw Vanessa suddenly smack Dwayne across the face. Dwayne grabbed Vanessa's arms tightly and had shaken her roughly in retaliation. Alicia forgot all about her pizza order and rushed across the street. She wanted to get to Vanessa and make sure she was alright. When Alicia approached Vanessa, her best friend seemed shocked and embarrassed to see her.

"Come on 'Nessa, let's get out of here," Alicia had pleaded.

Vanessa had tears streaming down her face. Her cheek also looked red and swollen, like someone had hit her. Vanessa stared hard at Dwayne.

"She's outta her damn mind!" he growled. "Get that bitch outta here 'Licia!"

Vanessa started to move toward Dwayne but Alicia grabbed her arm and tugged her back. Just then Lauren Ortiz came out of the bar and called for Dwayne. Vanessa glared for a moment at the curvy girl who stood in the doorway of the bar, then turned abruptly away, and started walking fast down the street. Alicia had to walk briskly to keep up with her. Vanessa refused to talk about what had happened so Alicia had taken Vanessa to her parent's home for the night. Alicia assumed it was just another spat between the emotional couple. Vanessa and Dwayne often argued.

Looking back Alicia wished she had forced Vanessa to tell her what had happened that night. If she had maybe things would be different. Maybe Vanessa would still be here.

~ ~ ~

Alicia had already combed the help wanted section of the newspaper once, but she was looking over it again to make sure she hadn't missed any jobs she would qualify for. Since Gram's passing Alicia had come to realize that she would blow through what little savings she had been left paying all the bills to keep the house going. She just couldn't afford it on her small Save-A-Bunch Grocer paycheck. At least she had Vanessa with her tonight. That was a blessing indeed, as her Gram would have said. Vanessa had fought with her boyfriend Dwayne yet again and had come over to spend the evening. Vanessa said it was best to give Dwayne some space when he was in one of his moods. Alicia was pretty sure she never wanted to date a man who had "moods". She really couldn't figure out what Vanessa saw in the creep.

Vanessa had crept up on Alicia as she scanned the newspaper. She wrapped her arms around Alicia's shoulders and gave her a squeeze hug.

"Stop staring at that newspaper Ali-Bee. I made us a big pot of spaghetti just the way Gram made it."

Alicia patted Vanessa's hand.

"Thanks 'Nessa."

Vanessa set a plate out for Alicia on the small kitchen table and the two friends ate in silence for a little while. Alicia was so drained she didn't know if she was coming or going lately.

"I feel like there is something I wanted to talk to you about, but I swear I can't remember," Alicia sighed.

"It's ok Ali-Bee. Just eat. I know it's hard on you. You know, with Gram being gone."

Alicia merely nodded. She really missed her grandmother. She wasn't sure how she had been getting though each day quite frankly. Vanessa had been a life saver lately.

"You can stay here as long as you like, you know 'Nessa?"

"Thanks, but...well, I'll need to go home to Dwayne tomorrow. If I don't he'll be unhappy."

"Yeah, heaven forbid he be unhappy." Alicia rolled her eyes as the sarcasm dripped off her tongue.

Vanessa frowned and looked like she might start crying. Alicia stared at her with concern, but then Vanessa smiled at her suddenly. There was something strange and *off* about Vanessa tonight. It was just a flash, but it unnerved Alicia. But as soon as she saw the strange behavior, it vanished. Her mood was like mercury. Now she just saw her bubbly best friend Vanessa. For the first time in weeks, maybe even months, Alicia looked at Vanessa. *Really* looked at her. She looked tired and thin. When had this happened? Alicia decided to file it away and bring it up later when she wasn't exhausted.

"You know, I see help wanted signs posted in Dwayne's, er, our neighborhood all the time. I'll start getting contact numbers for you. I know it would be a bit of a drive, but if it helps you save the house..."

Vanessa trailed off, suddenly uncertain.

"Thanks 'Nessa," said Alicia quickly, to assure Vanessa her help was appreciated.

Vanessa smiled and after dinner the two friends watched *Double Indemnity*, the way they had so many times before, cuddled up in big fluffy blankets snuggled together on the couch. Mid-way through the movie Alicia fell off to sleep.

When she awoke early the next morning, still on the couch, pale sunlight streamed through the living room window. She spotted a note on the coffee table. It was from Vanessa. She had gone back to Dwayne's. The blue house was quiet once more.

~ ~ ~

Alicia tried to shake off the memories of Vanessa and Dwayne after her quick dinner of two slices of cheese pizza. She had washed it down with a soda and then headed to the new hair salon. She was determined that if the cute delivery guy came back the least she could do was have some nice locks and a shirt without a mustard stain. Alicia entered the salon without realizing it was already closed. Even the dimmed lights didn't clue her in.

"Hello?" Alicia called from the front counter.

A beautiful woman stepped out from behind a curtained room. She was tall and attired in a bold zebra patterned dress that clung to her curvy hips. She had waves of caramel hair that spilled over her shoulders in a glorious display.

"I'm sorry, but Nubia Hair is closed."

"Oh." Alicia's face fell and crumpled.

"Now, now. It's just hair. I'm sure if you come back tomorrow -"

Alicia pulled her hair out of the large silver clip and let if fall around her shoulders. The woman gaped at her hair while stopping mid-sentence.

"Who did *that* to you?"

"Bernadette over at Weave Design." Alicia tugged at her braids nervously. She was embarrassed this elegant woman was seeing her messy hair.

"Mmm-hmm, I can see that. I seem to be fixing all her clients hair. That girl can't put in a decent weave for nothin'!"

Alicia must have looked either pathetic or desperate, or a combination of both, because the elegant woman let out a sigh and then motioned for her to come back. Alicia smiled her gratitude. She truly didn't want to face another day with bad hair.

"You just have a seat here, uh…"

"Oh, Alicia. Alicia Williams. I work at the bank next door."

"I'm Odessa Bryant. I own Nubia Hair. I hope you won't mind but my feet are killing me child."

Odessa kicked off her staggering four inch fuchsia heels and slipped on a pair of fuzzy leopard print slippers.

"Now, that weave has to go girl."

For the next two hours Odessa worked diligently on Alicia's hair. She had long maroon hued nails but not once did they prick Alicia's scalp or face. Bernadette scratched her face up all the time with her fake talons. Odessa also worked quickly and quietly. Alicia was used to hairdressers running their mouths non-stop. But Odessa was content to sway and sing along to the music coming out of the speakers perched high in the corners of the salon. Alicia didn't recognize the music at all.

"What…what kind of music is this?"

Odessa smiled at her in the mirror and laughed.

"It's country music. I can't play it much during the day. Could you imagine what all those hens would say?"

No wonder Alicia didn't recognize it. She thought only white people listened to country music. Odessa laughed again as she noticed the puzzled look on Alicia's face.

"I can tell what you're thinking."

"You can?"

"Sure. You're thinking, only white folks listen to country music."

Alicia's eyes grew wide as she stared back at Odessa in the mirror. Odessa proceeded to pull out a pair of shiny scissors and started cutting away at her hair.

"Well, truth be told, I did pick this habit up from my ex-husband. My third ex to be exact."

"You've been married three times?"

"Oh no! Four times," Odessa smiled. "My third husband was half black, half white. I guess the white genes determined his taste in music."

Odessa cackled as she ran her fingers through Alicia's de-braided hair.

"But you know what, I really like this music. Sometimes it's peppy and other times sad and soulful. Lots of broken hearts and rodeos."

Odessa hummed along to the music again until she finally said, "My last husband passed away two years ago. He was from Germany. Can you imagine that? I was crazy about him!"

For the next half hour Odessa told Alicia about her four ex-husbands. But somewhere along the way Alicia mentally checked out. Her mind wandered and dredged up painful memories. Why now, at this moment, she couldn't really say. Maybe she felt safe in Odessa's quiet, dark shop. She hadn't realized it but she had started crying and large tear drops ran down Alicia's tired looking face. She looked up when she realized Odessa had swiveled her chair around to face her and was gently shaking her.

"Alicia? Alicia! What's wrong?"

Alicia realized with a start that she was crying. Odessa handed her a tissue so she could dry her eyes. After she did that she blew her nose loudly.

"Odessa, I am so sorry! Shit! How embarrassing. I didn't mean to -"

"Shhh…Shhh…tell me what's wrong."

Alicia took a deep breath and then looked up at Odessa.

"I…I recently lost someone. And I'm just…I'm just really confused."

"I know. You told me when I first started on your hair. You said your grandmother passed away about a year ago."

Alicia shook her head; First yes, then no.

"She did. But then two months later my best friend Vanessa…she committed suicide."

The last part came out in a whisper. With her admission complete Alicia stared to cry once again.

~ ~ ~

Alicia had been killing time near the magazine rack when her grandmother finally tracked her down in Save-A-Bunch Grocer.

"Alicia Bertrise Williams!"

Alicia started and dropped the magazine that was in her hand.

"I have told you a thousand times not to run off on me! Have I not?"

"Yes Gram."

Alicia put the Teen Beat magazine back on the rack and followed her grandmother to the checkout lanes. They had almost made it to the front of the store when a lady with a squeaky shopping cart turned down their isle blocking them. Alicia let out a soft groan and Netty placed a firm hand on her shoulder to let her know that would be enough.

The older woman standing before them was Anita Russell. Alicia thought she dressed weird and smelled kinda funny. Today was no exception. Mrs. Russell wore a long, red straight skirt, an orange blouse with pink polka dots and royal blue pumps. She also had a purple wool coat tossed into her cart. All the color coordination, or lack thereof, wouldn't have been *that* bad – if it wasn't summer and ninety-eight degrees outside. Besides the winter coat Mrs. Russell also had her cart piled high with soup cans, crackers and a fifteen-pound bag of dog food. Mrs. Russell hadn't owned a dog in four years.

Alicia had been examining all this as Netty and Anita chatted. Near the end Mrs. Russell turned her attention to Alicia. She groaned again – except this time only in her head. She did not want to face her grandmother's wrath. That would consist of dish washing chores on top of her other chores for a month.

"Well, aren't you getting big Lisa."

Alicia opened her mouth to correct Mrs. Russell, but Netty gave her a look that would have made the devil shut his mouth.

"She's in the sixth grade this year," said Netty proudly.

"Is that so?" asked Mrs. Russell.

"Yes ma'am," said Alicia.

Once they had finally made it outside with their bagged groceries Netty calmly turned to Alicia.

"You need to learn to have patience with Anita," she said.

"But she is so weird Gram!"

"I know that's what you think, but have you ever stopped and wondered *why* she acts that way?"

Alicia thought about this while enjoying the sucker Netty had bought her at the register. Alicia just thought she was some tripped out old lady. Someone who had no color coordination skills? Maybe Mrs. Russell was color-blind? Alicia realized her grandmother was waiting for an answer so she shook her head.

"Anita lost her husband a few years ago and her health has been in decline ever since. It hadn't been so good before when her oldest daughter died in that car wreck five years ago. The other day Thelma caught Anita out in the middle of the street in her nightgown and slippers."

They had finally reached Netty's station wagon. As they loaded the paper bags into the back Netty continued.

"I'm going to tell you something Miss Alicia and I want you to remember this. No matter what anyone looks like on the outside, you never know what's goin' on inside. I want you to think about that. The next time we run into Anita you keep that in mind.

"You just think she dresses funny, smells bad and acts weird. But there's a reason for that. You can't ever tell what someone's goin' through or been through just by giving them the eye. You understand?"

Alicia stuck her sucker in her mouth and nodded as if she understood. But really, she didn't. Not yet at least.

Chapter Five

Cynthia Part I

Cynthia was walking home from work when the street lamp above gave a sudden flicker and went out. She was now plunged in darkness and still four blocks away from her apartment. Cynthia quickened her pace and looked around nervously. Usually she thought nothing of walking home alone late at night after work even though she lived in an old factory district. Cynthia had been a tomboy growing up. She had played soccer and softball in high school. She had an older brother who had taught her to throw a punch and break a nose. Cynthia could take care of herself. But at that very moment a cat darted out from behind a rusty waste bin causing Cynthia to jump and let out a shrill shriek. She clutched her chest, shook her head and told herself to get a grip.

Just fifteen minutes earlier Cynthia had been enjoying some peace and quiet at the office. She had been at the end of another long day, her co-workers already gone. Cynthia had slipped her heels off, slid down into her padded grey chair and propped her legs up on the corner of the polished wood desk. She still had two more items to complete on her daily to-do list before she could head home. Most of her co-workers would have been displeased to wile away an evening in this fashion, but not Cynthia. She worked for Pierce's Solutions, a mid-level ad agency. Cynthia often used this quiet time to contemplate how and when she could make the move to a premiere agency.

As she reviewed the latest budget report for an ongoing project the only sound she could discern was the faint hum of a vacuum cleaner coming from another wing of the fifth-floor offices her company occupied. This was the only time Cynthia could be alone in her office as she shared it with another junior associate, Holli Marshall. Or as Cynthia thought of her, Little Miss Perfect Boobs. Cynthia had silently given her this nickname because at one of those awful office-workshop-bonding-retreats Holli had laid down on the floor for a seminar titled 'Relaxation 101' but her boobs had not. They had stayed perfectly upright which led Cynthia to believe they were perfectly fake.

Holli was much admired around the office as she was tall, leggy, had blown-out blonde hair that obviously came from a bottle, and oh yes, the boobs. She had also matriculated from an Ivy League university. Why this inspired so much awe was beyond Cynthia, especially seeing as how she often had to correct Little Miss Perfect Boobs' copy mistakes. Shouldn't an Ivy Leaguer be correcting her mistakes? Not that she ever made those Cynthia noted to herself with a curt nod of her head. She may have graduated from a no-name college but she could write copy like nobody's business.

Cynthia pulled out a small mirror from her desk top drawer and held it up in her left hand to study her face. The tips of her right fingers lightly touched the area under her eyes where she noticed the beginning of dark shadows forming. It had *definitely* been a long day. Still Cynthia didn't think she looked all that bad. She had large soft brown doe eyes and cute little bow lips that produced dimples when she smiled. Cynthia brushed her long curly chestnut brown hair away from her face and examined her forehead. She was always waiting for wrinkles to form there. Probably because she always caught herself frowning at the computer screen when she was concentrating on writing. Cynthia always tried to make herself smile to erase the frown lines but that just looked utterly goofy so she would go back to frowning.

She turned her face to the right, then to the left, and then back again. For a brief moment she contemplated getting Botox, then pictured a long needle filled with poison in her mind. Cynthia mentally cringed and quickly shoved the mirror back into her desk drawer. Who was she turning into? Little Miss Perfect Boobs? Please.

Cynthia woke up each morning to a new day yet in her work it didn't seem to matter. The work day would contain the exact same problems from the day before; the only thing that changed was the client. Cynthia spent her days at the agency dutifully pulling necessary copy information from impatient clients, soothing graphic designer temperamental psyches and artistic frustrations, hustling printing vendors for better prices and faster turn-around time and stroking her bosses' egos. Cynthia was often requested by and worked with Pierce Goddard, the founder of the ad agency, yet she knew this didn't ensure her a place at the top. Especially when co-workers like Holli flirted with Mr. Goddard all day.

Cynthia often had to remember that she was exactly where she wanted to be. Hadn't she dreamed of a career like this when she was toiling her way through that no-name college while waitressing on the side? Cynthia would remind herself that she was only twenty-eight. She had plenty of time to wait for the right moment to make her move and jump to a big agency with her own private corner office.

After she had finished her last email Cynthia yawned and stretched. She shut down her computer, gathered her bags, flicked off the lights and headed for the elevator. As the door slid open her cell phone gave a sharp ring in the confined space.

"Hello?"

"Hey babe! You still at the office?"

The caller was Cynthia's fiancé Michael. He sounded slightly drunk.

"I'm just leaving."

"Great! Head down here pronto!"

"Michael -" Cynthia started to protest.

"No, no, Listen! Derek and Justin challenged me to sing that stupid song that comes on the radio all the time. You know the one, the one that has that…"

Cynthia's fiancée was currently getting plastered at that tacky karaoke bar down the street from their offices. Michael was a successful salesman for a start-up media company that occupied the floor directly below Pierce's Solutions. She hated karaoke and had insisted this morning that he go with some office buddies and enjoy himself later that evening. Now he wanted her to join in the festivities, but Cynthia was tired. She wanted the night away from Michael. Wasn't that the point of a boy's night out? No girls.

Cynthia sighed and interrupted Michael's description of the silly songs he had been singing while knocking back long necks and shots.

"I'm going home and going straight to bed."

"Why not go to my place and I'll meet you there in an hour?"

"Because I was there all night last night. I'll talk to you in the morning, ok?"

"Babe -"

"Have fun," Cynthia interrupted. "Tell the boys hello for me. Good night Michael."

He knew when Cynthia wasn't going to cave.

"Alright Cindy-Lou," Michael slurred begrudgingly, using the stupid nickname he had given her because she was southern.

Cynthia turned her mobile off once she exited the building. She most definitely did not want a booze fed two am booty call to wake her up later. A light summer breeze caressed her bare legs and she thought about how good it felt. It reminded Cynthia of the summers she had spent growing up in a sea-side tourist town in South Carolina. She now worked in a sprawling city several hours away.

Cynthia was still unsettled from the street lights going out so she continued her fast pace home. Cynthia tried to sort out why she had been wound so tight for the past few months. Work had been insanely busy, but she begrudgingly admitted her personal life was becoming more and more complex. Cynthia had been engaged to Michael for seven months and she often wondered if she had been too impulsive in accepting his offer. When he had pulled out an emerald cut ring during a last-minute ski trip it hadn't been all that hard to refuse. Little Miss Perfect Boob's eyes had bugged out when she first saw the impressive rock in the white gold setting.

Cynthia had met Michael two years ago at a company party. They had hit it off right away even though they came from very different backgrounds. He was a displaced Northerner enjoying the abundant cash he had been able to accumulate in the Southern economy. They casually dated for a few weeks then transitioned into a relationship. Cynthia still wasn't exactly sure how or when that had happened. Everything with Michael was always such a blur.

At first the relationship was exciting. But isn't that always the way at the beginning? Michael had broad shoulders that he covered with crisp Brooks Brothers dress shirts and an expensive haircut. They would meet mid-afternoon on the stairwell landing between their office floors and steal a few moments of company time for themselves. The bland grey stairwell was their backdrop for quickie make-out sessions that left Cynthia's hair mussed and her lip gloss smeared. Holli would cast a satirical eye her way whenever Cynthia would return to their shared office and fix her wayward gloss.

Now that the merge – Cynthia's label for her impending betrothal next spring; it sounded horribly Wall Street but how could that be helped? – was looming she was beginning to worry. A lot. Everything seemed to be moving much too fast for her comfort. Her stomach would clinch into knots whenever she thought about *the merge*.

Michael wanted her to move in with him at the end of the year when her lease was up. He lived in Alto Towers, a newly constructed high rise on Graystone Avenue near all the trendy shops. His apartment complex was all glass, chrome and marble. Cold. There was also a formal doorman that made Cynthia uncomfortable. She didn't feel it was necessary for anyone to open a simple door with such pomp while declaring her last name:

Miss Taylor. She didn't even live in the complex for heaven's sake! Cynthia had been raised in a middle-class home on the proverbial tree lined street. Doormen had been relegated to movies and nighttime legal TV series' until she had started dating Michael.

Cynthia was not sold on the idea of vacating her apartment once the lease was up. She lived in a tiny space in a converted candy factory. Everything about her building was pleasantly worn with its faded bricks, wood and plaster. Warm. It pleased Cynthia to think her miniscule living room and galley kitchen once produced sugary treats that had been hidden in brightly colored wrappers. She kept a bouquet of large pastel suckers in a lavender coffee mug on the sill of her kitchen window as a tribute.

The other day while cleaning her flatware she had absentmindedly stared at the spoon in her hand for a good five minutes. During that time she was trying to imagine this spoon residing at Alto Towers. Cynthia couldn't get the two images to mesh at all. Her flatware had yellow roses climbing up the stem. Michael's flatware was silver and functional. Flatware didn't need yellow roses climbing up the stems in order to function, but the sight was cheerful to Cynthia. The utensils had been one of her first purchases when she had moved into the old building.

Cynthia was now a block from the candy factory front door when the light spilling out from the Smithson Fish Market caught her eye. The owner had been remodeling the interior for the past two months and she noticed he was near completion. Cynthia halted her brisk pace to catch her breath and look in the window when something made her stop breathing altogether. She stared open-mouthed at the blue-grey sailboat model hanging from the ceiling near the display window. Cynthia had spent the best summer of her life when she was nineteen on a boat that looked exactly like the one gleaming in the light. A flood of memories suddenly washed over her.

~ ~ ~

Cynthia felt sympathy for her mother. She could tell her mom was distressed and trying to adjust to all the changes that were rapidly falling upon her head like sharp-edged bricks. Both Cynthia and her older brother

Charlie had returned home from college for their summer break. She had just completed her sophomore year and Charlie was now a graduate. Balloons and banners still hung around the ranch, a testament to the occasion.

Charlie had announced the morning after the graduation party that he would not be attending law school in the fall as originally planned. Instead he had signed on with the Peace Corps and would be leaving at the end of August for a tour in Paraguay. Charlie had also broken off his engagement to Sheila Lucas, who lived two blocks away. Her family always attended the Taylor's New Year's Eve party. No doubt that would be an awkward occasion this year.

While this Earth shattering news was being delivered, Cynthia slipped out of the house unnoticed and went to see Tina, her hairdresser. When she returned later in the day eight inches of her thick chestnut brown hair had been chopped off. Cynthia's hair now lay in bouncy curls above her shoulders. Her mother almost fainted when she saw how short it was. The final blow for Mrs. Taylor came when she asked her daughter why in the world she had cut off her beautiful locks. Cynthia had so far avoided telling her mother she would not be waitressing at The Pizza Palace as she had in the past. This summer Charlie had helped his baby sister acquire a job painting boats at The Landing, thus the necessary haircut. Cynthia had always waitressed, even during college in the evenings after class, and she wanted to do something new. Something different.

"Cynthia Taylor, you most certainly will not be painting boats all summer long out in that sweltering heat!" her mother declared in an exasperated manner.

"But mom, I -"

"No, no arguments! And now you've gone and cut off all your beautiful curls!"

"Mom, sis isn't like other girls. She plays soccer with all the neighborhood boys for heaven's sake! She can do this job. Can't ya sis?"

Charlie playfully nudged her with his elbow and winked at her. Cynthia opened her mouth to affirm her brother's statement, but took one look at her mother and closed it shut. Mrs. Taylor looked like she was about to burst into tears at any moment. She had already spent all morning sobbing over Charlie's decisions that she considered impulsive and inconsiderate. So Cynthia summoned all her courage and did what she always did during moments like these. She ran to her father.

It only took Cynthia a few minutes of pleading, a flash of her big doe eyes and she was given clemency to paint boats. She let her father worry about smoothing things over with her mother. He had a knack for it and she didn't waste another moment dwelling on the matter. She was much too excited about starting her new job tomorrow.

Cynthia had enjoyed her first exhausting week painting boats. The other guys had relegated her to trim work but she didn't mind. She was glad to be free of customers who whined for this or that and then shorted her waitress tip. Cynthia was out in the sunshine and fresh air all day. She didn't have to wear a stupid uniform of red and black checkers. Her work ensemble now consisted of cut-off jean shorts, tank tops and Chuck Taylors. Cynthia's tan had never looked better and her freckles washed over her nose and cheeks in a pleasing way. Life was good she thought late one Friday afternoon. And then, even though five minutes earlier she hadn't thought it possible, life got even better because she saw *him*.

Although Cynthia didn't know who *he* was. She had just finished cleaning a trim brush when the most handsome guy Cynthia had ever seen walked across the bright green lawn near the boat slips and greeted Charlie in a knowing and friendly manner. They gave each other one of those ridiculously complicated handshakes men often give each other. They chatted for a few moments then Charlie gestured over to where Cynthia stood. When he turned to look at her Cynthia realized she had been staring open mouthed at the striking mystery man with the shoulder length black hair. She quickly looked down and tried to turn away but somehow tripped over her very own sneakers and dropped her trim brush in a bucket of thinner. Cynthia hurried away with a burning face but not before she heard the two of them laughing.

Cynthia took her time cleaning up in the female employee washroom so she wouldn't run into her brother and his friend again. She had embarrassed herself enough for one day. Frustrated with herself for being such an idiot she swung open the door of the washroom with extra vigor and it immediately collided with something on the other side. As the door swung back into place Cynthia realized she had smacked Charlie's friend square in the face. He was bent over holding his nose. She froze where she was standing and stared at him in complete horror. After a long agonizing moment he straightened up and fixed Cynthia with his striking blue eyes. Then he let his hand drop and smiled at her. She let out a breath of relief, happy she hadn't injured him. He didn't even have a bloody nose.

"What were you doing standing *there*?" Cynthia asked, still in mild shock.

"I was waiting for you."

And then to Cynthia's astonishment he began to laugh. She was so relieved that she let out a shaky laugh to try and ease her nerves.

"I'm Evan Fischer," he said, as he held out a hand to her. "Your brother asked me to give you a ride home. He had to leave early."

Cynthia stared up at him – as he was about six inches taller than her – dumbfounded. She hadn't even realized she had placed her hand into his and had left it there. His hand felt warm and strong. Cynthia quickly decided that she never wanted her hand back. Really, who needs two hands anyways? She would learn to make due with just one. That was when she realized Evan was laughing at her again. Cynthia pulled her hand away, regretful to have it back once more.

In the weeks that followed Cynthia would learn that Evan had spotted her on her first day of work and had been intrigued by the petite girl who was painting boats with the boys. He had asked Charlie to introduce him one afternoon, but she had run away. Evan had then pleaded with Charlie to let him drive Cynthia home. Charlie hadn't objected because he had never seen his sister stare at anyone the way she had stared at Evan. The only thing he had ever seen her stare at with as much appreciation was a soccer ball.

Evan had worked at The Landing for the past six summers. His grandfather had sailed all his life and had taught his grandson everything he knew about boats. Evan was crazy about boats. He refurbished and repaired those docked at The Landing when owners requested the service. This coming fall would be his senior year at college. Evan was quick witted, funny and had an easy-going air about him that made him extremely likeable.

After the work day was done Cynthia and Evan would meet up and spend the balmy evenings getting to know each other. There were lots of things to do at The Landing after hours that kept them plenty busy. Not only did The Landing house hundreds of local and visiting boats whose owners were spending their vacation in the touristy South Carolina town, there was also a restaurant, a game room with an adjacent snack bar, an outdoor pavilion where bands played on Friday and Saturday nights, and a mini golf course. One particular docked boat, situated in a slip in a nearly empty cove, was Cynthia's favorite attraction at The Landing. This boat was older, in need of repair, and was painted a faded blue-grey color that was peeling off in numerous places. This sailboat belonged to Evan.

Evan spent most of his free time working on the run-down boat he had bought with the money he had saved over the past few years. He had purchased the dilapidated twenty-three-foot Ranger sailboat, built in the late seventies, from an estate sale in North Carolina this past spring. Evan was determined to use his skills and knowledge to return the shoddy sailboat back to her former glory. He knew if he put enough TLC into the boat it would become a jewel that would be able to ride the rough seas with him. Sometimes Cynthia was jealous of the way Evan would stare at his most prized possession, until one fine evening when she realized her was staring down at her with the same intensity and wonder. Cynthia wasn't sure what she had done to inspire such a look, but it made her pulse quicken.

That night Evan had pulled her into his arms tightly and swayed with her on the soft grass as a blues band in the pavilion played songs about love gone wrong and broken dreams left at some crossroads. Cynthia had no clue what they were singing about and didn't care. Evan smelled like a heavenly mix of soap and sun. Not even the most expensive cologne would have intoxicated her the way this man's scent did.

Cynthia rested her small hands on his warm chest as they swayed, his large hands wrapped firmly around her lower back. She was wearing a knee-length light linen dress, but the heat radiating from his body made her feel like she wasn't wearing one stitch of clothing. At one point Evan's left hand trailed slowly up her spine. The heat from his fingers seared her back, neck and then slid into her short curly hair at the nape. He tilted her head back and stared into her eyes for a long moment with a look Cynthia had never seen on a man's face before. He looked…hungry. Evan slowly lowered his face to hers, gripped her body closer to his and then claimed her lips with his own. It was light and wonderful at first, then deepened and intensified.

A surge shot through Cynthia's body as his kisses consumed her. She realized she was kissing him back with a passion she never even knew she possessed. His lips moved over hers and he tasted deliciously of salt and sea air. Evan pulled away, but not before slowly brushing his lips up her cheekbone to the edge of her ear.

"Cyn," he breathed.

"Yes?" Cynthia whispered.

But Evan never answered her. Instead he kissed her once more and Cynthia forgot they were surrounded by a multitude of other people enjoying the music that drifted off into the dark night.

Unfortunately the passion that Evan unlocked in Cynthia that night was not something she solely reserved for his kisses. Every now and then, maybe when the moon was full and hung so low in the sky it looked like it could dip right into the ocean water, a spat would erupt between them. When these passion filled episodes would occur, The Landing patrons would bear witness to their quarrels. Looking back in later years Cynthia could never quite recall what they had even fought about, but she remembered that it usually took one of them to cave before peace could be restored.

One evening Cynthia had become so mad at Evan she pushed him off his beloved boat into the murky water below. He in turn had chased her across the lawn of The Landing while soaking wet until he caught up with her at the empty pavilion. Evan managed to wrestle her to the ground where all thoughts of fighting were quickly forgotten. He had kissed her until Cynthia was laughing with gleeful abandon. His wet, wavy black hair fell across her bare shoulders and made her shiver even in the sweltering night air.

Thankfully most their nights were spent in more peaceful pursuits. They usually lounged on their backs on an old patchwork quilt on the deck of Evan's ramshackle boat and stared up at the shimmering stars. During these quiet, reflective moments they would talk about their future plans, hopes and wishes as young people often do. Evan wanted to travel the seas in his sailboat and explore exotic locations. His exaltations of life at sea always reminded Cynthia of Miss Austen's estimable Colonel Brandon confiding that, "the air is full of spices". As soon as she thought it though she had to remind herself that was the Colonel Brandon of the movies, not of Jane Austen's written word. There was a difference, as any Janeite could tell you.

Cynthia also shared her dreams of working in a large bustling city. A concrete jungle. It was a testament to their youth that they never realized their goals were not exactly compatible. Besides, neither was very good at compromise anyways.

The most magical night of that summer occurred as it was coming to a close. In a few days' time Cynthia and Evan would part and leave once again to pursue higher education. Cynthia had been lying on her side on the faded quilt, running her hand through Evan's dark hair absentmindedly, when she suddenly realized she was in love with him. She thought he felt the same way about her because the look that passed between them in that moment was heady indeed. Without words Cynthia knew what she wanted. What she would always want. Evan.

He slid over closer to her and tightened his arm around her waist as they lay facing each other on their sides. The way he kissed her made Cynthia believe he wanted all the same things she did. Evan got to his feet, pulled her up and then lifted her into his arms. He carried her below deck to the sparsely furnished room. There was a table, a built-in bench and a small bed in the corner. A few shelves and drawers tucked away here and there held everything else. He often spent nights on his boat and often dreamed Cynthia spent her nights there too.

They slowly removed each other's clothing, one piece at a time, and let them fall to the worn boards below. When Cynthia's soft green dress slipped off her shoulders and down her arms she shivered. Evan looked at her questioningly, as if she might have changed her mind. To dispel this thought Cynthia quickly stepped out of the dress so Evan could look at her. She had never made herself this vulnerable to anyone else and adrenaline rushed through her veins.

When Evan's last article of clothing was removed he wrapped his body around Cynthia's in a way that made her tremble. In that moment Cynthia knew that he wanted her. It was a powerful feeling. For the first time in her life she made love to a man. It was the most glorious moment full of new sensations and emotions. Afterwards Evan held her in his arms while the blue-grey sailboat swayed in the teal sea and he promised to love her forever.

~ ~ ~

Cynthia picked up the carton of milk, spout still open, and sighed. This was the fourth time in so many months that she had forgotten to put the milk back in the fridge before heading off to work. Since she had spent the evening before at Michael's place her galley kitchen now slightly reeked. As Cynthia quickly surveyed her tiny apartment she realized it had fallen into disarray. She was usually a neat freak so the thought of a messy apartment agitated her greatly. For a brief moment she thought about pulling out her cleaning supplies and rectifying the situation. Instead she pulled a bottle of wine from the fridge, poured herself a glass, and retired to her postage stamp sized bathroom.

As she settled into a warm, soothing bubble bath and began to relax, her mind drifted back to her earlier thoughts out on the street. She had remembered lying in Evan's arms naked under an old patchwork quilt on his boat as it had swayed on the water. It was one of Cynthia's most treasured memories. She took a sip of wine and tried to recall her first time with Michael. It took her a few moments to recollect a hazy night in a hotel room in Charlotte, North Carolina. Cynthia had been attending a conference and Michael had followed her. She had gone back to her room to retire after a long day only to find him sitting outside her door in the hallway with a colorful bouquet of Asiatic lilies and a bottle of champagne.

Cynthia swirled the fragrant liquid around in her glass and contemplated how very different the two men were. There must be some common denominator she mused. After all, don't people usually have types? Cynthia caught herself frowning as she lay back in the white porcelain, clawfooted tub. She was slightly disappointed by the thought that she didn't have a definitive type. Every girl needs someone who is her perfect match, she thought lazily, as her mind drifted once more.

~ ~ ~

It had rained all morning leaving the deck of Evan's boat slick. Cynthia was sitting rigidly on top of a storage container while Evan stood looking out towards the sea. They had been dating for over a year now, this was their second summer together, and she was convinced no one knew her the way he did. Unfortunately, Cynthia didn't understand him at all in the present moment and her stomach kept tightening in knots. She had a horrible feeling that this summer would not end as the last summer had. Evan had been restless ever since he graduated college in June and it had confused Cynthia.

Mid-July, on their anniversary, Evan had presented Cynthia with a nautical map as his gift to her. The map detailed a route that started in South Carolina and ended someplace she had never even heard of. He had excitedly explained that he had saved enough money for the both of them to be able to travel comfortably for a year. The gesture had been bold and romantic, but it also came attached with a price.

Cynthia would have to push her senior year of college back one year for her to follow along on his adventure. She had mulled over his offer during many sleepless nights. She knew her mother would be furiously disappointed as she already had one son off in the wilds of South America. Cynthia knew this was something even her father wouldn't be able to smooth over. In her mind she could see them sailing to various ports and spending their evenings below deck entwined in each other's arms. When she thought of this Cynthia wanted nothing more than to be on that sail-boat with Evan.

But as the time for departure drew near she began to have doubts and could not reconcile pushing her senior year off until they returned. Cynthia was a very pragmatic person, a trait she had inherited from her mother, and the time had finally come to tell Evan that she couldn't follow him. She had placed all her hopes on the fact that he wouldn't want to go with-out her and would postpone the trip until after her graduation.

"I don't want to do this without you Cyn."

"You don't have to if -"

"But I do," he interrupted roughly. "I have to do this now Cyn. I don't want to wait. I *can't* wait. I feel like I've been waiting for this my whole life."

Evan crossed the wet deck in an agitated manner and sat down beside her on the storage container.

"Why can't you understand?" he pleaded.

"Because I don't Evan," she said while shaking her head. "My educa-tion is important too! I worked hard to get into a great marketing program. I could lose my place if I leave for a year."

Evan caught her face between his warm hands and gently rubbed her soft cheeks with his thumbs. He then suddenly brought his lips down hard on hers. This was a kiss filled with longing and regret. It wasn't like any of their past kisses. When he finally pulled away he stared into her eyes then wiped away the tears streaming down her face.

"No matter where I go Cyn...it will always be you."

Throughout the fall and spring Cynthia would occasionally find post-cards from exotic places in her school postal box. Sometimes there would be a return address, but she never wrote Evan. She knew now that nothing she could say would bring him back. Cynthia wasn't even sure she wanted Evan back. She felt hurt and betrayed he had left without her. If someone really loved you, Cynthia often thought, they wouldn't leave you behind like a memory.

~ ~ ~

Cynthia combed the wet tangles out of her hair then slipped on soft cotton pajama pants and a worn tank top. Michael always teased her about her preferred sleepwear. She felt sure he wished she would wear silky slips to bed but, Cynthia thought that was highly impractical, not to mention quite uncomfortable. Michael only slept in boxers for heaven's sake so he really had no room to talk.

As she slid under the covers Cynthia recalled a bit of wonderful news her good friend Madelyn had called to tell her the day before. Maddie, as Cynthia called her, was getting married and she had asked Cynthia to be her maid of honor. The two women had been friends since their freshman year in college and Cynthia was thrilled to be asked. They had decided to meet sometime over the coming weekend to work out the details as Maddie had requested Cynthia's help in pulling the special day together.

When Cynthia finally drifted off to sleep she dreamt she was sailing all alone in the open sea on a blue-grey sailboat. She was lost at sea. Beside her lay a rolled map tied with a black cord. Cynthia would hazily recall the next morning that she had been too afraid to untie the cord and see the map's final destination.

Chapter Six

Rosemary Part II

Rosemary sat behind the wheel of the car and silently fumed. She could never figure out why this road courted so many wrecks. She had driven this road thousands of times and not once had she ever been inspired to collide with another vehicle. Rosemary glared at her watch again then leaned her head back against the headrest and let out a frustrated sigh. No one had moved for the last ten minutes. Rosemary had begun to despair that they would never move again when the delivery truck in front of her started crawling forward.

A surge of elation shot through her as she pressed her foot on the gas pedal gently. Only to stop once more ten feet later. At this rate Rosemary wouldn't arrive at The Blue Orchid until noon. She hoped Julia remembered the Pattersons would be coming in for their anniversary party order. Rosemary hadn't had time last night to put the finishing touches on the centerpieces, but she was confident Julia could take care of it. She was a blessing to have at the shop.

Rosemary flicked open her visor mirror and smoothed her newly cut bob. It was a bit too fluffy and perky for her taste right now. She thought she looked like a frenzied Doris Day, as if she had been out singing and dancing with Rock Hudson. But in a couple of weeks it would look perfect. Rosemary flipped the visor back up and stared out at the stationary traffic. She was trying to resist consulting her watch once more when sirens screamed down the opposite highway. An ambulance rushed past in a blur of flashing lights. Rosemary closed her eyes and took a deep breath.

~ ~ ~

Rosemary slowly opened her eyes and tried to focus on the white object above her. There was something wrong with this room. It was all blurry. Or maybe she was blurry. She couldn't focus enough to truly tell. Rosemary's head felt heavy and groggy. She tried to will her body to move, but when she barely managed to lift a hand her whole body reacted with a terrible ache. Rosemary felt like she had the flu, underwater. She rested her eyes for a few more minutes then opened them once more. This time the ceiling above her came into focus. Soft filtered light shone above. A machine to her left beeped and Rosemary twisted her head to look up at it. Suddenly she saw railings near her face. The bed she was in had rails! That's when Rosemary realized she was in a hospital. Of course she was in a hospital! She had come and gone during the last forty-eight hours, but she vaguely remembered flashes of x-rays and tests and many men in white coats bending over her to touch her. A young nurse with porcelain skin and strawberry blonde hair had pinched her arm during the night. The crook of her arm still felt sore from that.

Rosemary heard a soft sound to her right so she twisted in that direction to peek over the railing. Susan was curled up into a ball in the bed next to hers snoring lightly. Her machines were whirring and beeping too. Rosemary wondered what was attached to her but didn't have the courage to look just presently. Her head still felt heavy and she was afraid to sit up. Mostly she was afraid of the pain that might accompany such a bold movement. She turned her head to stare up at the ceiling once more. She wished that she could piece together the last two days, but all she could recall were fuzzy patches here and there. As she lay in the bed thinking Rosemary suddenly became aware of two voices drifting in from the hallway.

The voices were accelerating in volume and she realized they belonged to her parents.

"I don't know John! Phelps just said it didn't look good."

Mr. Phelps was their family attorney. His name caused Rosemary's skin to prickle. It hadn't occurred to her until just this moment that Susan could be in big trouble.

"Calm down Prissy. We'll think of something."

Her mother's name was Priscilla, but her father always called her Prissy, as she was just that. It was his pet name for her. It made Rosemary smile.

"John, she is in a great deal of trouble. I don't know how we'll get her out of this mess!"

"Have either of the girls woken up yet?"

"Only Susan, but she's sleeping now. I spoke with her briefly. Did you hear about the Reynold's boy?"

"Yes," said her father gravely. "His family was down the hall earlier. I felt for them so much. He was their only son."

"Oh John! I can't believe he didn't make it!"

Rosemary's chest gave a sudden squeeze at her mother's words. *He didn't make it.* Eric Reynolds hadn't made it?

"Oh my goodness," Rosemary whispered to herself. "He died."

Rosemary closed her eyes once more and warm salty tears streaked down the side of her face. Susan would be devastated when she woke up. She wondered if her parents would try to keep this news from them. Should she play along? Act like she hadn't heard? Rosemary's sluggish brain tried to figure out what she should do.

"The police investigator wants to talk to her when she wakes up and becomes alert Prissy. They have a lot of questions for her."

"Should we call Phelps to be present for that?"

Her mother sounded panicked.

"Yes, I think we should," her father replied calmly. "They may charge Rosemary then and there. If that happens she'll need Phelps."

Rosemary blinked rapidly as she tried to process the conversation she had just heard. Why would the police charge her with anything? She hadn't been drinking or driving. But suddenly a horrible suspicion crept over Rosemary's bruised and battered body. She twisted once more to look at Susan. Had Susan told them *she* was responsible? The answer popped into her head without hesitation. *Yes*, she had. The vision of two dozen goldfinches swarmed her mind until her heart monitor let out shrill, rapid beeps.

The day of Eric's funeral the sisters were not allowed to attend. Their mother had already fretted multiple times about all the "good society" gossiping about the car wreck and the tragic death. The Pope family had shut themselves away in their home. Mrs. Pope said she wanted to protect the girls from all speculation. Rosemary knew better. Her mother was just hiding out until all this blew over. But how could something of this magnitude just blow over?

Rosemary had been covering for Susan for over a week now. The police had determined that Susan had been intoxicated the night of the wreck and that Rosemary had not. Phelps had proclaimed his relief that it had been Rosemary driving and not Susan. The consequences would be much more severe if it had been Susan driving he had declared. As it was he felt confident he could persuade a judge to declare the whole fiasco an unfortunate accident. Rosemary had flinched at the use of the word fiasco. It seemed so inappropriate seeing as how a young man had died.

When the sisters had been released from the hospital Susan had begged Rosemary to stick to the story she had fabricated. Susan had broken down and cried on Rosemary's four poster bed. She had never seen her younger sister look so vulnerable. The noose of lies tightened around Rosemary's neck as the days passed, but she could see no way to loosen its grip without sacrificing Susan.

~ ~ ~

Rosemary parked her car in its usual space then checked her hair once more. She tried to smooth it down again before finally giving up and hurrying off to the shop. Perky Doris Day hair would just have to do for now. A few doors down from The Blue Orchid Rosemary slipped into a coffee shop to grab an herbal tea to-go. Her nerves were shot from sitting in that traffic jam for over an hour. When she had finally reached the scene that had caused the delay the two twisted cars had made her heart flutter. It brought back a memory she often tried to repress. It wasn't a memory she liked to linger on.

As she left the coffee shop with tea in hand the doorway was blocked by two young people in a full on make-out session. The young lady's back was pressed against the glass door. The establishment had quite a view of her low rider jeans and the fluorescent green thong that peeked out over the top of them. Rosemary couldn't figure out for the life of her why young people thought this was an appropriate form of attire. She could certainly appreciate trends but this was a bit much for her.

Rosemary tapped on the glass door with her index finger and the young man with the strange facial hair retracted his tongue long enough to pull his partner away from the door. Rosemary shuffled past the young lovers and thought that her mother would have quite disapproved of such a public display of affection. The word tacky sprang to mind. It would have been bad for business her father would have said. Rosemary smiled at the thought. Her father had passed away almost twenty years ago, but she could still remember his kind smile and whenever she heard anyone quote Emerson he was the person she pictured in her mind.

~ ~ ~

Rosemary picked at the vegetables on her plate with a fork. She was in no mood to enjoy this evenings dinner. Her mother had already chastised her twice about playing with her food but she didn't care. Trunks filled with Rosemary and Susan's school items had arrived today. The reminder that she had been kicked out of her beloved college had put Rosemary in a foul mood. Susan ate with gusto, as if she didn't have a care in the world.

This week Rosemary had begun to evaluate if her parents light hand and her own covering up for Susan had enabled her to become the selfish, spoiled person she was today. All those years Rosemary had taken the blame for Susan she thought she had been protecting her little sister. But now she wondered. She began to suspect she had done her sister a great disservice all because she had wanted to enjoy a few after-school activities. Rosemary was consumed with worry about her own future too. She was still very naïve as to where the tragic events that foggy night would lead her. Rosemary put her fork down and pushed her plate away at the same moment the doorbell rang.

Kay ushered Mr. Phelps into the formal dining room and John stood to greet him and offer him some dinner.

"Thank you, but I'm afraid I'm here on business. This visit is unfortunately not a social call."

Rosemary's stomach tightened. This was it, the moment she had been waiting three weeks for. Rosemary braced herself for the sure-to-be bad news.

"But before I continue I'd like to have a word with Rosemary."

Her father nodded solemnly and he invited Phelps to join them at the polished cherry wood table. The attorney sat down and placed the hat in his hands off to the side. He sized Rosemary up before looking her square in the eye.

"Rosemary, do you have anything you want to tell me?"

Rosemary stared at him blankly while her mind raced. What could she possibly tell him at this point that wouldn't implicate Susan? She slowly shook her head.

"Nothing? Nothing at all?" Phelps pressed.

"No, I…no." Rosemary clamped her mouth shut before the whole sordid truth came spilling out.

"Alright then. Maybe Susan has something she'd like to tell me?"

Susan looked at Mr. Phelps with big blue innocent eyes. At that moment a cold chill seized Rosemary as she realized what a flawless liar her sister was. Rosemary began to wonder if Susan actually thought the wreck was all her fault. She knew damn well it wasn't.

"I'm going to give you one more chance to come clean Susan."

"What in heavens name are you talking about Phelps?" asked Mr. Pope. "What more can Susan possibly tell you?"

"The truth."

Susan's innocent eyes grew wide and hope sprang in Rosemary's chest. Mr. Phelps knew the truth! But how?

"How, how do you know?" stammered Rosemary.

Phelps pulled out a manila envelope from the pocket inside his tweed jacket and lightly tossed it on the dining room table.

"The police just messengered this report to me."

"What report?" asked Mr. Pope.

"That is a forensic test John. It seems Rosemary wasn't driving the night of the accident. Susan was. Her blood was found all over the steering wheel, driver's seat and on the floor."

Mrs. Pope clutched her hand over her chest and looked from one daughter to the other. The girls did not dare meet her eyes.

"One of the investigative officers became suspicious when Rosemary injuries didn't match the blood stains in the Impala. Your daughters have different blood types. You see, when the girls arrived at the hospital in all the chaos they mixed them up. It wasn't hard to put together after seeing the blood samples."

Rosemary felt lightheaded and had to remind herself to breathe. After all these weeks of lies pressing down on her, the truth had lifted them off.

The next few months were not kind to Susan. Mr. Phelps tried to make a strong case but the judge had been most displeased with the lies the two sisters has tried to pass as the truth. Rosemary had felt the most shame the day she saw Eric Reynolds's parents sitting in the courtroom. They were overcome with grief and Rosemary mourned in spirit with them. Looking back, she realized they had tried to deny the Reynolds's family justice and closure.

Susan was sentenced to two years in girl's juvenile detention. The place was actually a home where girls aged twelve to twenty had to take classes, attend counseling and do chores. Rosemary knew Susan would hate being there. Who would she find to cover for her in there? Their mother was absolutely devastated the day Susan was dropped off. Rosemary noticed her mother laid around in her bedroom for months afterwards hardly ever coming out. Mr. Pope made the decision to send Rosemary away to college the next semester. Rosemary had never been so glad of anything in her life. The past few months at home she had been forced to peel back lie after lie to expose the raw truth of her and Susan's wrong doings. Well, Susan's wrong doings and Rosemary's attempts to cover them up. Going away to school was the balm Rosemary needed to heal herself. For four years Rosemary rarely came home. And for the first time in her life the shadow of Susan could not follow or loom over her.

~ ~ ~

"Rosemary, while you were out Finola left something for you."

Julia reached behind the front counter and pulled out an envelope. She handed the plain and unmarked item to Rosemary and then went to help some lost looking gentlemen in a business suit eyeing the white phalaenopisi orchids. Rosemary glanced at him and immediately thought *apology* then amended her thought to *betrayal* after watching him flinch at Julia's voice and stare repeatedly at the floor. He looked to be in his late thirties and his hairline had already started to recede. Why did men always try to hang onto their youth with such atrocious antics?

Rosemary tore open the envelope and saw an invitation to Harrison's second grade art class graduation. This was just getting out of control. Children today "graduated" from practically everything and usually received a ribbon or trophy to boot. She could still remember when Harrison was just a baby and Finola was a flustered young mom.

Rosemary tucked the invitation in her purse, picked up her herbal tea, and headed to the back office to get started on paying invoices.

~ ~ ~

The waiter looked apprehensive about approaching the table while Finola was in full on rant mode. Rosemary caught his eye and waved him over. She gave him a kind smile to let him know the intrusion was not unwanted. He smiled kindly back at her. Of course. As the waiter refilled their sweet iced teas Finola continued, oblivious to the interruption.

"He cried and cried then threw the nastiest temper tantrum I have ever seen a child throw. I swear, I thought there was going to be no end to Vincent's outburst!"

The waiter finished refilling their glasses and quickly scooted away in a hurry. Rosemary couldn't blame him. Finola looked quite the sight. Her dark hair, which she had inherited from her father, was pulled back into a sloppy ponytail. She had purple circles under her eyes and looked to be on the verge of collapse or hysteria. Neither was a pleasant option. Rosemary patted her daughter's hand.

"Well, welcome to motherhood dear. You wanted two children and now you have them. It's quite natural that Vincent is acting out. You are spending all your time helping Harrison with preschool projects so naturally Vincent is jealous. Children aren't big on rationalization or sharing."

"You are not helping mother!" Finola snapped.

Rosemary had treated Finola to a dinner out after her husband Matt had called. He told his mother-in-law that Finola and the two boys had spent the day alternately crying and he was at his wits end. Finola was about to have a nervous breakdown adjusting to now having two mobile children in the house. Now that Vincent was walking, and entering the terrible twos, both of the boys were competing for her attention. It had become a bit too much for poor Finola.

Matt's parents lived in Texas so they weren't around much to help, except for when they came to town to visit over holidays. Lucky grandparents thought Rosemary. She was stuck here trying to help them get through the daily grind.

"No wonder you only had one child mother."

Rosemary laughed.

"Well, I'd say that was more of a reaction to my *own* childhood."

"The thing is, I don't want the boys to grow up and grow apart the way you and Aunt Susan did. I had two of them so they would be good company for each other, so they wouldn't be lonely and isolated and -"

Finola suddenly stopped and looked up at her mother.

"Oh, please finish dear. So Harrison wouldn't grow up like you did, all alone in a flower shop, isolated in a back play room."

"That's not what I -" Finola broke off into a frustrated sigh.

"It's alright dear. We each do our best. What else can we do?"

"You're starting to sound like grandpa. Before you know it, you'll be quoting Emerson."

Rosemary laughed and continued eating her meal.

"Mom, why did you and Aunt Susan grow apart?"

"Oh Finola, you know the story. Sometimes life just takes you different places. Susie finally had her own places to go as did I."

"But you once said she came out so altered after her stay in that home."

"That was juvey dear. And yes, Susie came out quite altered. How could she not? Isn't that the goal? Truth be told I rarely saw much of her after she came home. She traveled a lot while I was busy getting my master's degree and then your grandmother talked me into that silly sham of a marriage."

"Oh yeah, to the doctor. Do you ever regret divorcing him?"

"Oh heavens no! Because of that divorce I got one of the greatest joys in my life."

"The Blue Orchid."

Rosemary laughed heartily again.

"No dear, *you*. I got you. If I hadn't divorced Stephen I wouldn't have met your father and had you."

Finola tucked a stray hair behind her ear and smiled at her mother.

"Thanks mom...for this. I needed to get out."

"Don't we all need to get out once in a while. Sometimes escape is our only option."

Finola gave a contented sigh and Rosemary was happy to see her relax finally. All too soon she would be thrust back into the world of toddlers and teethers.

"I heard about Aunt Susan. That's terrible."

"Yes, it is. I'm going to visit her at the hospital tomorrow and see what I can do."

"That's good. She needs you. When was the last time you saw your sister?"

"At your grandmother's funeral."

Finola grew quiet and contemplative. Rosemary could always tell because Finola had a horrible habit of chewing on her bottom lip whenever she was lost in thought. Rosemary decided to enjoy the silence and some more of the wonderful lasagna on her plate. She loved eating out. Everything always tasted better.

"Mom, have you ever thought about retiring?"

Rosemary finished her bite of lasagna while giving her daughter a perplexed look.

"Retire? Why would I do such a thing?"

"I don't know. I mean, you're at that age."

"*That* age? What does that mean?"

"You know, the *retirement* age."

"Really Finola, the things that come out of your mouth."

During the rest of their dinner the thought of retirement percolated in the back of Rosemary's mind. The idea of retirement had never occurred to her. Until now.

Rosemary had visited the hospital on many occasions. Babies were born, surgeries had success and yet others died all in this same building. Life and death all within a few floors of one another. Rosemary remembered the day Finola had been born. She had arrived early and was the tiniest thing Rosemary had ever seen. There had been touch and go moments when the doctors thought Finola wasn't going to make it. She also remembered the last time she had been in this familiar institution. Rosemary's mother had been admitted for minor chest pains and had passed on a few days later. It had been quite unexpected even though she had lived a great many years. The hospital was a fickle place.

She rode the slow elevator up to the seventh floor and looked for Dr. Jasmit's office. When Rosemary located it, she was shown into the Doctor's private office. After waiting a few minutes a tall lady with black hair and olive skin entered. She greeted Rosemary with a friendly hand shake.

"As you know Mrs. Melton your sister Susan has been diagnosed with chondrosarcoma, which I'm sure she told you was a form of bone cancer. Susan has opted to try stem cell therapy, which data shows can be successful in cases like your sisters. Of course, we need healthy stem cells for the treatment and cells from a sibling are a desirable option. I've heard you are willing to donate as Susan's sister."

"Yes. Is Susan here now?"

Dr. Jasmit gave Rosemary a puzzled look.

"Yes, she's in Ward D. Did Susan not tell you this?"

"No, I...I only spoke to her husband José briefly on the phone."

"I see."

"Will I need to stay overnight for the procedure?"

"No, it is relatively simple. You will be given a medication to increase the number of stem cells released into your blood stream. In a few days you will return and your blood will be removed from a large vein in your arm. The blood will go through a machine that will remove the stem cells and then the filtered blood will be returned to you. I will tell you now the procedure may take four to six hours."

"And then..."

"The stem cells will be frozen until we can give them to Susan. After radiation she will need your stem cells to help her produce new blood cells."

Rosemary squirmed in her chair.

"Now, I have some paperwork for you to review and then I'll have one of my assistants set up an appointment time for the procedure. How does that sound?"

"That sounds...fine. It's fine."

"Perfect. Please review this paperwork and then we can discuss any further questions you may have."

Rosemary nodded then took her glasses out of her purse.

Rosemary decided to grab a sandwich and lemonade before she headed back to The Blue Orchid. She needed to decompress. She had gone by Susan's room but her sister had been asleep and Rosemary decided not to wake her. All the talk of blood removal plus the ever-present hospital smell had made her queasy. She didn't want to get back into her car and the oppressive summer heat just yet. Rosemary thought she might pass out. She had never had much tolerance for the sight of blood. It was the reason why she could never watch all the horror movies the kids today liked so well. It may have been fake but her brain did not process it that way.

She had just taken a bite of her sandwich when a shadow fell over her table.

"Rosemary?"

Rosemary looked up and saw José Alvarez standing before her. The last time she had seen Susan's husband was at her mother's funeral. He looked ten years older today. His dark hair was streaked with grey and he had that haggard look people get when they care for someone with an illness. Their life becomes the patient's life.

"José! How nice to see you. Please, sit."

Rosemary gestured to the seat across the table and José sat down. He had a cup of coffee in his hands and Rosemary wondered how he could drink a warm beverage on such a sweltering day. Air conditioning be damned, it was near a hundred degrees outside. In the shade.

"You look well Rosemary."

"You look good too José," she lied.

"It always amazes me each time I see you. Your eyes. They are Susan's exact eyes. The same light blue."

"They come from our mother's side of the family. They are her eyes. Our father had hazel eyes."

José smiled warmly at her. He had always been a friendly man. Rosemary liked him a great deal. She was glad her sister had found such a nice man to settle down with. No matter what Susan's past transgressions had been, Rosemary wanted Susan to be happy. She had always wanted that for her.

Susan had met José shortly after her release from the detention home. She had taken the money their parents had set aside for her college education and used it to travel. Susan had wanted to breathe and be free. She had made this declaration when she had returned home. Rosemary had a suspicion her sister had done a lot of thinking about her travel plans during her confinement. Within a few weeks she was gone. One day a few months later their parents received a letter letting them know she had married a man in California. This was interesting and shocking seeing as how Susan was supposed to be working on a horse ranch in Colorado. Apparently she had skipped out on her mucking chores and ran off to the sunny beaches of Cali. Beach Boys songs could be awfully persuasive when your boots were mired in horse poo day after day.

José Alvarez was a realtor and he loved his family very much. It was obvious in the way he looked at Susan, had helped raise their two sons, provided for them as Susan never worked and always put their needs before his own. He thought Susan with her blonde hair, blue eyes and pale skin had been an angel. Rosemary figured he must be in love to be so blind. The pain in his tired eyes was heartbreaking. It was so real. In a world of jealous, adulterous and stalked orchids it was nice to see, even though the occasion was anything but nice.

Susan's husband pulled his wallet out and extracted two photos. Their two sons had managed to find some time last year so they could all go on a cruise. José proudly showed the pictures of a smiling and sun burnt family. Well, Susan was sun burned. The two boys had been blessed with their father's dark complexion. Over the years Rosemary had rarely seen Susan's two boys. Finola and her two cousins barely knew one another. This always made Rosemary sad.

"Did Dr. Jasmit review the procedure with you?"

"Yes. It seems very simple. I'm sure it will help Susan a great deal."

After José inquired about her family a silence descended between them. If you only saw someone once every few years it was hard to make conversation last. Mutual topics were bound to recede quickly. Rosemary decided this was her cue to leave.

"Wait Rosemary. I wanted to tell you something I think you should know."

Rosemary sat back down and looked tentatively at José.

"I know my wife better than anyone Rosemary. Sometimes I think I know her better than she knows herself. I know you two have had a rocky relationship ever since…well, that accident. But I want you to know my wife doesn't blame you."

"Doesn't blame me?" Rosemary's voice shot up an octave.

"I'm sorry. That came out all wrong. I certainly don't mean that she did blame you, but she has made peace with what happened. She harbors no ill feelings towards you."

"Well, that's something isn't it," said Rosemary as she let out a short derisive laugh. "It must have been hard for Susan to forgive something imaginary. I suspect those are the hardest things to forgive after all."

Rosemary stood up suddenly.

"I'm sorry Rosemary. I didn't mean - my intentions have come out all wrong. I just wanted you to know that Susan takes full responsibility for that dreadful car wreck."

Rosemary stared at José for a moment before saying, "Please give your sons my best wishes. And tell Susan…send Susie my love."

José nodded and stood to give Rosemary a parting handshake with both hands.

"Thank you Rosemary. And not just for today, for the donation -"

"Of course," Rosemary cut José off. "I'll help Susie however I can."

Rosemary exited the hospital and made her way back into the afternoon heat. It was going to be a long, sleepless night. She could already tell. Rosemary could always tell.

~ ~ ~

Rosemary tucked the bright yellow potted Cattleya orchid into folds of soft peach organza fabric. She gathered the folds up to the rim of the container and tied a sage green silk ribbon around the package to pull it all together. The customer stood off to the side watching her work. This used to bother Rosemary, years ago when she had first opened the shop, but it had been ages since it had pricked her notice. Having an audience no longer perturbed her. Besides, the customers were merely curious about their purchase. It wasn't every day that one bought an expensive orchid.

Rosemary was the last person in the shop today. Julia had just left to go home so Rosemary could close up the store and get the deposit ready for tomorrow. Rosemary was thoughtful as she pulled together the presentation for her last customer of the day.

As she worked Rosemary tried to get a feel on the middle-aged man waiting for the finished product, but for some reason she couldn't. There were usually tell-tale signs. Cheaters always paced, as if they were afraid to stand still for fear of being caught. But this gentleman didn't look like a cheater. He stood perfectly still and made eye contact with the other customers in the shop. Cheaters hated to make eye contact. Liars always had a self-satisfied smirk plastered on their face. As if they were unduly pleased with themselves for their nefarious acts. Liars were always habitual. Rosemary saw the same liars repeatedly. Liars were good for the flower business. But this man had a kind look about his face. Rosemary was having a devil of a time trying to figure out why he would want the exquisite orchid. So finally, when it was ready, she decided to just ask him.

Usually Rosemary had a policy in her shop not to ask customers the reason for their purchase. But curiosity about this man pushed her beyond her normal ethics. The man's cheeks flushed red and immediately Rosemary pegged him as an apologist. What for though she had no clue. She waited for him to tell her.

"This is for my secretary Debbie."

Ah. The illicit affair with the much younger secretary. Classic. Rosemary mentally shook her head.

"She's retiring today."

"Retiring?"

"It's a few years earlier than I had hoped but, well, her husband has cancer. She wants to spend some time with him before..."

The man trailed off and looked down.

"Debbie has been a good friend to me. She was with me when my wife had cancer. My wife recovered but it was Debbie who really held the office together when I was gone all the time."

The man looked back up at Rosemary.

"It's rare you meet someone like that, you know? She's been a real good friend. I'm really going to miss her."

The man smiled at Rosemary. Not as a sexual conquest or as a grandmother figure. Just as a person. Rosemary smiled back and gave the man the orchid for free. Who knew people gave exotic, expensive orchids just for being a friend? Certainly not her. The thought sustained Rosemary for the rest of the evening.

~ ~ ~

"Julia, I'll be back in about an hour. Are you comfortable keeping an eye on the shop?"

"Sure thing Rosemary! We have three more orders to complete, then some inventory to log in."

Rosemary gathered up the bundles of wrapped roses in her arms. Vibrant reds, oranges and purples spilled over her sleeve.

"Do you need any help? Where are you going?"

"I have to make a few deliveries. I won't be long."

Rosemary was glad fall had started to settle in. She could walk down the street now without her blouse clinging to her body from the sticky humidity. She wouldn't even need to use the air conditioner in her car soon. She would simply be able to slide the sun roof back and let in a nice breeze. The thought cheered Rosemary up.

Twenty minutes later Rosemary made her way across the carefully manicured grounds. Hardly any other visitors were here today and this was the reason she often chose to visit during this time. She could enjoy the quiet and spend as much time as she liked without being bothered or disturbed. Rosemary hiked up a small slope and her breathing became heavier. When had that started? She used to run around here and there and never became winded. As much as she hated to admit it Rosemary acknowledged that her age was starting to catch up with her. She slowly made her way back to the far corner of Bay Rock Memorial Cemetery.

She stopped in front of a double bronze grave marker that was flush to the ground with a bronze vase standing erect in the middle. Rosemary bent down and placed the orange roses on her father's side of the vase and the red roses on her mother's side. She brushed away bits of twigs and leaves that had been resting on the marker. Several times a year she gave the marker a proper cleaning, but she had already completed that maintenance last month so it looked pretty good. Rosemary spent some time with her parents then moved down the row to locate another marker.

Rosemary kneeled before her last delivery of the day and placed the regal purple roses in the vase on the grave marker. She brushed some grass off Susan's name then left her fingers pressed to the marker. Her sister has passed away just last year. Her death was still fresh in Rosemary's heart and it tugged and pulled in an awful way.

"Oh Susie, what should I do?"

She played with her sister's flowers and rearranged them several times. Rosemary often visited her parents and sister and asked them for advice, or support, or just to chat about nothing. The graveyard was a peaceful place for Rosemary, though at times a sad and mournful place too. That was to be expected though.

"Should I retire from The Blue Orchid Susie? I know you only spent a little bit of time there after your first recovery. I was so glad we got to spend that time together. I don't know what to do. Just yesterday I was setting goldfinches lose in the church sanctuary and today here I am."

Rosemary thought a moment and then burst out laughing. Even to this day she sometimes thought she had done the things she had covered up for Susan. Reality could get awful confusing once enough time had passed. The truth became blurred. She left a half hour later still unsure what she should do about her future. Rosemary settled back into her car and wondered which direction she should go.

Chapter Seven

Cassandra Part II

Cassie stood outside Ethan Carson's door at Ivey Gardens. She had been standing there for ten minutes. All she had to do was reach up and knock softly on the door. That's how all unexpected guests should knock. That way it gave the resident the option of saying later, 'Oh, I'm sorry, I never heard you knock', even if they did. Cassie took a deep breath, gripped the basket of muffins tightly in her left hand and raised her right hand for the twentieth time. Cassie had bought the muffins, not baked them herself. She was hopeless at baking. She often felt bad for her children, especially during school parties or bake sales. Her kids always showed up with something horrid from the grocery while their classmates came with expertly piped designer cupcakes. Cassie let out a sigh. Why was she even here?

She had been mulling that over for the past ten minutes. Over the last few weeks Cassie couldn't seem to get Ethan or his offer of theatre out of her mind. She would be folding warm towels fresh from the dryer, or cooking spaghetti and find herself picturing his face in her mind. One night she even recreated the accident between her van and his bicycle in a dream. She had woken up startled. Not because it had been frightening, as it had in real life, but because it *hadn't* been frightening. What did that mean? Cassie had decided years ago that dreams meant nothing. Although to be fair her determination was more personal than based on any sort of science.

Cassie hoped Ethan wouldn't be too weirded out – as her son Joseph always said – by her unexpected appearance on his doorstep. Would he wonder why she was here? She sincerely hoped he didn't ask because she hadn't quite figured it out herself. Finally, Cassie shook her auburn hair out, gave a swift rap on the door – Shoot! There went the soft knock – and waited with some sort of emotion akin to breathless anxiety. Someone yelled, "Just a minute", then she heard feet shuffle towards the door. Cassie stood as still as a statue in a park.

The black apartment door swung open and Ethan stood there wearing faded jeans and a bright orange short sleeve polo. The color was so bright it made Cassie blink. He stared at her for a moment, as if trying to place her, then his face turned sunny and he smiled.

"Well, Cassie Smyth. This is a surprise. How are you?"

"Hello. You remembered my name."

"How could I forget the name of the woman whose van I collided with?" he laughed.

Cassie gave a small smile and held up the basket of muffins.

"These are for you. I was just...I had hoped...I mean to say -"

"I tell you what, why don't you come in, have a seat and figure out what you mean to say."

Cassie let out a long breath, relaxed her shoulders and stepped over the threshold. She peered nervously around Ethan's apartment. It was furnished nicely for a single man – if he was single, Cassie really had no clue – although there did seem to be a too many varying shades of blue and some strange blue jean-esque covered furniture. Surely this wasn't a new style, was it?

"Are you amused by something?"

"Excuse me?" asked Cassie.

"Well, as you've been looking around you seem to have a sort of smirk on your face."

Ethan grinned at her as if he were amused himself.

"Sorry, it's just, uh, it's a *lot* of blue."

"Yes, I suppose it is," he laughed. "Blue is my favorite color. I leave the design skills at work I suppose."

Ethan removed the basket of baked goods from Cassie's hands and motioned for her to take a seat.

"I guess I just wanted to check up on you. I was curious I suppose."

Ethan held up his arm.

"Oh! Your arm is healed!"

"Yep, got the doc's blessing three days ago. I'm back to all my normal routines. It's nice. There's a lot of work to be done down at the theatre."

"There is?"

"Oh yeah. Well, you would know having been involved in theatre in the past. We're about a month away from opening *Three Sisters*. You should come down and check it out."

"Really?"

"Sure, why not? What, uh, what did you do in the theatre?"

"Mostly acting. But, I also spent a semester in college learning costume design. I'm not great but I'm not terrible either."

She may not be a baker, Cassie thought, but each year her children had the most amazing Halloween costumes in their neighborhood.

"Huh. You know, our costume mistress is always in need of assistance. I'm sure your help would be appreciated."

"I never thought - I guess I assumed my theatre days were behind me."

"Can one ever really put away the theatre? Isn't it always there, bubbling beneath the surface, ready to rise to the top."

Cassie had been staring at Ethan with fascination and realized he was staring back just as intently. It caught her off guard and she felt her face flush. Why was he staring at her like that? Ethan finally chuckled and broke the tension.

"Why don't you meet me at the Playhouse around eleven next Tuesday? I'll show you around and introduce you to Eve Little."

"Who's Eve Little?"

"The costume mistress. What would the theatre be without mistresses?"

Ethan winked at Cassie and once again her face grew hot. She made a hurried exit a moment later, then sat in her van wondering what had just happened.

Later that evening Cassie was stirring a large pot of stew for dinner when she heard the door leading to the garage slam shut. A moment later Marc came into the kitchen, kissed her on the cheek and took his blazer off.

"Dinner smells great Cass."

"Stew, bread and salad."

"Perfect. Hey, the air in your tires looks low. I'll check them later tonight."

Cassie smiled at Marc and went back to stirring the stew. Marc was already flipping through the newspaper to find the sports section.

"Marc."

"Hmm..."

"I was thinking of volunteering at Weatherwood Playhouse for the season. Maybe help with the costumes or something."

"Say what?"

"You know, that beautiful old theatre in the North District downtown. They need volunteers. I was thinking about doing that."

"Oh. Well, sounds good."

"Yeah?"

"Sure. You need a break from here. Hey, weren't you involved in the theatre before we met?"

"Yeah, something like that," she muttered.

"Where are the rug rats?"

Cassie held up the baby monitor she had sitting beside her on the counter. It crackled with static.

"Arguing about which cartoon to watch next."

Marc laughed and went off to find them. Cassie smiled to herself. She was growing excited about the possibility of immersing herself in the world of theatre once more.

"Mom!"

Joseph ran into the kitchen out of breath.

"Dad wants to know when dinners gonna be ready."

"Tell him five more minutes."

"Ok!"

Her oldest ran off with glee. They always got wound up when Marc came home from work. He would roll around on the floor with them and watch silly cartoons. Cassie didn't have much patience for absurd cartoons. Yes, the opportunity to get away from it all and have a break was looking very good to Cassie.

A few days later Cassie stepped through the doors of the stark white building into the darkness. She was so nervous and excited her hands were trembling. She had realized over the last few days this could be a chance to recapture a bit of her past; A bit of herself that had been hibernating for the past few years. Cassie walked through the lobby slowly as her eyes adjusted to the dim lighting inside. Her footsteps echoed across the marble floor. Suddenly a door among many other doors flew open. Ethan and a stout man walked out into the lobby.

"I'll be back in a few," the man said to Ethan.

Ethan nodded then saw Cassie standing near the ticket booth.

"Cassie! Welcome!"

"Hi. Thanks Ethan. I had forgotten how beautiful this lobby was. All this cherry wood and marble."

"Yeah, it's a great building. The original Playhouse burnt down in the forties. This building was its replacement. Well, let's get this tour started, shall we? Eve will meet us downstairs later."

During the next hour Cassie saw every nook and cranny in the theatre. It was a beautiful, majestic building that smelled of paint, dust and lacquer. So many feelings rushed back to her as they wandered from room to room. The main stage and seating area was set up in a Wagner style. The seats fanned out and gently sloped upwards from the front of the theatre near the stage to the back of the auditorium. The stage floor looked worn. She remembered that Eli had once said that was the sign of a well-loved theatre. So much of today reminded her of Eli. Cassie did her best to stay in the present and block those thoughts and feelings out. It wouldn't do for her to have a breakdown amongst all these strangers she thought wryly.

"And this is our costume department."

Cassie stepped into the long, wide room that was housed in the basement of the theatre. It looked like a bomb of clothing, fabric, hats, gloves and other accessories had exploded everywhere. Cassie had always been quite meticulous about organization so her balance was immediately thrown off.

"I have no clue how Eve finds anything in here,' Ethan muttered.

"I find everything quite well thank you."

Cassie spun around and saw a petite woman with a white-blonde pixie haircut staring at her. She looked to be in her early twenties. Her right eyebrow was pierced.

"I'm Eve Little. You must be Cassie."

"Yes, hello. It's lovely to meet you."

"So, you wanna help huh? What can you do?"

"Oh, a little of everything. It, umm, looks like you need some help with organization first. Would you mind?"

"Mind? Heck no. Help yourself."

"Oh! Well, great! What about tomorrow? I could come in a couple of days a week to pitch in if that's alright."

Ethan laughed, reached over and gently squeezed Cassie's arm. She gave a little jump which made him laugh even more. Cassie noticed Eve raised her pierced eyebrow as she examined them. Cassie hadn't remembered the theatres of her past being anything quite like this.

Over the next two months Cassie adopted a new routine. For the past seven years, since they had moved to Marc's hometown in upstate New

York, her days and nights had not altered much unless it was the addition of another child to their brood. After all this time Cassie had hardly made any real friends. She hadn't ever really been good at that anyways. Eli had always been her best friend. And then Marc, although he was more of a husband than a best friend. The only people Cassie knew on a social level outside her children's schools were the other ladies at church. They had taken up with Marc's church since returning. Somehow she had become a catholic.

Ah well. She was going to convert to Judaism when she married Eli. Cassie truly didn't understand either religion anyways so what was the difference? None as far as she could tell. She liked that Sunday service was performed in Latin. It gave her a full hour of uninterrupted quiet time. That was rare to get when one has multiple children running amok under your feet all day. For one blessed hour she could zone out and let the mysterious words run over her body and through her mind like a cleansing ritual.

At first Cassie had visited Weatherwood twice a week. But as production deadlines drew near – not only for Chekhov's *Three Sisters*, but also two children's pieces – Eve had quickly come to rely on Cassie's help. She now spent three or four days a week at the theatre. If she wasn't trimming satin dresses in lace she was sewing buttons onto jackets or fashioning mouse ear headbands out of grey felt. Cassie had also organized the chaos of the costume department so that even the lowliest scrap of fabric had a home. At first this had confused Eve greatly, but she was slowly adjusting. Cassie would see her white-blonde pixie head bobbing around looking for this or that and Cassie would have to direct her.

The funny thing was, even though Cassie and Eve were nine years apart in age, the two had grown quite close. Cassie liked Eve. She was smart, witty, funny and said the most outrageous things. One day Eve had declared that Shakespeare was really a woman, but a huge conspiracy had taken place to cover up this fact. No doubt men had been at the helm of such an awful trick. Anything to deny a woman her rightful place as one of the greatest playwrights that had ever lived! Eve had told her all of this with such conviction that she believed her. Cassie wasn't sure she believed the conspiracy, but she believed in Eve. That's why one day it shocked her when Eve said something that threw Cassie for a loop.

"I'm glad you're here Cass. I'd be drowning in lamé if you weren't!"

Cassie laughed, "But it's such shiny gold lamé."

"Gawd, it looks like fat Elvis ate one too many fried peanut butter banana sandwiches and exploded in here."

Cassie and Eve were cutting the slippery fabric. Both women were trying not to get their fingers chopped off.

"Anyways, I'm really glad you are here. I guess I thought you were one of *them* at first. But, I guess I was wrong…"

Eve was concentrating so hard her face was scrunched up.

"I'm sorry, one of what?" asked Cassie.

"Huh?"

"One of what?"

"Oh, one of *his* women."

"Whose women?"

Eve looked up from the gold fabric.

"Ethan's women of course."

"I don't understand."

"I shouldn't have said anything. None of my business anyway."

"Well, it's too late now Eve! Spill!"

Eve sighed.

"Look, Ethan has a reputation as quite the ladies man. He often parades 'volunteers' through here until they quit. You know, once he's done with them."

"Oh."

It was the only response Cassie had been able to make at the time. The truth was Cassie wasn't friends with Ethan the way she was friends with Eve. The women shared iced lattes, wraps from the deli, and reality TV talk. What she had been sharing with Ethan was quite different and definitely not as innocent.

Cassie had run into Ethan in the back hallway a few weeks earlier. The collision had caused her to drop the pile of fabric that had been in her arms. Ethan had helped her retrieve the wayward velvet and when he had looked into her eyes her stomach had tightened. Since Cassie had been volunteering at the Playhouse she hadn't seen that much of Ethan. Both of them had been busy with the hectic schedules and rapidly approaching deadlines. But two days after the hallway run-in, she had met Ethan again. Eve had a dentist appointment that day and Cassie had nothing to do until she returned. She had wandered up to the main stage area and found it deserted. She had assumed no one was around so Cassie had climbed up on the stage to have a look around.

A mirror was propped up against a wall in a far corner and it had caught Cassie's eye. She wandered over to it and looked at her reflection. Over the past few weeks she had been so busy running around the theatre she had dropped eight pounds. Cassie admired her slimmer looking figure in the long mirror. She still had another few pounds to go, but Cassie thought she looked pretty good all things considered. She thought she looked curvy now instead of lumpy. Even her fair complexion looked rosier somehow, healthier.

"Well, well...aren't you a sight for sore eyes."

The voice behind Cassie had startled her. She had jumped and spun around on the worn stage. Ethan was standing there grinning at her.

"You look very beautiful today. Very much like The Lady of Shalott."

Cassie recalled the Arthurian legend and it gave her a sudden jolt. Was that who she was? The Lady of Shalott?

"I can see where some might think -"

"But Lancelot mused a little space", He quoted, "She has a lovely face."

Ethan slowly made his way over to her and was looking at her with admiration. His eyes on her made Cassie blush. She walked away from him towards the center of the stage.

"Your set is looking great," she said.

"You think so?"

"Yes, this over here is amazing. It actually looks like real bricks and real carved wood."

"Just a bit of Styrofoam. Smoke and mirrors and all that jazz."

Ethan edged closer to Cassie once again. She took a deep breath and inhaled the scent of him. He smelled musky. It was a very manly sort of smell that suited him well. Cassie had watched him measure and cut boards one day and had marveled at how precise his technique was. No wonder the sets looked so amazing, she had thought at the time.

"Do you like this color?"

Ethan motioned towards a wall that was painted a light rose color. Cassie moved closer to the wall to inspect it.

"Yes, it's lovely. Very soft."

"I was thinking it might need to be richer, darker, *bolder*, maybe the color of your hair."

Ethan picked up a lock of Cassie's hair and she held her breath. Marc never touched her hair. Somehow her husband had never made that fiery piece of her a part of their intimacy. Eli had loved to touch her hair. Ethan wound the long strand around his finger and then let it go. He gazed into her eyes and for some reason Cassie couldn't make herself look away. He leaned in towards her slowly and kissed her softly on the lips. Ethan pulled back and gazed at her once again. Cassie knew this was wrong, knew she should have run off that stage and out the door, but she didn't. Instead she let him kiss her a second time. And so for the past few weeks she had let this man, this absolute stranger, continue to kiss her and wind his fingers through her hair.

Cassie didn't know what the hell she was doing but something in her had woken up. Even though she now knew Ethan's true nature, as Eve had let his womanizing ways slip, Cassie didn't care. He was using her, but she was also using him. At home things had grown so tense. Marc and Cassie were fighting more than they ever had before. He was upset that she kept forgetting things like groceries, church bake sales, dry cleaning drop off and pick-ups. Marc was especially upset that she had missed a school conference meeting because all her time was now spent at the theatre. Her husband didn't like having to go alone. But as Cassie had told him, he'd get used to it, she did lots of things alone.

One day he had suggested that maybe Cassie should cut back on her volunteer time at the theatre. In that moment Cassie had become consumed with guilt. But Cassie couldn't let go of her new escape just yet. She needed the escape. The part of her that had been in hibernation did not want to go back. Cassie was so tired of going back; of looking back.

~ ~ ~

The sun had set over an hour ago, but stagnant heat was still rising from the pavement. Cassie sat on the low concrete steps of her front porch and waited for Eli. He had taken a job in the city for the summer but came back to Jersey every Friday night so he could spend the weekend with her. Cassie's father had finally caved and let her get a part time job at the library as a page. She thought being surrounded by books and quiet all day was pretty boring, but her father thought it would be educational. That was his mandate for everything in her life, safety in education. Cassie had mainly wanted a job so she could save up some money for the coming school year. She and Eli were going to sub-lease Brady's apartment. They would need the extra money to cover the utilities.

Cassie spent her days shelving dusty books at the library daydreaming about her and Eli's future home. It was going to be absolutely perfect. At least, that's what Cassie told herself. It wouldn't actually be perfect though until she told her father. He wasn't ultra conservative, they weren't even religious, but she knew he wouldn't approve of his little girl living with her boyfriend just yet. Maybe someday, after graduation, but not today. She knew her father would worry and Cassie hated that feeling. She never wanted to worry her father. Ever since her mother had died it was like their life equilibrium was off, that her father felt life wasn't as sure or safe anymore. It had pervaded their household. Eli had been pressuring her to tell him over the last few weeks. He said it would make everything so much easier if her pop was cool with it. Eli would not be pleased to learn she still hadn't told her father about their future living arrangements.

A moment later Cassie heard Eli coming down the street. He had bought a used, cheap hatchback and it rattled – everywhere. The car puttered to a stop in front of the Mueller house. Eli jumped out, slammed the car door, and ran up the sidewalk to greet Cassie. He pulled his left arm out from behind his back. In his fist was a bundle of wildflowers.

"Hey doll," he said, as he handed the bouquet to Cassie.

She accepted the beautiful, if slightly wilted flowers, and gave Eli a huge hug. She had missed him so much this week. The days were so lonely without him.

"These are lovely Eli," she said as she pulled back.

"Not as lovely as you, Cassiopeia."

Eli pulled her close again and gave her a long, slow kiss. Cassie melted in the heat as he wound his fingers into her thick hair. He gave her hair a gentle tug and Cassie giggled. They sat down on the concrete steps together.

"So, what do you wanna do tonight?" he asked. "The club is having a cool ska band from the village come in. Or, there is an outdoor jazz trio playing down at the park."

"I don't care what we do."

"You sure are easy to please."

Cassie sighed and rested her head on his shoulder.

"Hey, I'm gonna say hi to your pop before we head out."

Eli stood up but Cassie quickly grabbed his hand and pulled him back down. She looked into his eyes warily and Eli's face hardened.

"You *still* haven't told him about the walk-up yet?" he hissed in a low voice.

"I'm so sorry Eli. I will. I promise! I just need more time -"

"You said that last week. It's almost August Cassie. You've had a whole summer to tell him."

"I know, but -"

"I don't want to hear it. Dammit Cassie! I have to tell Brady something next week or he's gonna give the place to Casper."

Cassie stared down at the concrete and felt so ashamed.

"Maybe…maybe we should just forget it Cassie."

"What?"

"Well, you're never going to tell your pop. All I can think is…you've changed your mind."

Eli frowned and looked sad. His disheveled hair framed his pensive pale face.

"I haven't Eli! But you know my father. He'll freak out! Ever since my mom passed he's been so wary of, well everything."

"I get that Cassie. I understand that. But if you want this – *us* – you have to fight for us. Anything worth having is worth fighting for."

"I know Eli, but -"

"In life you have to make choices. I've chosen you. I love you Cassiopeia. I will fight for you with every last breath I have. What do you have in your life that's worth fighting for?"

Cassie stared into Eli's dark, deep eyes and in that moment she knew the choice she would make. She knew *who* she would fight for. Cassie knew Eli was right. Some things in life were definitely worth fighting for.

~ ~ ~

Footsteps echoes down the hall and Cassie held her breath. Guilt washed over her in the most awful way. Ethan's hand tightened around her waist. They were hiding out in the black box stage on yet another secret rendezvous when they heard two people, probably actors, walking their way. Cassie was terrified someone in the theatre company would catch them, but Ethan just laughed. Of course he did. According to Eve he did this sort of thing all the time.

The past couple of weeks Cassie had been asking herself why *she* was doing this. Was she really this desperate; this lonely? Was her life really all that bad? Enough to be sneaking around the Playhouse with Ethan? What was she trying to fill in her life with this affair? She most certainly wasn't nineteen anymore so why was she acting like she was nineteen? Cassie had asked herself so many questions lately that she had no answers to, leaving her frustrated with herself. Cassie only knew she felt *something* when she was sneaking around with Ethan. But it wasn't about Ethan.

Truthfully, he could be replaced with any man. Cassie wondered if she could get this same what-the-hell-am-I-doing feeling from sky diving or white water rafting.

Cassie didn't have the connection with Ethan that she had with Eli or Marc. So why couldn't she get that secret-kissing-in-a-prop-storage-closet feeling with Marc? He was her husband after all. Last night she had lain awake in bed and stared at Marc's face as he slept. His face had looked so peaceful and content. Lately he didn't look that way when he was awake. They had been arguing on and off for the last few weeks and it had taken a toll on her handsome husband. Cassie longed for *him* to pull her into the pantry or den one night, grip at her blouse as if he wanted to rip it off and kiss her desperately. Marc hadn't acted that way with her in a long time. When had they lost that passion? After the second child? The third? Cassie couldn't pinpoint the exact demise of their passion.

Secretly Cassie feared their intimacy issues lay entirely with her. Even though he worked long hours, often had to travel out of town and spent most of his evening hours watching sports, she had suspected their problems lay mostly with her. Maybe after Eli died she had rushed too fast into a relationship with Marc. Without a doubt Cassie knew she had never fully given all of herself to him. How could she when she still felt the loss of Eli so intensely? None of this was fair to Marc. Not her continued love for Eli, or this fling with Ethan. Cassie felt sorry for Ethan even though she now realized he was playing his usual game. He obviously had a thing for married, so-called unobtainable women. She knew he would be disappointed when he realized it was he who was being used and discarded this time.

The footsteps died away as the pair turned a corner and the hall outside was silent once more. Ethan pulled Cassie tighter to him.

"So, what do you say?" he whispered in her ear.

His hand ran down her back, over her waist and down her hip. Ethan had been trying to persuade her to take their illicit relationship to the next level for the past week. But Cassie now realized, in the dark of the black box, that he was just another man who couldn't fully have her. The only man who had ever really had all of her was Eli.

"Ethan…I can't. This has to stop."

"You said that yesterday and yet here you are."

His hand reached up and lightly caressed her cheek.

"But this time I mean it," she said firmly.

"Mmmm…"

His other hand encircled her waist and he kissed her eagerly. Cassie waited until the kiss was finished.

"I'm sorry Ethan."

She kissed him gently on the cheek then turned to leave the room.

"Cassie, what are you doing?"

"I told you. I can't keep doing this. It's not right."

"For who? For us it is. For your husband? He doesn't appreciate you. Not the way I can."

Cassie laughed. Ethan certainly was well versed in what bored, lonely housewives needed to hear. Or what he thought she needed to hear. He was probably a better actor than most of the people that read lines each night on Weatherwood's main stage.

"Actually, he does. You've got it all backwards. It's me who hasn't appreciated him. Not really."

Cassie left the Playhouse and made a hasty retreat to her vehicle. She had finally realized she couldn't keep doing the things she was doing. Things couldn't keep going the way they were. Something had to change. Cassie drove aimlessly around town while a million thoughts swirled in her mind. Did she still want to be married to Marc? Had she ever really wanted to be married to him? What about the children? How would all this mess affect them? Cassie drove around for a long time when suddenly she knew what she had to do. She made an illegal u-turn on Hanover Street and hurried home.

Marc had the day off so he was at home watching the kids. When Cassie pulled up to their house she saw her children playing in Mrs. Keller's

yard across the street. She was an elderly widow who lived in the neigh-
borhood. Mrs. Keller loved all the neighborhood kids and they loved her.
She always had an endless supply of icy pops on hand. Today was no
exception. Cassie waved to Mrs. Keller and heard Joseph exclaim "Mom!"
He was waving blue finger-tipped hands excitedly. She was glad Mrs.
Keller was watching them. Cassie knew what she had to say to Marc
would be difficult and unpleasant. The children didn't need to hear this.
Regardless of anything that had happened, or would happen after today,
Cassie loved her children fiercely. Since she was an only child she hadn't
known a life that included a large family until now. She loved Christmas
with the children, especially when her father stayed with them. The children seemed to fill a space in him too that had been empty for a long time.

Cassie shut the door to the garage softly and quietly entered the
kitchen. Marc was sitting at the table reading the sports section of the
newspaper as usual. Cassie's heart ached as she looked at him. She felt
like she hadn't seen him – really seen him – in years. His soft brown hair
gleamed in the sunlight that poured in through the kitchen window. Suddenly he looked up, spied her near the kitchen entrance and smiled at her.
Cassie remembered that smile. How had she forgotten it? It was the smile
he had given her the very first day they had ever met. He had been the first
person since Eli to make her feel something. Back then, after Eli's death,
she hadn't thought that was even possible.

"What are you doing home Cass? I thought you were going to be at the
theatre all day?"

Cassie crossed the room and sat down at the kitchen table. She didn't
know how to begin to say what had happened over the last few weeks.
Over the last few years really. She didn't know how to tell Marc it was
over.

"Cass? What's wrong?"

Cassie opened her mouth and the whole horrible truth came spilling
out.

~ ~ ~

The sun glared down on Cassie's notes. She was cramming before next periods Environmental Science exam. She should have studied for it last night, but instead Cassie had laid on the bed in her dorm room and stared at the ceiling. This was how she had spent most of her senior semester so far. All her classmates were busy celebrating their final year but Cassie felt she had nothing to be celebratory about. It had felt so hollow coming back to college without Eli. Her sole reason for being here was gone. Some days Cassie wondered what her purpose for living was. How could there be any life or light in the world without Eli? Some days it was unbearable to even get out of bed.

Yet here she was, cramming in front of the Science and Mathematics building on a sparkling, blustery late fall day. Leaves coated in red, orange and buttery yellow floated to the ground around her. Even in her current frame of mind she couldn't deny the beauty of it all. It was sort of depressing to realize that no matter how crappy your life was the world continued to be a place of beauty and wonder. Mother Nature obviously didn't care enough about the human condition to let it stop her from showing off. Cassie felt there was a lesson to be learned here but ultimately just didn't care. That was a lesson better suited to poets and artists anyways.

Cassie had ceased studying her scribbled notes and zoned out for a few minutes while looking at a pile of scattered leaves on the ground. A strong wind was blowing, tossing the leaves and her red curls in the air.

"Excuse me...erm, uh Cassandra?"

Cassie started at her name and looked up from her spot on the outdoor bench to see a tall man staring down at her. It took her a moment to realize he was a fellow student. When Cassie had looked up at him a slow but winning smile had broken out over his face. The stranger had the most charming, warm smile. Cassie stared at him stupidly for a moment.

"Are you Cassandra Mueller?"

"Yes. How did you know?" she asked in amazement.

"Well, er, it says so on this piece of paper."

"What piece of – hey, wait a minute! That's my Enviro notes! Where did you get that from?"

"From over there."

Cassie looked around and realized all her loose-leaf notes had blown off her lap and were now scattered on the lawn in front of the school building. Apparently during her zen leaf moment the pages had made a break for it.

"Oh no!"

Cassie bolted from the bench and began collecting the dispersed papers. The handsome man also began picking up her notes. Cassie tried not to stare at him, but there was something about him that made her want to look. It unnerved her.

"I believe these are yours."

"Thanks, umm…"

"Oh, Marc. Marc Smyth. Can I ask you something?"

Marc leaned in towards Cassie. She unconsciously leaned in too.

"What were you thinking about just now?"

"What do you mean?" asked Cassie.

"Well, when I came up the walk I saw you and you had this *look* on your face. Seemed pretty intense for such a beautiful girl."

Cassie blushed and Marc laughed.

"What's so funny?" she asked.

"Your cheeks match your hair."

Marc winked at her which made Cassie blush even more. He was still staring at her and she had no clue why. No man had flirted with her since Eli. If that's what he was doing it seemed so strange. Foreign.

"So?" Marc pressed.

"So, uh, what?"

"What were you thinking about?"

"I was thinking…I was thinking that the fall leaves on the trees are lovely now, but soon they'll all be dead."

"It's only temporary, until spring. The leaves will come again next spring when it's time. Most things in life are temporary anyway. You just have to wait for the next thing to happen."

"Is that good or bad?"

"It's both I guess. But probably mostly good. Well, it was nice to meet you Cassandra."

"Oh, it's Cassie."

"Maybe I'll see you around Cass."

Marc winked at her again and made his way to the entrance of the building. He paused at the door, then turned back to look at Cassie. Marc smiled at her once more and this time Cassie smile tentatively back.

Chapter Eight

Danielle Part II

A warm breeze wafted through the open window. The brick building had baked in the hot Georgia sun all day. Dani was having a hard time adjusting to the lack of air conditioning in most of her classes. Her dorm room didn't even have air. All she had to keep her cool was a large white plastic fan wedged in the window. All her energy was slowly being sapped away by the ever-present heat. Late in the afternoon, when English Lit rolled around, Dani's concentration was shot. She would be glad when November arrived. Her classmates had assured her the heat would break by then and the campus would be awash in cooler air. That seemed a million years away on this stifling September afternoon.

"What did Emily Dickinson mean when she wrote, 'Hope is the thing with feathers, that perches in the soul'?" asked Professor Carver.

A petite girl with short blue hair raised her hand.

"Well, um, I think it's a metaphor. Like, hope is in bird form here."

Dani rolled her eyes. It was so uncomfortably hot she was close to mentally checking out. She thought Dickinson was so eleventh grade. Professor Carver urged the class to dig deeper. A long silence settled in among the stuffy hot air.

Finally the tall boy in the front said, "Isn't she saying that hope is always caged or locked in our soul?"

"Can you lock away something like hope Andy?" challenged Professor Carver.

Andy gave the teacher a blank look.

"You can't cage hope," snipped a girl with curly red hair in a bright pink tank top. "Hope is an abstract concept. It is eternal and everywhere at once. Dickinson is telling us there is always hope, ready to burst forth at any moment, even in the bleakest days."

"Thank you Mary Ann," said Professor Carver. "That echoes the sentiments of the last few lines of the poem…"

Dani glazed over, glad someone had finally figured out the beautiful poem. She didn't think it was all that hard to understand. In fact, she had always held the poem to the highest truth. Dani was currently roosting a mighty hope on the perch of her soul. Since classes had started she had barely been able to devote any time to her true purpose of being all the way down here. The past few weeks had been so hectic and confusing. The campus was spread throughout the town and Dani was just now figuring out where all her classes were located without getting lost.

Plus, she was sharing her dorm room with a complete stranger. Casey was nice enough but they hadn't become friends yet. She wasn't sure they would ever be that close. Casey had posters of industrial metal bands on the walls of her side of the room. Dani wasn't exactly down with that. Casey did have a large stuffed pink rabbit on her bed though. That softened her tough girl image up considerably. She also shared her candy fetish with Dani. Bags of candy and chocolate bar wrappers littered their room. In return Dani had been helping Casey with her history assignments.

Dani had been resting her head in her hand when her arm slipped. Her elbow knocked her notebook to the floor. Dani reached down to retrieve it when a masculine hand darted out and picked up the notebook first. This startled Dani out of her heat daze and she looked up to see a guy smiling at her. He had tousled blonde hair and a few strands were covering his right eye. His one visible eye was a deep green color. He flipped Dani's notebook open and inserted a piece of paper. Then he handed the notebook back to her with a large grin plastered on his face. Dani mouthed 'thanks' and grabbed her notebook.

She swiveled around in her seat to face the front of the classroom and opened the notebook. The piece of paper that had been inserted was a flier advertising a party in Johnston Hall this coming Saturday. In the upper right corner of the flier the message, 'You should come, Trace', had been scribbled. Had that cute boy just invited her to a party? Dani stared in shock at the flier then closed the notebook. The party – any party for that matter – would have to wait. Dani had more important things to do. She would make friends later. This upcoming weekend would be the first one she had free from required freshmen seminars and she already knew what she was going to be doing. Dani had been making these plans for a long time now.

~ ~ ~

Dani pushed open the door to Frieda's Pizza and quickly made her way to the booth at the very back, near the kitchen. This is where Becca and she always sat. Most customers didn't like that booth because of the constant swinging door that led to the kitchen, but that never bothered the two friends. Since hardly anyone sat there it was always clean.

"Sorry I'm late! I had to drop Chelsea off at the football game. I'll have to pick her up in a few hours."

"That's ok, I already ordered for us."

"Triple cheese, large?"

"You know it!"

"This is why you are my bestie!"

Becca almost took a sip of her bright yellow drink when her eyes got wide and she slammed the drink back onto the table.

"Did you hear Tom wrecked his dad's police cruiser?" asked Becca.

"What? No way!"

"Cindy was in here a few minutes ago and she heard it from Kimmy, who lives next door to Tom and his family."

"What was he doing in the cop car?" asked Dani.

"Joy riding! How dumb can you get?"

Becca let out a huge laugh then finally took a long sip of her neon soda. She was already buzzed on caffeine. Becca could practically inhale caffeine.

"Oh! Before I forget. I have an early birthday gift for you!"

"What? No, Becca. My birthday isn't until next week. Just give it to me at my party."

"I can't silly. Your whole family will be there."

Dani gave Becca her arched eye-brow, what-are-you-up-to, look. Both girls laughed and Becca handed Dani a small square package wrapped in the Sunday funnies.

"Nice wrapping," said Dani wryly.

"Hey! I never said I wasn't cheap. Plus, I am doing my part to save the environment. Being green and all that."

Dani ripped the newspaper off and saw a folded map. The concept of a paper map seemed so old-fashioned. It was hard to believe people used these for navigation. How did travelers in the past not get completely lost?

"Open it up!" Becca instructed impatiently. "Start unfolding!"

Dani began unfolding the map. She soon saw it had been marked in various places. It was a map of the town where she was going to attend college.

"Those marks are all the places we've investigated. Your birth mom could be at any one of those locations right now!"

"This is amazing Becca! I don't know what to say…"

Dani trailed off and looked at her best friend. This was such a lovely gesture. Dani thought she might cry.

"Oh, don't tear up on me! Just think of me when you use it, ok?"

"Sure thing Becca."

Their triple cheese pizza arrived just then and the girls dived in.

~ ~ ~

Dani sat down on the bus stop bench, closed her eyes and took a deep breath. When she felt calm she opened the yellow binder, pulled out the map and marked an X over yet another spot. For the past five weekends Dani had combed the town using the map Becca had given her as a birthday present. So far she had been unsuccessful in finding her birth mother. No one seemed to know anything about Shelby Perry. Dani had grown increasingly frustrated. She wasn't sure what she had expected when she had moved to the little college town, but it hadn't been this. Dani hadn't thought it would be this hard.

She checked her next location on the map and then her watch. The bus wouldn't come by for another fifteen minutes so Dani put the map and binder back in her messenger bag and tried to relax. This Saturday was breezy and crisp. Her classmates had been right. November had brought cooler weather. She still didn't need a coat though. Back home in Virginia they would be breaking out the coats, scarves and mittens right about now. Apparently, you didn't need those items down here until December, sometimes January.

As Dani waited for the bus she thought about Becca. She missed her best friend. Dani wished Becca were here to help her with the search. It would've been nice to have some company on this journey. Everywhere Dani looked these days everything was new and strange. It was an unsettling feeling. She had been missing home for the past few weeks. She hadn't expected that. Dani laughed at herself as she sat on the empty bus bench. She had spent years yearning to leave home and find her real family. But so far she had found no one and in the process she had begun to miss her parents and sister greatly. Surely Professor Carver would call this dramatic irony or something like that.

Dani gave a sigh and looked up the street once more for the bus. She had become quite adept at traveling the public bus line. Some of the drivers were even beginning to recognize her. If she went out searching at night Dani hired a taxi, but during the pleasant fall days she preferred to take the bus. So far Dani had visited over a dozen locations. Not one of those places had turned up Shelby Perry. She was lucky if she got weak leads and the location wasn't a total dead end. Some places had provided her with forwarding addresses, and others could only give her a shake of the head and a sympathetic "sorry".

One of the places she had visited last weekend was a brightly painted Victorian house about ten minutes from where she now sat. The current owner was a little old lady who had been quite deaf. She had practically yelled her questions about Shelby Perry to the woman. Dani had been standing on the front porch, the owner had stood in her cracked doorway, and somehow during the interrogation the lady's cat had escaped. Dani had spent the next hour looking for the truant pet only to find it trapped in a street gutter. It had then taken her another twenty minutes to pry the cat out. By the time she returned to her dorm room she was filthy and tired. Plus, she had multiple cat scratches on her arms.

The weekend before that Dani had visited a temp agency. The office manager had refused to give Dani any information about Shelby Perry even though it had seemed like she knew something about her birth mother. That same day she had also visited a food bank and a homeless shelter. The food bank volunteers couldn't recall a Shelby Perry gracing their doorstep. The homeless shelter had been very busy with people in need and no one seemed to have time for Dani's usual game of twenty questions. One lady who worked there told Dani so many women had come and gone it would be almost impossible to track her birth mother.

Sitting on that bench Dani had begun to wonder just who Shelby Perry really was. She had visited quite a few places that helped destitute and in need people. She wondered if her birth mother's life had always been like this. Dani couldn't help but think that this was the reason she had given her up for adoption. She had lain awake last night and wondered if she should call the search off. Knowing what she now knew, well maybe Shelby Perry didn't want Dani to find her. An unwanted child certainly wouldn't fit into her vagabond lifestyle. But then again, maybe her birth mother needed her help? These confusing thoughts had been running through Dani's exhausted mind all night and day.

The last few weeks had given Dani a new appreciation for the stable home she had grown up in. But as Dani sat on that bench she knew in her bones she couldn't give up the search until she found the mysterious and always out of reach Shelby Perry. She didn't want to live the rest of her life wondering. Dani had done enough of that in the past. She hadn't realized until now how weary she had grown. Now she understood why a lot of people gave up looking for their birth parents. Maybe it wasn't because they wanted to stop looking, but because they had eventually run out of leads, out of time, out of hope. Those people had no other choice. Their long-lost family members might as well be ghosts. Was the thing with feathers in her soul losing its hope?

Dani heard the bus rumbling down the street and she vowed to herself with determination that she would look into each and every lead until she had no more paths to travel down. She paid her bus toll and took a seat near the front. She was on her way to visit a Habitat for Humanity home building site. This lead had been provided by a local pastor. Dani guessed her birth mother hardly ever attended the church because the pastor didn't know much about her. This whole journey, the places she had visited, was so strange to Dani. She didn't understand any of it. Shelby Perry had obviously needed a lot of assistance. What would this lady think when she met her? A daughter Shelby hadn't looked for since giving birth? A daughter that was attending the college in her hometown. A daughter who had grown up in a very comfortable middle-class existence. Maybe they wouldn't have anything in common but genes. Dani shivered at the bleak thought.

Dani exited the bus at her stop and began walking the four blocks to the build site. After she rounded a corner she saw a flurry of activity up ahead. Dani heard hammers pounding and saw blades whirring. It was a beautiful day to be building a house no doubt. Dani approached a lady taking a break underneath a shady tree and asked if she knew who Rachel Moore was. The resting lady pointed to a woman in a plaid flannel shirt and jeans splattered with paint.

"Excuse me, Mrs. Moore?"

The middle-aged lady turned around and said, "Yeah?"

"Hi, I'm looking for information on someone. I was hoping you could help-"

"Hey! Make sure that's grounded! I don't need any accidents today!"

Mrs. Moore marked a piece of paper attached to her clipboard then looked up at Dani.

"You were saying?"

"Oh! Yes. I'm looking for someone, a Shelby Perry. Do you know her?"

The woman in plaid thought for a moment.

"Nope. Sorry."

"Are you sure -"

"Hey! That goes over there!"

"Mrs. Moore -"

"Look, I'm sorry but that name rings no bells. I've been managing these jobs for quite a while too. I have to get back over there before someone does something stupid and gets hurt. Excuse me."

Dani, disappointed once again, watched the lady direct a load of dry wall.

"She's kinda like sandpaper sometimes."

Dani turned around and came face to face with the cute boy from her English Lit class. He pushed his disheveled blonde hair out of his face and smiled. Dani had to look up to see him. Usually she was as tall as or taller than most boys, but this guy was a few inches taller than her.

"What?"

"She's rough. Like sandpaper."

"Umm…ok. I'm sorry, you're…"

The guy laughed.

"You've been in a class with me for two months now and you still don't know my name. My feelings are hurt."

"I'm sorry, I've been – oh, you're joking."

The guy laughed again and put out his hand.

"I'm Trace Moore."

"Moore? Is -"

"Is that grouchy lady related to me? Yep. That's my mom."

Dani reached out and tentatively shook Trace's hand.

"And you -"

"Help out at build sites on the weekends."

"Oh. That's nice."

"So Danielle, what are you doing here?"

"How do you know my name?"

"English Lit...two months...I sit two desks behind you off to the right..."

"Right. Sorry. And it's Dani. Just Dani."

Dani blushed. She felt silly standing in front of this cute boy looking so stupid.

"So, you're here because..." he pressed.

"I'm looking for information on someone, but your mom didn't know her. Just another dead end."

"Another? You working on a mystery?"

Dani looked sharply at Trace.

"Sorry, bad joke," said Trace. "I spend a lot of time reading mystery, who-done-it novels. It's kind of a hobby of mine."

"You do? Most people our age won't admit that. Because, well, it's..."

"Dorky?" asked Trace with a hint of humor.

Dani laughed. This made him smile for some reason.

"Yeah. Well, good luck on the house. Uh, see you in class."

"Well now. That's the problem. I'll see you but you won't see me. You never came to that party I invited you to."

"Party?"

Dani thought hard then remembered the flier he had placed in her notebook.

"Oh, that's right! Well, I'm sure you invited more girls than just me."

"Actually, no. Just you."

Dani stared at Trace's handsome face. His green eyes looked luminous. She most certainly didn't believe she was the only girl he had invited. Boys like him at her old high school never gave her a second glance.

"So, this lady you're looking for. Maybe I can help?"

"Help? How?"

"Well, being the son of that lady over there barking out orders I have access to certain databases. I could, say, run a name through. See what turns up?"

Dani looked up at Trace hopefully but cautiously. She wasn't sure why this handsome guy wanted to help her out.

"Really?"

"Sure."

Dani pulled a piece of paper out of her messenger bag and wrote down her birth mother's name. She then handed it to Trace.

"Shelby Perry, huh?"

"Why do I feel like we're becoming characters in a mystery novel?" asked Dani.

"Better yet," said Trace as he leaned in towards Dani, "if we were in a suspenseful movie we'd be hearing the duhn duhn duhn music in the background right about now."

Dani laughed. It felt good. She hadn't laughed, *really laughed*, in a while.

"I'll let you know what I find next Tuesday after English Lit. Sound good?"

"Sounds great! Thanks Trace."

"You're welcome Dani."

Sunday and Monday crawled by at a snail's pace. Dani was impatient for Tuesday afternoon to arrive. She was desperate to know if Trace had found any information about Shelby. Dani was running out of leads. Her hope was beginning to lose its feathers.

When Tuesday afternoon finally arrived Dani hurried off to English Lit. She loved the classics but was no fan of Professor Carver's hand holding teaching style. The students in her class should've already known the material the professor was throwing at them. Most of the time Dani zoned out in English Lit. She was happy her science and math classes were more progressive.

When Dani entered the classroom her eyes immediately darted around to see if Trace was there. He wasn't. Dani's spirits sank. She dropped in her seat and opened her notebook so she could pretend to take notes on today's lecture. Five minutes after class started the door creaked open and Trace quietly entered the classroom. He ducked down and made his way over to his usual seat. Dani couldn't help but wonder why he was late. She swiveled in her seat to glance back at him. Trace gave her a friendly grin like always.

Dani couldn't wait for class to be over with. When the bell finally rang she gathered up her books and waited for Trace out in the hall. He was still inside apologizing to Professor Carver for being tardy. After a minute he emerged from the classroom.

"So, what did you find?"

Dani looked at Trace eagerly and hopefully.

"Hello to you to."

"Oh, sorry. I mean, hi. So, did you find her? Did you find Shelby Perry?"

"Do you like coffee?"

"Coffee?"

"Yeah, coffee, lattes, mochaccinos. There's a great coffee house just down the street. My treat. What do you say?"

Dani stood in the hall and stared at Trace. Why in the world was he talking about coffee?

"We can talk about what I found there."

"Oh! Ok." said Dani. "Well, let's go."

As they exited the brick building Dani noticed Trace only wore casual cargo pants and a fitted short sleeve t-shirt. She also noticed for the first time that his arms were very muscular. Must be from all the house building she thought.

"What are you staring at?"

"Huh?" muttered Dani.

"Why are you staring at me like that?"

Trace had a hint of a smirk on his face. Dani flushed and turned away. The wind rushed down the tree lined street blowing her long bangs into her eyes. The rest of her long blonde hair was up in a twisted knot. She was glad for the distraction.

"I was just thinking, er, wondering if you were cold," she lied. "You don't have a jacket on."

Trace laughed. Nothing ever seemed to faze him.

"No, I'm warm blooded. I rarely get cold."

When they reached the coffee house Trace held the door open for her. Dani stepped inside and looked around. It was a charming place. The coffee shop was toasty inside and Dani was glad as she shivered. She hadn't realized she was chilly.

"I figured the cold wouldn't bother a Northerner like you."

"I'm not a Northerner!" Dani protested. "I'm from Virginia. That's the South too."

"You don't have much of an accent."

"Neither do you."

"I was raised by my dad in Michigan. I came down here for college to spend some time with my mom."

They ordered caramel lattes and sat at a table by the window facing the street.

"So, I kinda have some bad news," began Trace.

"Bad news?"

"Yeah, I couldn't find anything on Shelby Perry. I checked both databases and even searched the file cabinets. But I turned up nothing on your mystery lady."

Dani's face fell. It really was another dead end. The usual disappointment filled her.

"I'm really sorry Dani."

"It's ok. Thanks for trying. I should get going."

Dani stood up to leave and Trace stood up so suddenly he almost toppled his chair over.

"No! Stay…please."

"Why?"

"Well, I thought we could get to know each other."

"Oh, I don't know…"

"What else are you gonna do? Go hide in your dorm room as usual?"

Dani sat back down in her chair and glared at Trace. He too sat down to see what she would say.

"Excuse me? How the hell do you know anything about me?"

"I have Chem with your roomie Casey. She says you don't hang out with anyone and spend all your time obsessing over a bunch of maps and stuff."

"That's none of your business!"

"Actually, you made it my business when you asked me to help you look for that lady. What's going on Dani?"

"I've gotta go."

"Fine, go. But college life is pretty tough without any friends. Is that how you want to spend the next four years? Isolated with no friends?"

Dani looked down at her latte. The truth was, she was terribly lonely. She was tired of looking for her birth mother all by herself in a strange town. Dani had put off making friends so she could concentrate on the search. But now she was home sick and several times she had even thought about calling it a day and heading back home to Virginia.

"You can talk to me Dani. I won't even interrupt. I'll just listen."

Trace made a pretend show of zipping, then locking his lips shut and throwing away an imaginary key. Of course, immediately after he spoke.

"I've seen you around campus you know," he said softly. "You're always by yourself. You always look sad. Why? Is something wrong? Because if there is -"

"Just shut up! Didn't you just say, or mime, or whatever that you were going to zip it? Are you gonna listen or what?"

Trace nodded, pretended to zip his lips once more, and for the next hour Dani told this absolute stranger all about her search for Shelby Perry and why it was so important to her. She even told him about the outfit she had bought back in the summer. That outfit was still hanging in her dorm closet, unworn. It depressed Dani each time she saw it.

Trace was true to his word. He merely listened as Dani spilled her story. It felt so strange to tell someone besides Becca about all her hopes and fears. Dani had been carrying this heavy emotional load for so long it was a relief to unburden herself. Finally, two lattes later, Dani had talked herself out.

"Look, I know this isn't my place Dani but, why don't you let me help you?"

"Help me? How?"

"You said you still have a few more leads. I spent two months every summer growing up visiting my mom in this town. I know it pretty well. You said there were a few places you couldn't find, right?"

"Yes, but," Dani sighed, "You know what, screw it. I'd love some help. I'm tired of doing this on my own."

Trace laughed that hearty assured laugh. For some reason his laugh appealed to her.

"Thank you so much Trace. Not just for helping but, for listening."

"No problem. So, let's see that map. Looks like I'll be taking a break from building houses this weekend."

"Ok. And this time lattes are on me! Deal?"

As they shook hands hope fluttered in Dani's soul once more.

The motorcycle raced down the hard-top road, veered to the left and lurched onto the pedestrian sidewalk. A few feet later the machine screeched to a halt on a dusty patch of land. Dani unlocked her iron grip from around Trace's waist and hopped off his bike. She removed her helmet and looked around.

"What are we doing here? This isn't on the map."

"We've been hitting spots on the map for the past three hours. It's lunch time and I'm starved. I'm a growing boy Dani. I've gotta eat!"

Trace smiled and winked at her.

"You already eat like you're a bottomless pit!" Dani teased. "How is it you never gain any weight?"

"Basketball with the boys three times a week at the gym."

"So, what? We're eating in this shack?"

"For your information, this so-called shack serves the best tacos in town. You have to try these things."

For the past few weeks Trace had been helping Dani with her search. It used to take her several hours to map a location and then figure out how to get there by bus or taxi. But now that Trace was a part of the scheme they went everywhere on his bright red motorcycle. The first time he had pulled up to her dorm on it her stomach had lurched. Her parents had forbidden her from riding on motorcycles in high school. They had called them death machines. At first Dani had balked at accepting the ride, but Trace had persisted and finally wore all her arguments down. He knew the town so well that it took them no time to arrive at the mysterious locations. It was definitely a thrill inducing time saver. And so far, Trace had proved to be a safe driver.

Dani's first time on the motorcycle had been exciting in a make your palms sweat and hair stand on end sort of way. The bike had flown down the street and Dani had clung to Trace for dear life. But now she was used to, ok *getting used to,* the fast ride. She even had her very own matching red helmet that Trace had picked up for her. Of course, she had made sure not to mention Trace's motorcycle to her parents. They would have flipped out! In fact, Dani had kept Trace a secret from her parents altogether. She couldn't exactly explain to them who he was and what they did on weekends. Trace let Dani keep her helmet in her dorm room when they weren't racing around town. Her roommate Casey was even jealous of it!

"I wish I had a boyfriend who bought me cool shit like this!"

"Trace isn't my boyfriend. He's just a friend."

"Yeah, right. I've seen the way he looks at you. Plus, he spent the first few weeks in Chem asking about you all the time."

"The way he looks at me? No, you've misunderstood. He's helping me with a project."

"Is the project trying to get into your pants?"

"Casey! He would not! He's never even made a move on me!"

"That must be disappointing. Besides, why not? Is he gay? I don't really get a gay-vibe from him."

Dani rolled her eyes and continued folding her laundry. As far as she could tell Casey never did laundry.

"So, do you think he's hot?"

"Well, yeah." said Dani. "He's cute. So?"

"And you like hanging out with him?"

"Yeah, he's a lot of fun. We get along really well."

"But you don't want to date him?"

Dani hesitated.

"It's just not like that between us. We're just friends, I think. Besides, he could date anyone on campus. I'm sure there is no short supply of girls who think he's hot."

"Uh-huh…whatever. You better just hope those girls don't beat you to it."

When the tacos arrived at their table Dani had to admit they were really good. Probably the best tacos she had ever eaten. Halfway through their meal Trace's cell buzzed. It was his mom and she needed his help on a home build site. One of the volunteer electricians hadn't shown up and if Trace didn't pitch in the house would fall behind schedule.

"I'm really sorry Dani."

"That's ok. I understand. We can do these next three locations later this week. Well, actually just these two. This address doesn't even exist."

"Let me see. Hmmm…oh! You just have it spelled wrong. It's Highland Street, not High Land Street. One word."

"Really?"

"Yeah, see, here it is on the map."

Dani bit into another taco and tried to remember where she had originally gotten that address.

Later that afternoon Dani put the final touches on her English Lit paper that dissected revenge and the character of Hamlet. Once the paper was finished Dani realized she had completed all her weekend homework assignments. She leaned back in her chair and wondered what Trace was up to at the build site. Dani made a promise to herself that if she were successful in finding her birth mother, or if they finally ran out of leads, she would repay Trace for all his help by volunteering for his mother's Habitat for Humanity crew. She figured she could handle a hammer or a nail gun as well as the next person. Of course, someone would have to show her exactly how to use one first. Plus, she could spend more time with Trace. You know, if he wanted her to.

Dani pulled her map out and began crossing off the locations Trace and she had visited today. All dead ends as usual. If Dani found a lead that went somewhere she wasn't sure how she would react. She would probably pass out from surprise. Dani was almost finished marking the map when she remembered the Highland Street address. Suddenly Dani remembered how she had acquired that particular address. It had been one of the first leads Becca had traced to this town. These past few months Dani had thought it was a false lead. But now it was an active lead again.

She looked at the clock on her desk. She still had a whole evening to fill by herself. Dani hadn't realized until recently how much of a presence Trace had become in her life. Most of her free time was now spent with him studying, searching for her birth mother or playing air hockey in the student lounge. Dani and Chelsea used to play air hockey all the time as kids so she frequently beat Trace. Lately they had taken to making silly bets. Yesterday the loser had to buy the winner a brownie sundae supreme. Trace had won that round, but he had split the gooey treat with her. He was always doing little things like that for her. Trace really was a great guy.

After staring at the wall in her dorm room for another five minutes Dani realized she didn't want to spend her evening like a zombie. She called a cab, gathered her yellow binder and map, placed them in her messenger bag and headed out the door. She doubted Trace would be too pleased when he found out. He had been concerned for her safety when he found out about her nighttime expeditions. Trace didn't like Dani traveling alone to unknown locations. But he was busy and she couldn't keep relying on him. After all, wasn't college about learning how to function in the real world like an adult?

The cab picked Dani up in front of her dorm and then they were off as the sun began to set. She wrapped her coat around her tightly. A cold front had moved into town. Twenty minutes later the cab pulled up to the curb on a quiet residential street. Dani peered out of the dirty back window and looked around. She noticed it was a very nice section of town with large, expensive looking houses lining the street.

"This is Highland Street miss."

"Can you wait for me? I'm sure this will only take a minute."

"It's your dime, just remember the meter is running."

Dani nodded at the cab driver then slipped out the back door into the chilled night air. She stood on the sidewalk in front of another three story Victorian house with intricate scroll design work. As she stared at the house nervously she noticed for the first time that someone was standing on a step-ladder on the front porch. Dani approached the house cautiously and watched the figure in the shadow work on a light fixture near the door. Dani cleared her throat.

"Hello? Excuse me."

The figure gave a startled jump and gripped the ladder.

"Didn't you see the sign?" asked a gruff man's voice.

"I'm sorry. The sign?"

"The no soliciting sign. Whatever you're selling I don't want."

"Oh! I'm not selling anything. I'm looking for someone."

"Yeah, who's that?"

The man continued to work on the light fixture. He hadn't turned around so Dani couldn't see his face.

"I'm looking for a woman named Shelby Perry."

The man stopped tinkering with a wire and stood still for a moment. Then he shook his head and said, "No one lives here by that name."

"Are you sure? Maybe she lived here before you. Do you have any records of the previous owner?"

"Look lady," the man began as he climbed down the step ladder holding a screw driver and another tool Dani couldn't identify, "no one lives here by that name."

The man reached the porch floor and turned to look at her for the first time. Dani could see he was an older gentleman, probably a few years older than her father. His hair was mostly grey and he had a face full of two day old stubble. He wore jeans and a worn looking work shirt. When the man looked at Dani he muttered, "Sweet mercy" and dropped all the tools in his hands. The tools clattered to the wooden porch floor as the man continued to stare at her.

"Are you alright?" Dani asked.

Her palms started to sweat she was so nervous. His strange actions put her on edge.

"You're her," he whispered.

"I'm sorry. Do you know me?" asked Dani confused.

The man moved closer to Dani. He studied her face intently and then smiled at her. It was a warm and affectionate smile.

"I know someone who looks an awful lot like you."

Dani's heart began to race and her mind went into overdrive.

"Who is that?" she asked, her mouth suddenly dry.

"I wondered if you'd ever show up."

The man held out a hand to Dani.

"I'm Patrick Derring by the way. But everyone calls me Pat. I reckon you should too."

Dani gripped the man's rough hand in her trembling hand.

"I'm Danielle James. Everyone calls me Dani. Do...do you know Shelby Perry?"

"I sure do. She was my wife for thirteen years. Best years of my life. Go get rid of that cab and come in for some coffee or hot cider. Your choice."

Pat ambled into the house and Dani stared after him in shock.

Pat Derring had met Shelby Perry fifteen years ago in Tennessee. They had fallen in love quickly and married a year later. It was Pat who had brought them to Georgia seven years ago when his job transferred him. According to Pat their life was near perfect and Shelby was his soul mate.

Listening to Pat Dani had grown increasingly excited and anxious to meet the woman he was describing. All her fears about Shelby vanished and were replaced once again with the overwhelming need to meet the woman who had given birth to her.

"Where is Shelby now Pat? I just want to meet her! It's all I've ever wanted. If…if she wants to meet me."

"Sweetheart, Shelby would have liked nothing more in her whole life than to meet you. In fact, she dreamed of it quite often. She just wasn't sure how you would respond."

Pat poured Dani another cup of warm cider and suddenly looked sad.

"Pat, what's wrong?"

"Dani, I hate to be the one to tell you this, but Shelby passed away three years ago. She had a stroke and never recovered."

Dani could barely breathe and went into some sort of shock. All her hopes and dreams had come crashing down in her chest. Dani put her hand on her chest as though it might collapse. Dani could not believe this was the end to her long search.

"I'm so sorry. Your mother never forgot you Dani. She always hoped you'd come looking for her one day. She often mentioned trying to find you."

"Why didn't she?" asked Dani hoarsely, while holding back tears.

"Ah, Shelby was scared."

"Scared?"

"She knew the James' were good people. Shelby had met them briefly. She didn't want to disrupt your life. It always haunted Shelby that she couldn't give you a home all those years ago. When she had you she was young. She had barely known your father. They had dated only briefly.

"At that time she had no money and no job. She didn't think she could give you the life you deserved."

"How did you meet her?"

"I had already been married once before. I was a good decade older than your mom. We met while working for a non-profit that helped refugees find housing, work and education. Your mother was a very charitable soul. Maybe…well, I always thought she was trying to atone for her past mistakes or something. She was a good woman Dani."

Suddenly all the locations Dani had visited in the past few weeks fell into place like the pieces of a puzzle. They had all been places that helped people down on their luck. Shelby hadn't needed the assistance; she had been helping others find assistance.

"This is for you Dani."

Pat had pulled out a beautiful light pink album. He handed it to Dani.

"What's this?"

"Items your mother collected for you over the years. She had hoped to give it to you herself one day."

Pat cast his eyes downward. Dani could tell her loss had affected him greatly. It was obvious he had loved his wife.

Dani opened the cover of the album and gasped. A woman who looked almost exactly like her was staring up at her. The resemblance was remarkable.

"She sure was pretty, wasn't she?" said Pat.

Dani could only nod her head in agreement. She reached out a trembling hand and ran a finger along her mother's long blonde hair. It was the exact same color as Dani's hair. After the shock wore off a little Dani continued to flip through the album her mother had made for her. It was filled with pictures of relatives she had never known and even medical information. Pieces of Dani's puzzle began to click into place. It was overwhelming, but also oddly comforting. When Dani reached the back of the album a manila envelope fell out. It was sealed. Dani picked it up and looked at it.

"Is this for me too?"

"Yes, that there is information about your father."

"My father? You mean, my *birth father*?"

"Shelby collected leads on him throughout the years. She wanted you to be able to find him one day if that was your wish."

Pat chuckled.

"What?" asked Dani.

"Well, that was just like Shelby."

"What do you mean?"

"Oh, well, Shelby always did love a good mystery."

Dani stared at Pat as a grin broke out over her face. Tears escaped the corner of her eyes. Dani loved a good mystery too, but this one was finally solved. It hadn't ended the way she had hoped but a large piece of the puzzle of her life was now complete.

Chapter Nine

Alicia Part II

The first time the phone rang Alicia ignored it. No one she knew would call her this early on a Saturday morning. The second time the phone rang she rolled over and looked at the alarm clock beside the bed. It was only eight-thirty. When the phone rang the third time Alicia answered. It was Odessa wanting to know if she would like to grab some lunch at their favorite spot. These days, in her life, good company was in short supply. Good food and even better conversation was just the temptation needed to get her moving on a weekend morning.

Alicia threw off her bed covers and made her way to the cramped bathroom. After a quick shower she wrapped a towel around her body and then wiped steam off the mirror above the sink with her hand. Alicia pulled her plastic shower cap off and fluffed out her hair. Odessa had given her a dramatic Cleopatra look. The braids were gone and in their place she had sleek straight hair that was cut just above her shoulders. She also had heavy bangs that fell to the top of her eyebrows. Alicia loved this cut. Not only was it easy to style, but damn did she look good!

Alicia and Odessa had formed a tight bond since that first evening she had come into the salon for weave life support. Alicia hadn't realized before that night just how isolated she had become. It was a revelation to her to find friendship in the older woman. The two were from different generations and backgrounds but they had a lot in common. After the deaths of her grandmother Netty and her best friend Vanessa she had cut herself off emotionally from other people. At times during the past eight months it had taken all her energy just to make polite, banal conversation with her co-workers at the bank. It was nice to have someone to talk to again about the real things that make up life. Alicia could confide in Odessa.

Odessa liked to talk anyways. When she was in a good mood she could be a non-stop chatterbox. Over the last two months Alicia had learned a lot about the elegant lady that owned Nubia Hair. Odessa had been married four times to four *very* different men. Husband number one had been an accountant. They had married very young and had a son. Husband number one had cheated on Odessa with his secretary.

"Your typical shit," Odessa had said while smoking a cigarette. "Text book. Almost a cliché. The sex-retary for heavens sake! A car hit him a few years back and he died. Karma's a bitch."

Alicia had recently begun to try to get her to stop smoking but it was slow going. Husband number two had been a plumber.

"I guess I was rebounding. Once I woke up I realized we had neither spark nor future. Plus, pipes were the only thing he could snake honey."

Husband number three had been of mixed race. He was a chef who had taught Odessa how to run a business. But one day he hit Odessa and that was all it took.

"I wasn't gonna wait around for the second hit, and so on. Those dumb women who stay always end up dead. I was gone so fast girl!"

The fourth husband had been a linguistic professor. Friedrich had been born in Germany but his family had immigrated to America when he was a teenager. He had a quiet but intense love of languages. Friedrich had died from a sudden massive heart attack three years ago.

"He's been the hardest to get over. I guess I still haven't. I loved him the most."

"Why?" Alicia had asked.

"Because he loved me the most. He always told me I was his special language. A secret language only he could decipher. You know what, he was right. He understood me, all the parts of me; the beautiful and the ugly."

The tight bond the ladies shared had started to cement the first night they met.

They began as confidants about something that was rarely spoken of in their community. Odessa's youngest brother had committed suicide when they were both in their twenties. The night Alicia had met Odessa they had talked into the early morning hours at the salon. Not only had Odessa comforted Alicia, but she had opened up to her and shared a piece of her past that she rarely talked about.

"They always tell you in those damn brochures to look for all the signs but, to be honest, I don't recall seeing any of those signs in Jarell. That's what makes it so scary. By the time we found him it was too late. He was gone."

Jarell had hung himself with his belt in a closet.

"You won't hear anyone talk about it either. It's taboo or some stupid shit like that."

Odessa had wrinkled her nose in distaste.

"It's a shame. If more of us would talk about it we might save more people like Jarell or Vanessa."

Odessa had been trying to get Alicia into counseling down at the Community Health Center, but she wasn't interested. The idea of counseling scared her. She didn't like the thought of being open and vulnerable with a stranger. Besides, Odessa's friendship had been the best therapy for Alicia as far as she was concerned.

Alicia rounded the corner and saw Gloria's Café up ahead. The atmosphere was casual with no pretense and the food was all home cooked. The only people who ate there were locals who lived in the surrounding neighborhoods. Sometimes the cook would sing snippets of old Sam Cooke or Otis Redding songs to the ladies. He thought he was smooth. Soul food had never been tastier.

An elderly couple was exiting the glass door to Gloria's Café. The man held the door open for Alicia and she thanked him. She always thought it was nice when a man had manners. Not that you saw much of that anymore. Alicia spotted Odessa tucked away in the corner of the restaurant. When she approached she realized Odessa was on her cell.

"Yes, I do know that Benjy. Your momma has been around the block a time or two…mmm-hmmm…look Benjy, I've got to go. Come over later tonight for dinner and we can talk about this some more…love you too baby."

Odessa snapped her cell shut and rolled her eyes.

"That boy is a mess. In all other aspects of his life he has it straight. Job, nice townhouse, school, hobbies. But when it comes to women he just can't seem to find any good ones. He spent most of his life in my salon surrounded by women. You think he'd be better at picking them. But no, he always picks those heart breakers."

"That's your son Benjamin?"

Odessa nodded yes and took a long sip of her sweet iced-tea. Alicia saw a tall empty glass near the silver napkin holder and guessed this was her second one. The table was also littered with empty sugar packets. Today was a day Odessa was trying to not smoke, so sugar filled the empty nicotine space.

Lemarr the cook came out of the kitchen carrying two plates full of steaming food. Vondra the waitress was too busy flirting with a cute boy sitting at the counter. Lemarr was crooning *You Send Me* and on his way back to the kitchen he spied the two women.

"Ladies, ladies, you are both looking mighty fine today."

Alicia blushed and looked down, but Odessa just laughed.

"All the singing in the world won't sway us Lemarr," Odessa cackled.

"Is that so? Not even this fine sister right here?"

Lemarr was staring appreciatively at Alicia. She was baffled why he was paying any attention to her. Lemarr usually reserved his compliments and songs for the pretty girls in the Café.

"You get out of here! Get back in that kitchen!" Odessa admonished him.

Lemarr laughed at Odessa's orders, winked at Alicia then made his way back to the kitchen while singing *Ain't Too Proud To Beg*.

"I swear, all men think about anymore is sex. Whatever happened to romance and wooing a sister? You don't have to be embarrassed Lemarr was hitting on you. With that new 'do and all the shopping we've been doing lately men were bound to notice honey."

Odessa picked up her sweet iced-tea and was about to take a sip when she stopped and looked at Alicia as if she were seeing her for the first time.

"Why didn't I think of this before?"

"Think of what?"

"You haven't been dating for a while. It's time for you to get back out there."

Alicia was getting uncomfortable. She hadn't dated anyone in almost two years. The last person she had gone on a date with had been Mick Kelly. He had taken her to the movies then tried to stick his tongue down her throat and unhook her bra in the car afterwards. Alicia had made sure that was their first *and* last date. What a creep!

"I don't think I'm ready to date anyone right now."

"Why not?"

Odessa was looking at her in an accusatory manner.

Alicia lowered her voice, leaned across the table and said, "You know why! I had to take care of my Gram and the house. And then with Vanessa…"

Alicia trailed off, leaned back in her chair and sighed.

"It's time and I have the perfect man for you."

Alicia looked towards the kitchen apprehensively.

"Not Lemarr! He's a bit fast and too much player for you. No, I mean Benjy!"

"Your son?"

"Yes my son. *He* needs a date with a nice girl. *You* need a date with a nice boy. It's perfect. Besides, you said he was cute. Actually, I think the word you used was 'hunktastic'."

Alicia couldn't recall saying this about Odessa's son. She had never even met him.

"When did I say that?"

"The other day when he delivered a package to you."

A sudden vision of a tall, handsome black man dressed in a fitted brown delivery uniform filled Alicia's mind. *He* was Odessa's son? Alicia was speechless. Odessa cackled in delight.

Alicia tried to talk her way out of the date during the rest of their lunch but Benjamin was Odessa's son. She didn't want to hurt the feelings of the one true friend she had these days. By the time Alicia returned to her apartment later that afternoon she went and laid down on her bed while the cool waves from the air conditioner washed over her. She had a date next Friday night. Alicia thought she might be sick.

Alicia pulled up to the curb, turned the station wagon off and stared at the blue house. Her renter, Mrs. Phan, couldn't figure out why the back-screen door that led to the small, square wood deck wouldn't open without a lot of effort. Mrs. Phan had wanted to call a handy man but Alicia had told her that she would be right over. Not only would a handy man charge double because it was a Sunday, but Alicia already knew how to fix the screen door. It came off its tracks easily if it was pushed open too fast.

Alicia got out of her vehicle and walked onto the front lawn. She examined the exterior of the blue house. Mrs. Phan wasn't taking care of the home the way Gram had. Weeds were growing in the flower bed and the gutters looked clogged with debris. Alicia skipped up the stairs as she had done many times as a child and knocked on the door. That was a strange feeling. Knocking on your own front door and waiting for someone else to answer it. Alicia felt like she was having an out of body experience.

Mrs. Phan answered the door in her floral print kaftan and red slippers. She was divorced and had two young children. Kids that now lived in Alicia's peach colored bedroom. As she walked through the house to the dining room and the errant screen door she wondered at how alien someone else's furniture looked inside. Alicia had placed most of the home's original furnishings in storage. She hadn't liked the idea of strangers sitting on Gram's favorite chairs, storing their clothes in her dresser.

Alicia quickly fixed the screen door and warned Mrs. Phan not to open the door too quickly the next time. As she was getting ready to leave Mrs. Phan asked her to stay for a moment. She had something to give her. The tiny woman came back into the room carrying a plain cardboard box.

"This was address to you Miss."

Mrs. Phan handed the medium sized box to Alicia. There was no postage or address on it, just Alicia's name.

"I found it on the front porch one night after work. See, that's your name."

Mrs. Phan pointed to Alicia's name. She smiled at the petite lady then left the house with the mystery package. Once inside the station wagon her curiosity got the best of her so Alicia ripped off the packing tape and opened the box. When Alicia saw the contents inside she held her breath until she thought she might pass out. The box contained items that had once belonged to Vanessa. Before Alicia knew what was happening she was sitting in front of her old house, crying into a box of Vanessa's belongings.

Alicia laid the box on her bed later that afternoon and peered inside. A bundle of letters and cards tied with a purple ribbon were sitting on the top of the other contents. Alicia picked the bundle up and immediately recognized the card she had given Vanessa on her last birthday. She knew the inside sentiment wished her many more. Alicia's heart clenched tightly in her chest and she felt slightly nauseous. She laid the bundle down and once again looked in the box. This time she saw a silver music box. Vanessa had kept her favorite pieces of jewelry inside. She opened the lid and *Over the Rainbow* floated out. Nestled inside were several necklaces, bracelets and rings.

Alicia snapped the box shut and the tune vanished instantly. It finally occurred to Alicia that Vanessa's parents must have wanted her to have these items. She had not seen them since the funeral, but Alicia had a connection to most of the items in the box. There were crafts they had made together as kids at church vacation bible school, some CDs, a bottle of Tommy Girl perfume (Vanessa's favorite) and an album of photos. Alicia didn't dare open that. She couldn't handle seeing Vanessa's smiling face at the moment.

She kept rooting around in the box until she felt something slick near the bottom. She pulled the object out and realized she was holding one of Vanessa's old journals. *Her journal.* Alicia quickly searched the box and found all five of them. The bright colored journals now lay on Alicia's bed. She stared at the covers for a long time until she couldn't bear to look at them anymore. She shoved everything back in the box then tossed it into an empty chair. Alicia threw herself back onto her bed and covered her eyes with her arm. She was too exhausted to cry anymore and soon she fell into a restless sleep.

Several days passed before Alicia thought about the box and its contents. She had methodically erased the thought of the box from her mind. If the image of it popped into her head she shoved it right back out. She did not feel like dealing with the box and all the memories she knew the items inside would bring back. But on Thursday morning she was making a deposit at the bank for a local business when she had a sudden thought. What if the last journal held a clue as to why Vanessa had committed suicide?

Truthfully Alicia still didn't understand *why*. It was a mystery to her and others who had been close to Vanessa. Her parents and brother had been devastated by her suicide. They too felt like they were living in the dark where their daughter and sister was concerned. Unlike Netty's passing, Vanessa's death had no answer. To possibly get some answers Alicia would have to read Vanessa's private thoughts. Alicia wasn't sure she could do it. She hadn't even been able to look at the bundle of cards and letters without feeling distraught and she already knew what they contained. How would reading Vanessa's journals feel? She imagined it would be a grave invasion of privacy.

As the day wore on the idea stuck with her. When Alicia's shift was over she resigned herself to reading the last journal. She slowly ascended the stairs to her apartment, put the key in the door reluctantly and then entered as a feeling of dread washed over her. She knew she needed to do this. She *had* to do this. Alicia needed answers.

She collected the journals from the box in the chair. She took them over to her worn couch and laid them on her side table except for the turquoise volume. This had been Vanessa's last journal judging from the date inside the cover. Alicia took a deep breath, then tucked her feet under herself on the couch and opened it up. Vanessa's lovely cursive handwriting stared back at her and she began to read.

~ ~ ~

Alicia playfully screamed as Vanessa took a flying leap off the playground swing. She landed on all fours in the sand and laughed. Alicia was always too scared to leap from the swings. The thought of jumping out into the air, with no one to catch her and landing on her own scared her. But she didn't mind watching her friend enjoy herself. She was glad to have a friend in her new neighborhood and Vanessa was so happy all the time.

Vanessa ran over to Alicia, shoved her hands into the pockets of her corduroy pants and pulled out a handful of wrapped candy.

"You want one?"

Alicia nodded and Vanessa handed her a round candy in a shiny red wrapper.

"Where did you get those?" Alicia asked.

"My Mama," Vanessa answered as she shoved a large chunk of butterscotch into her mouth. "She gave it to me 'cause Taye shoved me."

Taye was Vanessa's older brother by three years. He could be a bully at times.

"Why'd he do that?"

"Cause I caught him stealing from Papa's change jar. And I told Mama. He called me a baby big-mouth bitch so he got grounded."

"How long for?"

Vanessa shrugged her shoulders. She didn't seem to have a care in the world.

"Mama told Taye to stop saying bad words."

"Which bad words?"

"I think big-mouth."

Alicia thought about this for a moment. She didn't have any siblings. She was used to always being on her own.

"I'm glad you told me," she finally said.

"I'll tell you everything!" said Vanessa. "We're best friends now. Hey! Let's go look at the birds in the pond! We can give them some of my candy!"

The two girls scampered off delighted by their plan of feeding butterscotch drops to the ducks.

~ ~ ~

The lunch room at Wilson High School was packed as usual. The old school was becoming overcrowded and there was hardly any place to sit. Some students sat on the floor with their backs pressed against the wall, while others perched in long, wide windowsills. Wilson High did not have a lunch-off-campus policy so you couldn't leave. The hallways were also off-limits due to fighting. Alicia had eaten the lunch her Gram had packed and now she was bored. She wanted Vanessa to entertain her, but she was busy writing in her journal. Alicia wasn't sure how she could concentrate with the volume of noise all around them in the overcrowded room.

"Let's go get some ice cream 'Nessa," Alicia pleaded.

But Vanessa ignored her and continued writing.

"Did you hear me?"

"Yes, I heard you. But I'm busy right now. Go get ice cream with someone else."

Vanessa had just broken up with Jeff so she was pouring her heart out into the pages of her journal. She always did this whenever she split with her latest boyfriend.

"But Beth is out sick and Corrine is sitting with Andre today. Come on 'Nessa!"

Vanessa gave a loud sigh and looked up at Alicia.

"Why don't you just talk to me? You don't need to write it out."

"Yes, I do Alicia. You don't keep a journal so you don't understand. I can't tell you everything! And you know what? I don't want to tell you everything."

Alicia stared at Vanessa in shock as she gathered up her books and stormed off. Alicia sat at the lunch table by herself as she watched Vanessa sweep out of the room and run off to the restroom. Alicia knew she would pick the stall at the end, shut herself in and write in that damn journal until the bell rang. She had found Vanessa there several times in the past few weeks. Alicia sat by herself stewing until the bell rang. She didn't see Vanessa for the rest of the day.

~ ~ ~

The image in the mirror had ceased to exist. Alicia had stood still in front of the mirror attached to the back of the bedroom door for the past five minutes. She was supposed to be checking out her royal blue knee-length wrap dress to see if it was appropriate for tonight's date with Odessa's son Benjamin. But her mind was a thousand miles away. She kept seeing Vanessa's handwriting floating before her eyes.

I'm pretty sure Dwayne is cheating on me. He was gone most of last night. When he finally came home to our apartment he reeked of alcohol and weed. I was so tired and cried out over that player that I just didn't have the energy to confront him.

Alicia tried on a pair of black flats, then remembered how tall Benjamin was. The last time he had dropped off a delivery at the bank he had looked a good six inches taller than her. Alicia kicked the flats off and slid into her black velvet heels.

Mama and Pop have decided to get a divorce. Taye told me before they had a chance to. He's still a jerk as always. Why didn't they tell me first? I just saw them two weeks ago. How does Taye matter to them more than I do?

The royal blue dress had short-sleeves so Alicia pulled a black shawl out of her bottom dresser drawer. She wrapped it around her shoulders and looked in the mirror once more.

I know that bastard is cheating on me now. I caught him coming out of the movies with Lauren. That ho had her arm around his waist and Dwayne had his arm slung over her shoulder. I swear I screamed at that low life for two hours straight. He doesn't have a heart. He couldn't. If he did he would never treat me this way.

Alicia placed her black beret on her head and looked in the mirror over the bathroom sink. Too cutesy? Too French? Too artsy? Just too wrong? Just too much. She took it off and tossed it back into her bedroom. Alicia fluffed her hair back out and smoothed her heavy bangs. She made sure she had no lipstick on her teeth.

I'm so lonely. My Pop left for Phoenix today and Taye skipped town. No one has seen him for two weeks now. Mama was a mess. She looked so old today when I saw her. Dwayne has moved out for a few days. I guess he's with that stupid ho Lauren. She'll be sorry one day when he breaks HER heart. If she's got one...

The air conditioner blew on Alicia's body in cool waves. She was standing in front of it trying not to sweat through her dress. She was so nervous her body had gone into hyper-drive. Shit! She hadn't been on a date in two years. During a panicked moment she thought about turning out the lights and not answering the door. Surely he'd go away. Why should she be going on a date anyways? Especially after she had read Vanessa's last heart wrenching journal. Alicia now realized she had been so caught up in taking care of her grandmother that she had completely neglected her best friend. And now it was too late. Vanessa hadn't mentioned any wrong doing on her part in the journal, but she might as well have. Alicia hadn't really grasped how depressed Vanessa had been until she read her own words. At times Vanessa had even sounded desperate. Why hadn't she *seen* this?

The doorbell buzzed and Alicia jumped. Her heart was racing! She waved her hands frantically in front of her face trying to cool herself down. Alicia shut her eyes and tried not to see Vanessa's handwriting in her mind. She walked to the door, took a deep breath, and then opened it.

Benjamin Bryant was one handsome man. When he entered a room women sat up and took notice. This evening he wore a black suit and a smart purple tie. In a lot of ways, he reminded Alicia of his mother Odessa. They both had a certain way of carrying themselves. As if they knew they were a good thing. Alicia often caught herself slouching. But really, after a lifetime of slouching it was hard to fix a bad habit like that in one evening. Each time she caught her shoulders hunching inward Alicia would mentally command herself to straighten up! That would last about a minute.

They ended up at Bombay Restaurant, one of the nicer places in town. The candles on the tables cast shadows across the dimly lit room. Dinner was halfway over but Alicia had barely touched her food. Normally she would have dived into a meal as fine as this, but she wasn't particularly hungry this evening. She had way too much on her mind. Between her nerves, the posture issue and Vanessa's last thoughts her date might as well be sitting with a zombie. Alicia doubted she had said more than fifty words the whole night. Sometimes she caught Benjamin – or Ben as he asked to be called – staring at her with a strange expression on his face. He was probably wondering when he could bolt.

"Alicia? Alicia?"

Alicia recognized her name and looked up startled. Ben had obviously been speaking to her, but she had no idea about what.

"I'm sorry, what?"

"Would you like dessert?"

"No. I mean, no thank you."

Alicia was so embarrassed she could have laid her head on the table and cried. This date was officially DOA. If this date was a vampire a stake would be sticking out of its chest where it had been plunged into its dead heart.

"Do you mind if I ask you something?"

Ben had finished his meal and was laying his cloth napkin on the edge of the table. Alicia just nodded.

"Are you not having a good time?"

Was this a trick question? It must be. How was she supposed to answer?

"Yes, I mean, of course I am. I'm sorry, I'm...I'm just a little distracted."

"A little?"

Alicia looked at Ben and realized he was smiling at her kindly.

"It's alright you know. My Ma told me some of the stuff you've been going through."

"She did?"

Ben nodded. Alicia was so embarrassed. This was obviously a pity date. Is this how Odessa viewed her? As a charity case?

"I've been having a pretty hard time lately," Alicia admitted. "Sometimes I feel like I'm trying to swim, but the current wants to tow me under. You know?"

What was she saying? Why was she telling this beautiful man these things? Alicia thought she sounded pathetic.

"Actually, I do know. I think we all feel that way at one time or another."

Ben ordered after dinner coffee for both of them, then began to tell Alicia about the past year of his life. He had been dating a woman at his workplace for a couple of years when he caught her cheating with another delivery driver. "Yeah...in the back of his van...that was a sight to see, talk about an eye opener..." He had been devastated. But thankfully he had his mother for emotional support. For the past year Odessa had taken it upon herself to fix her son up on a multitude of blind dates in an effort to get him "off his butt". Alicia laughed at this. She could hear Odessa saying just that.

Ben wanted to be a high school teacher one day so he was going to college part time in the evenings. Currently he coached a middle school basketball team down at the local youth rec center on the weekends. In turn Alicia found herself opening up to Ben about her job at the bank, Gram, how she wanted to finish her associate's degree and how much she missed the little blue house. Until that very moment Alicia hadn't realized how much she truly missed her home.

Ben helped Alicia drape her shawl over her shoulders as they left Bombay Restaurant. She made a mental note to be sure and return there one day. Hopefully with Ben. Under the most impossible of circumstances she had just had one of the best dates of her life. There hadn't even been a good night kiss yet and she was still buzzed. The thought of Ben giving her a good night kiss made her blush so she turned her head away from him as they walked down the street.

But when Alicia tilted her head away she spotted Dwayne's red Jeep parked across the street. It was in front of the jazz club Vanessa had liked so much. Alicia stopped walking and stared at the vehicle.

"Alicia? What's wrong?"

Alicia ignored Ben and walked across the street. Her shawl slipped and fell from her shoulders. Ben scooped it up off the street and followed her. A sudden rage flooded Alicia's mind. That asshole was out having the time of his life, probably getting jacked up on whiskey in Vanessa's favorite club, while her best friend lay cold in a grave across town. Before she even knew what she was doing Alicia had approached the Jeep, opened the back-swing door and found Dwayne's baseball bat. She slammed the door shut, got a good grip on the bat and walked to the front of the vehicle. Alicia glared at the Jeep for a long seething moment then lifted her hands and swung hard at the passenger side head light. A loud crack echoed down the dark street.

Suddenly a strong pair of arms encircled her, restraining her. Alicia hadn't realized it but she was crying. Tears were streaming down her face as Ben held her. He was probably in shock. Somewhere in the back of her mind she knew she had ruined their salvaged date by acting like a complete psycho. A crowd of by-standers had gathered. Alicia heard someone shout something unintelligible and then she saw Dwayne break through the mass of gawkers. He was staring at the damaged Jeep in complete and utter shock. He looked over at Ben and Alicia and the expression on his face morphed. Dwayne was pissed!

"You killed her!" Alicia screamed from the confines of Ben's arms. "You killed 'Nessa you bastard!"

Alicia struggled to free herself from Ben's grasp but he held her firmly against his body. She still held the baseball bat tight in her hands.

"I'm gonna kill you next bitch! Look what you did to my ride!"

Suddenly Dwayne lunged forward towards Alicia. Ben quickly spun her away from him, let her go, jerked his right arm back while curling his fist, then let it snap forward and punched Dwayne right in the nose. Another crack echoed down the street as Dwayne fell backwards landing in a pile of glass from the broken headlight. The crowd burst into applause and cheers. A fight in the street on Friday night was always appreciated. It was free entertainment.

Ben pulled a card from his wallet and tossed it on top of Dwayne who was still lying in the street, his face smeared with blood.

"I'll pay for the damage to your Jeep. You might want to put some ice on that nose bro."

Ben pulled the baseball bat out of Alicia's hands and tossed it at Dwayne who flinched away from it. Ben then took Alicia's hand in his and guided her to his truck. A minute later they were gone.

Ben slid Alicia's finger under the cool running water. It stung so she winced. Somehow Alicia had managed to cut her finger. Ben had been quiet for most of the ride to her apartment and this had scared her. She couldn't tell if he was mad or not. Maybe he thought she was a freak. If he did it was probably because she was a freak. Now that she didn't have all that rage pouring through her veins and the baseball bat in her hands she found it hard to believe she had smashed Dwayne's headlight. Alicia's head was throbbing so she pressed the palm of her uncut hand to her forehead.

"Hey there, are you ok? Feeling faint? Do you not like the sight of blood?"

"No, I'm fine. It's just my head really hurts."

Ben shut the running water off, grabbed her hand towel and carefully dried her finger.

"Do you have any bandages?"

Alicia pointed to her medicine cabinet. Ben located the band-aid box and her bottle of aspirin. He then led her to the bed and made her sit down. He fetched a glass of water, gave her an aspirin, and then proceeded to put a band-aid over her cut finger as gently as possible. When he was done Ben grabbed the box of tissues off her nightstand, pulled one out and began to dab at her face. Alicia thought she must look a fright. Why was he being so nice to her? She figured he would drop her off then drive off as fast as he could. Ben wiped her tears away and probably cleaned up the mascara that had run down her face.

"That was intense, huh?"

"Oh Ben, I'm so sorry! What you must think of me…"

"Was that about your friend Vanessa. Mom told me…well, my uncle he…you know."

Alicia nodded. She briefly explained about Vanessa's suicide and what she had found in her journal yesterday and today.

"That guy sounds like bad news. I think you need to stay away from him Alicia. Do you think he'll come after you?"

"No. Dwayne talks a big talk, but he don't walk no walk. You know what I mean?"

"That's good. I'd hate to leave you alone if -"

"No, he doesn't know where I live so he won't come here."

Ben nodded and Alicia realized he was still holding her hand gently.

"You know what's sad? I called Lauren yesterday and told her off for seeing Dwayne while he was with Vanessa. And do you know what she had the nerve to say? "It's almost over anyways." What the hell does that mean?"

Ben grabbed another tissue from the box and handed it to Alicia. She dabbed at her moist eyes and felt so tired.

"None of them cared about 'Nessa the way I did. She was my best friend."

Ben scooted over closer to Alicia then pulled her into his arms. He stroked her hair and rubbed her back until her tears subsided once more. Alicia was worried about messing up his nice suit but Ben didn't seem to mind. When she finally pulled away Alicia dried her eyes with another tissue then looked at Ben.

"I can't imagine what you must think of me."

"Now or when I first arrived here tonight?"

Alicia thought for a moment then said, "What did you think earlier tonight?"

"The truth?"

Alicia nodded yes.

"Well, on the way over I really didn't want to come. My Ma keeps fixing me up on these blind dates. They never work out."

Alicia's heart sunk. Of course. What else could she really expect? This date had been a total disaster. No man in their right mind would want to date some woman that went around busting up headlights.

"But then you answered your door and I thought, I wish I had brought some flowers with me."

"Why?" Alicia whispered.

"Because you were so beautiful. More than beautiful. Someone like you deserves flowers."

Alicia stared at Ben in shock. No man had ever given her flowers. Hell, no man had ever called her beautiful.

"But...but now what do you think?"

Alicia braced herself for the dump.

"I think you gotta lotta moxie girl. Damn. Can I ask you something?"

Alicia nodded.

"Why the baseball bat and the headlights?"

"I heard it."

"You heard it?"

"Yeah, in one of those country songs your mom is always listening to."

"A country – wait a minute, those crazy sad songs my Ma is always playing?"

Alicia nodded yes again. To her surprise Ben let out a hearty laugh. Alicia playfully shoved him.

"What are you laughing at?"

"You sure are some woman. I ain't never seen anything like that."

Alicia started laughing too. Then, suddenly, Ben reached over, cupped her chin gently with his hand and gave her a light kiss on her lips. Alicia was so shocked that she froze. Ben pulled back slightly to look at her face, so she smiled at him. Then he leaned in once more and this time he really kissed her. Alicia couldn't recall ever being kissed like this before. When it was over she was sorry.

"Can I tell you something?" Ben asked.

"What?"

"Well, it just seems like maybe you're holding on to too much stuff from the past. Maybe it's time to let some of that stuff go. You're still here…even if they aren't."

Alicia didn't know how to respond to that. This evening was a lot to take in.

"I'm gonna get going if you're sure you're ok?"

"Yes, I'm…"

Alicia was going to say 'fine', but didn't, because she wasn't. She walked Ben to the door. He leaned down, kissed her forehead lightly, and told her goodnight. After Alicia closed and locked the door behind him she sat on the couch thinking for a long while. Mainly she thought about what Ben had said about letting things from the past go. He was right. She needed a new start. But how? It was scary to think about taking a risk, jumping into the air, and hoping she would land somewhere safe.

Chapter Ten

Cynthia Part II

Cynthia and Maddie had been staring at swatches of glossy fabric for the past hour while sipping spiced green tea smoothies at their favorite bakery. At this point both women had discussed the pros and cons of each swatch but had not come to any decisions. It seemed they were getting nowhere.

"I can't believe you like those colors," Maddie snorted. "You will look like a plum or a radish if we make a dress from those fabrics!"

"Yes, but I will be standing beside you," Cynthia snickered, "and you will look like a large snowball pastry."

"I most certainly will not! I told Madame Suzette to scrap the plans for the Princess Diana gown in favor of the Jacqueline Kennedy. I like the idea of no sleeves, just caps. But please do keep up the snowball pastry talk and I will order a replica of Scarlett O'Hara's poofy gown and make you wear a tacky, flowery, flouncy dress with a rib shattering corset!"

Both women burst out laughing at this thought and ordered yet another round of smoothies. Cynthia and Maddie had been best friends for the past eight years. They had met while in college at the local sports bar. They had been the only two women in the whole run-down place watching international soccer. The girls had bonded over veggie burgers and deep-fried onion rings.

Cynthia had even brought Maddie home with her during spring break of their junior year. That trip had been extremely fortuitous for Maddie as she had met her fiancé during the visit. Jackson had been traveling with his family. There had been major sparks between the two of them immediately. Unlike Cynthia and Michael, Maddie and Jackson came from the exact same world.

Jackson's family came from old Southern oil money and Maddie's father worked in international trade. Maddie had spent her childhood being shuttled back and forth between her father in England and her mother in America. She had the strangest accent to prove it. After college graduation Maddie had followed Cynthia and in turn Jackson had followed Maddie. All three had lived in the same townhouse for a couple of years so they knew each other quite well. Cynthia was very happy for her two friends and honored to be a part of their special day.

It had come as quite a shock to Cynthia that Maddie had chosen The Landing as the location for the wedding. With both families money she knew they could wed anywhere they damn well wanted to.

"Because it is romantic love!" Maddie had declared. "A bit of returning to the scene of the crime and all that!"

Cynthia had purposely avoided The Landing as much as she could after her break up with Evan. She had returned to waitressing and upon graduation had left her home town completely. It hurt her to see the bright colorful sails waving in the wind so happily. They whispered promises that had never been kept.

Two weeks later Cynthia was in a car traveling home. Maddie kept up a steady stream of her usual zany banter but Cynthia barely heard a word. She was too distracted thinking about all the sights, sounds and smells from her past that were about to assault her senses. Her only saving grace was the knowledge that Evan was off sailing the seven seas – or however many seas there were – probably having the time of his life. Cynthia's stomach rolled and she realized Maddie was staring at her.

"I'm sorry you, uh, you were saying?" stammered Cynthia.

"Umm, hello! Where are you? You are like a million miles awa-ohhh!"

"No. No 'ohhh'. There is no 'ohhh'."

Maddie gasped as the remembrance of something long forgotten had occurred to her.

"I'm so sorry Cyn-a-buns," said Maddie sympathetically, using the silly nickname she used to call Cynthia in college. How did she collect so many absurd nicknames?

"Ok, first, do *not* call me that. Cyn-a-buns is not dignified."

Maddie laughed. "And second?"

"Let's hear it," Cynthia sighed in resignation.

"*This*," said Paige while gesturing around Cynthia as if she were buffing an invisible aura. "This is about Evan isn't it?"

Cynthia stared straight ahead at the road as she drove.

"I thought…I thought you were over him," said Maddie gently. "When you got engaged to Michael, I just assumed…"

A few moments passed before Cynthia spoke again. "I am" was all she said.

This first thing Cynthia noticed as she walked across The Landing's bright green lawn (even in all the late summer heat!) was the many improvements that had been made. At certain turns Cynthia barely recognized the place.

"Yes, they have new management," said Maddie proudly, as if she owned stock in the establishment. "I saw it all on their website! The old snack bar and game room have been remodeled into a celebration hall. That's where we'll be meeting the event coordinator."

Cynthia laughed at her friend's obvious enthusiasm and felt a release of pressure. Now that she was here it wasn't so bad Cynthia realized. The tension she had been carrying in her shoulders lessened and when they entered the celebration hall she understood why Maddie wanted to get married here. She barely recognized it as the same place where she used to play air hockey and drink cheap beer as a college student. Everything from the past had been torn down, gutted and refurbished to resemble an expensive New York City tea room. The walls were drenched in dark glossy red, the trim had been gilded, the cherry floors refinished and the china sparkled. Cynthia noticed Maddie beaming as she scanned the interior and she finally resigned herself to the mission.

"I was wondering when you would show up. I've been waiting for you all morning."

The soft low voice originated behind Cynthia and she immediately froze. If she thought she had imagined the voice, that the hall was playing with her memories, the wide-eyed look on Maddie's face as she stared over Cynthia's shoulder told her the voice belonged to a living, breathing person and not a specter from her past. Cynthia slowly turned around and saw a tall handsome man in a tailored suit, short black fashionable hair and striking blue eyes staring at her.

Evan Fischer had returned home very much the prodigal son two years ago. He was now the general manager of The Landing and had implemented a rigorous overhaul of the place where he had spent most of his childhood and teenage years. Evan had seen numerous ports over the last few years and had made a bet with himself that he could turn The Landing into a premiere destination for tourists visiting South Carolina. The game room had been replaced with an elegant hall, the mini-putt course had been removed to make way for the newly erected luxury spa, and the restaurant's line cooks had been replaced by a noted chef. As Cynthia had passed the water's edge earlier she noticed larger and more expensive looking boats lining the slips. Evan's new regime was the very reason Maddie had been drawn to hold her wedding at the place where she had first met Jackson.

Unfortunately, Maddie had no clue that Evan had been responsible for the luxurious facelift of The Landing. As he gave them a tour of the improved facilities Maddie silently mouthed the words 'sorry', 'so sorry', and 'shit' to her best friend who looked pale, waxy, and in shock. Later Maddie would say the scene reeked of *awkward*. As for Cynthia, she couldn't exactly say who she was more out of sorts with – Maddie or Evan.

Hell, maybe it was with herself. Cynthia barely spoke as they toured and when she did she chose her words with extreme economy.

Evan behaved professionally and friendly towards the two ladies. He seemed somehow pleased that the event coordinator had been called off to some mysterious meeting. It wasn't until the tour was coming to a close that he addressed Cynthia with more informality. Maddie was using the powder room while Cynthia checked her cell messages. Work was still moving at a brisk pace during her absence and there would be many fires to extinguish when she returned tomorrow. As she placed the phone in her purse Cynthia realized with a start that Evan was standing beside her. They were alone for the first time.

"I've wanted to congratulate you."

Evan was staring at her intently and it unnerved Cynthia.

"Excuse me?" she whispered.

Why was she whispering? Cynthia immediately chastised herself mentally. Whispers were for shared secrets. She had none of those with this man.

"On your engagement. That is a beautiful ring."

Evan was now staring at her hand. Cynthia became self-conscious and tucked her ring finger hand in closer to her body.

"Thank you," she responded at a normal vocal level.

"He's a very lucky man. I saw your mother in town a while back and she, ah, *informed* me of your engagement."

Cynthia tried to hold back a smile at his emphasis on the word 'informed'. She could see her mother doing just that. Mrs. Taylor had never been fond of Evan. She felt he influenced her daughter to act in an impulsive and irrational manner. Mrs. Taylor much preferred Michael. Her mother always said he had good breeding. As if he was an animal. Cynthia made a mental note to have a word with her mother later over dinner even though she knew it wouldn't make any difference. She could already hear her mother calling Evan *that boy*. That was how she used to refer to him when they had dated.

"You're smiling. You find that amusing eh?"

Evan grinned mischievously at her. For the first time that day Cynthia thought he looked, well, like himself. Or at least the person she used to know. Cynthia acknowledged she had no clue who he was now. He looked like a very elegant man in an expensive suit with a stylish haircut. Not at all like the wharf rat from her memories.

"Yes, I was thinking of my fiancé," Cynthia lied.

The mischievous grin faded from Evan's face. And then suddenly the two ex-lovers were staring at one another intently. They were taking in the changes each of them had undergone in the years since they had last laid eyes on one another. Cynthia had always thought of Evan as a man, even back then, but now he truly was one. He was more devastatingly handsome than her memory had recalled him to be. The night Cynthia had lounged in the bubble bath revisiting her memories she had realized Evan's face had grown blurry around the edges. It had made her sad. She knew in that moment she didn't want to forget him, but in so many ways she already had.

~ ~ ~

Cynthia quietly slid her key into the back-door lock, twisted it, and then gently pushed it open. The door gave a tiny squeak. The kitchen was dark and relief washed over her.

"You sure are late getting home."

Suddenly a light flickered on over the kitchen sink. Cynthia jumped in surprise. Charlie was leaning back against the cabinets, a bowl of sugary cereal in his hands. He was quietly laughing.

"Hush!" whispered Cynthia. "You're gonna get me in trouble!"

"And just where have you been off to at this hour, past curfew? Out with Evan I reckon."

"Dad said to ignore mom's curfew. It's silly at my age."

Charlie laughed again while shoveling a spoonful of cereal into his mouth.

"Anyways, I just had an unforgettable evening on Evan's boat. He has a telescope and he showed me all the constellations. That's how all the sailors used to know where they were going. They would be guided by the stars! It was so beautiful. I'll don't think I'll ever forget it."

And with that statement Cynthia drifted off to bed in a blissful stupor.

~ ~ ~

"I'm just going to say it," said Maddie. "It's all your fault I can't enjoy this arugula salad. It even has raspberry vinegarette. *Raspberry vinegarette!*"

"My fault? How is that my fault?"

"Because I feel so damn guilty about what happened last Friday."

Maddie threw down her fork and sighed deeply. Cynthia suspected her friend just didn't want to eat her boring lunch. She had vowed to lose ten pounds before her wedding in November. But Maddie was never very good at economizing – even when it came to food.

"Madame Suzette kept telling me to 'suck eet een' at my fitting yesterday. A lady can only hear that so many times before her self-confidence is in tatters on the floor next to all the empty Snickers bar wrappers."

Both women laughed and picked some more at their food.

"I really am sorry, I didn't know -"

"It's alright Maddie," Cynthia interrupted. "I'm fine."

"Anyways, I don't want you to fret a bit love. I already met with the caterer yesterday and took care of everything."

Cynthia stared at Maddie in amazement.

"You went to The Landing all by yourself?"

Maddie nodded yes, a wad of leafy greens peeking out of her mouth. Her short blonde hair bouncing up and down.

"But I didn't mean, oh, I feel awful Maddie. I am the worst maid of honor ever!"

Maddie swallowed and said, "Look, I don't want you to have to torture yourself by seeing Evan. I know he broke your heart into a million Reese's Pieces. I was there, remember? You came back to school that semester like a dejected little matchstick girl."

Cynthia sighed and placed her head into her hands while her elbows rested on the table.

"I only have to meet with the florist and event coordinator once more to pick out my flowers and table settings. I can do that without you. Don't worry a bit. We can take care of everything else from here."

Maddie gestured around the bistro in the city as if it held all the answers.

"Thanks Maddie. I don't know why it was so hard to see him."

"You don't?"

"I'm engaged now. I've moved on. What we had was so long ago. I mean, us meeting again, it had to happen sometime this century, right?"

Maddie nodded once more, her mouth again full of leafy greens.

Several more weeks passed and Cynthia tried to forget about Evan. But occasionally, his face would steal into her thoughts and disrupt whatever she was supposed to be thinking about or working on. Little Miss Perfect Boobs suggested, with a little too much acidic glee, that Cynthia might be cracking under the pressure and needed a break after she sent the wrong files to the printer – twice. The error would set Cynthia's project back a day causing her client major distress. Mid-morning Cynthia slipped away to the high-rise roof to get some fresh air and perspective. As she stared over the city skyline her cell buzzed.

"Hello?"

"Cynthia? It's Jackson!"

Jackson was in an absolute meltdown. He had treated Maddie to a night out at their favorite restaurant, The Panda House, as a reward for being so diligent about her diet. But things had gone terribly awry. Maddie had eaten some funky sushi and now had food poisoning.

"It's like something out of *The Exorcist*," he lamented. "I keep expecting her head to spin around at any moment."

Cynthia was laughing until Jackson begged for her assistance. Maddie was supposed to meet with the florist and event coordinator later that afternoon but most definitely wouldn't be able to make the appointments now. Cynthia's stomach twisted into knots at the thought of having to return to The Landing and possibly seeing Evan again. But Jackson sounded so desperate, and Maddie was her dearest friend, so she caved. Cynthia secretly wished she had eaten the tainted sushi.

Cynthia arrived at the florist shop in her old hometown just before they closed. She had raced all afternoon and was becoming weary. She quickly reviewed Maddie's flower selections and took cell phone pictures for her best friend so she could decide if she liked the arrangements. Once that task was completed Cynthia headed to The Landing. Fall had finally arrived but it wasn't noticeable yet in the tourist town. The stale heat clung to the edges of night as it slowly descended in a spectacular cherry sunset. Cynthia walked to the water's edge and admired the beauty of it all.

A warm breeze ran through her hair as she ran off to meet the event coordinator at the celebration hall. Her footsteps echoed throughout the elegant room as she crossed it. Cynthia was alone so she sat down at one of the round tables to await Mrs. Tilman's arrival. She noticed the table before her was already laid out with various china and stemware for her to choose from so she began to examine each piece.

"The glassware is full leaded crystal from Italy. I picked it out myself with Margaret's help."

Evan's voice startled Cynthia and she almost dropped the fragile champagne flute in her hand. He was dressed once again in a fine tailored suit.

"Where is Mrs. Tilman?"

"Margaret had to pick her daughter up from choir practice so I volunteered to fill in."

Cynthia's spirits sank and her psyche was suddenly awash in butterflies. Evan seemed to notice her distress.

He quickly sat down, leaned across the table, and said, "This doesn't have to be awkward Cynthia...we were over so long ago..."

Evan trailed off and leaned back in his chair. He looked down dejectedly. Cynthia stared at Evan and a surge of determination flooded her. She had promised to help Maddie and she would fulfill her duties as meticulously and admirably as she would take on any work project. Cynthia was most certainly alive to how awkward the situation was, but she was determined to not let it get the best of her.

Cynthia squared her shoulders and said, "Let's begin the review, shall we? I don't have a lot of time to spare."

For the next hour Cynthia and Evan took inventory of the multiple place settings The Landing had to offer. Cynthia called Maddie several times to consult with her and finally they settled on a lovely Waterford fine china setting with delicate Indian motifs on the edges and in the center.

"Yes, of course...oh, poor Maddie. Get some rest, ok? I'll check on you once I get to my parent's house...yes, I'm going there tonight. I'll send you the photos of all the flowers...yes, I like the parrot tulips in white especially...it's perfect Maddie..."

Cynthia laid down her phone after the call and rubbed her eyes wearily.

"You must be tired."

Cynthia looked up at Evan and realized she was exhausted.

"I wanted to show you one more thing, but...well, Madelyn had mentioned to Margaret that she wanted wedding day photos taken in the gazebo on the South lawn."

The very gazebo suddenly sprang into Cynthia's mind. It had been old and worn when she was a teen. She couldn't imagine that it looked much better now. Why would Maddie want photos taken there?

"The old gazebo was torn down a while ago," said Evan, as if reading her thoughts. "But I am having a new one built in the same location. It should be finished by now. Perhaps, if you will be in town tomorrow I could show it to you. You could take some photos and share them with Madelyn to see if she approves."

And so Cynthia and Evan decided to meet at noon the next day to inspect the new structure.

~ ~ ~

It had been raining non-stop on the quaint tourist town for the past three days so Cynthia and Evan had little work to do. They spent their time watching movies at the restored cinema on main street and cooking rudimentary meals on Evan's boat. Neither of them were good cooks and the boat only had a tiny kitchen shelf and ancient stove that smoked. That evening the smoke had forced them out into the rain to seek shelter until the tiny cabin cleared. This was how they ended up in the gazebo during the rainstorm.

No one else had the courage or stupidity to be wandering The Landing's grounds in the down pour so they had the gazebo all to themselves. Evan picked Cynthia up in his arms and swung her around. She laughed until she felt dizzy. He fell back on a bench in the shelter with Cynthia cradled in his arms. The raindrops in his black hair glimmered. He kissed her until she melted along with the rain.

Cynthia wasn't sure where it came from but suddenly Evan produced a rolled piece of parchment paper that was tied with a black cord.

"I was going to give this to you later tonight, but my plans for a romantic dinner kinda went awry."

Cynthia laughed, "Kinda?"

Evan smiled mischievously at her and placed the bundle in her hands.

"What is this?"

"That is your anniversary gift."

Cynthia and Evan had been dating for almost a year. They were still as crazy about each other as they had been on the day she had slammed a door into his face.

"What is it?" Cynthia wondered.

"The beginning of our future," Evan whispered in her ear.

~ ~ ~

Cynthia stared up at the newly built gazebo and was in wonder at how different it was from the one in her memory. The old gazebo had been ramshackle with peeling paint. This new structure was bright white with intricate lattice work.

After examining it for a few moments Cynthia said, "It's lovely. I'm sure Maddie will approve. I'll let her know it's available for photos."

"Perfect. I was hoping you would like it."

As she looked at the new gazebo Cynthia wrinkled her nose ever so slightly but Evan's keen eyes caught the movement.

"You don't like it?" he asked cautiously.

Today Evan wore corduroy pants and a light sweater. He looked more like the person she used to know than the man in the elegant suits.

"Oh no," said Cynthia, embarrassed as she realized she had been staring at his clothes for too long. "It's just…it doesn't look like…nothing. It's really beautiful and…intricate."

"But it doesn't look like the *old* gazebo that used to stand here?" Evan gently prodded.

Cynthia felt her face grow hot and turned away quickly.

"I'm sorry, I shouldn't have -"

"No, it's fine," she cut him off. "It's fine."

"Well, shall we give it a test drive?"

"A test drive?" Cynthia turned around to face Evan once more.

He gestured for her to follow and once inside the large gazebo she noticed a picnic basket tucked away underneath one of the benches.

"Oh," said Cynthia startled. "No, I can't."

"What? Have some lunch? Why not? It's lunch time after all and Margaret went to a lot of trouble. She even had our four-star chef make your favorite."

"My favorite?"

Evan opened the picnic basket and produced a wrapped object. When he opened the wrapper it contained a whole wheat peanut butter and apricot jelly sandwich. That sandwich had been her favorite. As an eight-year-old child. Her mother had always packed it in her school lunches. Cynthia looked at the sandwich and burst out laughing. How had Evan remembered that? Thank heavens her palate had grown much more sophisticated since then.

"And how did Mrs. Tilman know that was my favorite?" asked Cynthia slyly.

Evan was now embarrassed and he looked down at his shoes. He finally muttered that he *may* have helped. Cynthia took a seat on the gazebo bench and dived into her impromptu lunch. Mrs. Tilman had also provided fresh strawberries and sliced pears in a sweet juice, a selection of raw vegetables accompanied by a delectable seasoned dip, and a mango and cucumber salad. For dessert, they had peach crème bars. A sweet lime soda washed the meal down. Cynthia found herself relaxing and enjoying the beautiful day out of doors.

Most of the lunch had been consumed before Cynthia realized the strangest thing had occurred. Something she hadn't even thought possible. She was conversing freely with the man who had broken her heart all those years before. They talked about their old friends, her job and life in the city, and his exotic travels on his sail boat. Cynthia also realized there was something noticeably different about Evan. All the restless energy he used to radiate seemed to have vanished. In its place was a secure, confident and relaxed man. He seemed happy to be where he was. Cynthia could tell he really liked his new job, enjoyed the challenge of it all. An hour passed before Cynthia recalled the time.

"Oh! I have to go. I promised my father I would meet him at the putting range."

Evan smiled warmly at her.

"Do you miss them?" he asked suddenly.

"Miss them?" Cynthia repeated.

"Your family. Now that Charlie has moved back to town with his wife and new baby. I just wondered if you miss them since you live so far away."

"Well, of course I miss them," she replied becoming uncomfortable again. "But I'm only a few hours away and…I have another life now."

Evan didn't say anything but he stared at Cynthia in the strangest manner. As if he was trying to find the answer to something that was hidden on her face. Cynthia thanked him for the gazebo lunch and left with a peculiar feeling in her stomach.

The next day was Saturday so Cynthia was relaxing at her parent's house. They were at the farmers' market so she slipped back into a six-year-old version of herself, chowing down on cereal while flipping through cartoons as she sprawled out on the den couch. When her cell phone rang she didn't even look to see who was on the other end before she answered.

"Hewwoo?" she said, mouth stuffed full of cereal.

"Hello? Cynthia?"

Cynthia stopped chewing and her spoon fell into her bowl with a loud clatter. It was Evan. He wanted to know if she could come down to The Landing this evening. Margaret had ordered some outdoor hanging lanterns and he wanted Cynthia to look at them and see if Maddie would like them placed up the path leading to the gazebo for her wedding.

At seven that evening Cynthia made her way to the new gazebo once again. She was astonished to see a long double row of glowing orbs that cast peach and rose shadows across the meticulous lawn. The lanterns were absolutely magical. Cynthia knew instantly that Maddie would love them. She loved them!

A movement caught Cynthia's eye and she saw Evan step out from inside the gazebo. The sight of him made her catch her breath. He wore a pair of dark jeans and a fitted navy t-shirt. His hair was in casual disarray. On other man this look would have been passable. On Evan Fischer he looked as if he just stepped out of the pages of a J. Crew catalog.

"Quite spectacular, isn't it?" he said, as he came to a stop in front of her.

Cynthia merely nodded yes, then realized he was talking about the glass lanterns. At once she felt a blush creep up her neck and spread across her face.

"So, since you are here how about some dinner?"

The offer surprised Cynthia, but the idea of eating once more in the brightly lit gazebo appealed to her. After a moment's hesitation she agreed to be his dinner companion. When Evan began leading her away from the gazebo she was temporarily disappointed. Then she remembered the restaurant had a new chef and she consoled herself with the thought of a four-star meal. But when he veered off the path that led to the restaurant she became confused. It took her a moment to understand they were heading towards the boat slips.

"Where are we going?" she asked nervously.

"I want to show you something."

Cynthia's curiosity was now piqued so she followed quietly along. When they reached the last slip Evan walked all the way to the end of the dock. Cynthia found herself looking around for the blue-grey Ranger but didn't see it anywhere.

"So, what do you think?"

Evan was staring up at a very expensive looking forty-foot cruiser. She couldn't imagine why he would care what she thought of the luxurious boat.

"It's umm…nice?"

"Nice?" Evan let out a hearty laugh. It pierced Cynthia's heart. She hadn't heard his laugh in years. It sounded so good.

"Well, come on. Maybe after a tour on deck you'll change your opinion to something less cavalier. I have a meal waiting for us that is much more sophisticated than peanut butter and apricot jelly sandwiches."

"But, where is your boat?"

Evan looked at her strangely. "This is my boat Cyn."

She looked at the stark white cruiser once more.

"But where is the Ranger?"

Evan let out another laugh. "You thought I'd still have that old tug boat? She gave out on me about eight months into my very first trip. I was lucky to bring her into a port before she completely fell apart on me."

Cynthia wasn't sure why but the idea of the blue-grey sailboat no longer existing in Evan's world saddened her. It almost felt like an important piece of *her* past had been taken away. She suddenly felt empty. Cynthia had been so lost in thought mourning the old boat that she hadn't seen Evan come up to her.

"What's wrong Cyn?" he asked gently.

He was looking at her with such affectionate concern that she felt a part of herself snap loose.

"Don't you miss it?" she whispered.

After a long moment of him taking her in, a solemn look etched on his handsome face, he finally answered, "Every single day of my life."

And for the first time since Evan had re-entered her life, Cynthia realized he wasn't talking about the boat. She knew instinctively that he was talking about her. He missed her. As much as she had missed him? Her breathing quickened and a rush of blood sounded in her ears. Cynthia closed her eyes and a thousand images from years past flashed through her mind. All the thoughts, sounds, smells, touches and tastes were of Evan. He flooded all her senses and Cynthia felt like she was drowning in him.

She slowly opened her eyes to see that Evan had captured her face with both of his strong hands. She stared into his blue eyes and realized he was staring at her the way he had one night long ago. In a flash of memory Cynthia recalled a blues band playing songs about love gone wrong. All those years ago she hadn't understood what those sad yearning lyrics were about. But she understood now. *Now.*

Suddenly Cynthia broke free of Evan's light grasp and turned away from him. What was she doing here? She had another life now. She had Michael. Hadn't she told Evan that? Didn't he understand any of this? Did she?

"I can't be here. I can't..."

The last thing Cynthia heard before she took off running into the night was Evan call her name. "Cyn."

~ ~ ~

Cynthia's sleep had been disturbed for the past five nights. She yawned as she waited for her order to arrive. There was so much noise in the crowded restaurant her mind was having a hard time filtering all the sounds. It took her a moment to realize someone was speaking to her.

"Isn't that right hon?"

Cynthia looked up to find all her lunch companions starting at her.

"I'm sorry, what?"

Holli Marshall giggled and Cynthia shot her a frosty look.

"I was just saying that we were hoping to get married at Augustine Hall. Fred and Belinda's wedding was so over the top there. I'm not sure how we'll beat it babe."

Derek and Justin had also joined them on their lunch outing at Jorge's Bistro. Michael loved this place. There was a cigar bar in the back where he liked to indulge occasionally. Cynthia detested cigar smoke. It gave her a headache. Quite like the one she was nursing.

"You really should take a vacay Cynthia. You've looked like hell these last few days."

Cynthia stared at Little Miss Perfect Boobs and wished a waiter would come by and drop split pea soup in her blown out blonde hair. She was in no mood for her plastic diatribes today.

"Cynthia's just a little tired," said Michael soothingly while rubbing her back. "She's been helping some friends of ours plan their wedding."

"You mean the one you told us about at that tacky little port on the coast?" Holli sniffed. "Can you imagine getting married there?"

"There is nothing wrong with The Landing," Cynthia snapped. "In fact, I don't want to get married in Augustine Hall."

"You don't?" asked Michael perplexed. "But, I thought we had discussed -"

"No! *You* discussed. I just agreed and I'm not sure why."

The entire party at the table stared at Cynthia like she had lost her mind. She suddenly felt boxed in, so she threw her linen napkin on the table and went outside to get some fresh air. Cynthia realized ruefully that lately all she seemed to be doing was running away from everything.

Cynthia wasn't sure what had possessed her to be driving down the highway like a madwoman in the dead of night. The only thing she was sure of was that she had to know. Until she did her head was never going to clear. Her thoughts would remain an unending tangle of questions she had no answers to.

When Cynthia arrived at The Landing the moon was in full bloom overhead. It cast silvery shadows over the water and created shimmery ghosts along the water's edge. The sight did not distress her. She had spent many a night with these ghosts.

Cynthia rounded a corner and spied the slip she was looking for. She practically ran down the dock as it swayed slightly beneath her. Her equilibrium was thrown more than it already was. Cynthia was so tired of her balance being off and this was the only way she knew how to find solid ground once more. As she climbed up the side of the sleek cruiser she was almost to the top rail when her foot slipped. Suddenly a hand reached out and grabbed her arm.

"Cyn? What are you doing here?" Evan asked, sleep thick in his voice.

"Help me up!"

When Cynthia was on deck she took in the sight of Evan. He wore only cotton pajama pants and his hair was disheveled. His feet were bare. She had woken him from his slumber. While looking at him a surge of emotion rose within Cynthia.

"Why are you here?" she cried. "Why did you come back?"

Evan hesitated and said, "I came back for the job Cyn."

"Stop lying!"

"What do you want me to say?" he pleaded.

"I want you to say what is true! Why did you come back?"

Evan ran his hand through his midnight hair and looked down at her. His face looked torn. But then his expression cleared as he continued to stare at her.

"I came back for you Cyn. But you already knew that or you wouldn't be here right now. At night. Alone with *me* on *my* boat."

Cynthia took in a sharp breath of air and sat down. Her legs felt weak. She felt weak. Evan crossed the space between them and sat beside her. Neither of them spoke for a long time. Cynthia watched the moon dance on the water.

"I know this seems like a mess," Evan finally said, his voice barely a whisper. "Why are you even with him Cyn? Do you love him the way you loved me? Because...you belong with me. Don't you - can't you *feel* that?"

For the first time in years something powerful built up inside Cynthia until she was back on her feet yelling.

"Belong with you? If you thought we belonged together you wouldn't have left me behind in the first place! I can't belong to you! You don't even -"

But Cynthia didn't get to finish her passionate plea. Evan was suddenly on his feet and he pulled Cynthia into his arms. His mouth came down hard over hers and he kissed her like a man who had been starved. His hands and arms clutched her to his body and Cynthia once again drowned in his touch, taste and smell. He breathed her name in between kisses and Cynthia felt electric. Alive. The same energy that had always flowed between them made the moon pale in comparison.

Suddenly stable ground found purchase below Cynthia's feet and she pulled away from Evan. He tried to reach for her again, the look in his eyes filled with want. But Cynthia backed away and she warned him not to touch her. She needed to breathe. To really breathe.

"I told you," she whispered unsteadily, "I don't belong with you."

"Cyn, of course you do. Why would you say that?"

"Because that's the truth."

"That can't be the truth Cyn. If it is, it's made a liar out of me."

"You are a liar. You told me you'd always love me and never leave me. And then you did. You just left. How could you do that?"

The hurt look that flashed across Evan's face pierced Cynthia's soul. Tears spilled down her face as she realized she only had one choice. To follow the truth.

Chapter Eleven

Part III

Rosemary took a small sip of the margarita, tasting the cold rush of fresh lime as it coated her mouth. A burst of salt hit her lips and she licked them automatically. Her mother would not have approved of this ill-mannered move. Ladies were supposed to blot their lips with proper linen napkins. The remonstration of Prissy Pope in her head made Rosemary smile. She relaxed her shoulders and thought that every afternoon should start this way. Any why not? A new chapter in her life had started.

A rush of cool air entered the door and Rosemary let it fill her lungs. It was late fall and she was glad. No more sticky shirts and fake air inside sub-zero shops. This was the season that always felt the most real to her. Her sister Susie had always loved the summer months. She had liked the heat and pent up energy. Rosemary preferred the ease and casualness of fall. As she looked up at the blue sky Rosemary let her mind wander.

"That sure looks good. Are you going to share?"

Rosemary's reverie was broken by the teasing voice off to her left. When she turned away from the alley door she saw Julia standing there with a sly grin on her face. The woman with the purple streaks in her hair and the pierced nose was oddly beautiful. Rosemary felt a mixture of emotions as she stared at Julia. In a matter of moments she felt anxiety, confidence, sadness and relief wash over her.

Rosemary had decided to sell The Blue Orchid to Julia. However, the transfer came with provisions. Rosemary would sell her flower shop if – and only if - Julia agreed to train with her for two years. This turned out to be agreeable to Julia as she had never owned a business before. Rosemary wanted to make sure that whoever took over The Blue Orchid could properly manage it. There was a lot to learn. Rosemary would ease into it at first and as the time wound down she would amp up the training. The two years would also give Rosemary a fair amount of time to let go of something that had given her much joy throughout her life. Besides Finola, The Blue Orchid had been her greatest achievement.

Rosemary had nurtured thousands of rare, exotic orchids that had passed through the flower shop over the years. In return, the business had nurtured her need for freedom, independence and self-worth. Rosemary had a large part of her identity wrapped up in The Blue Orchid. Selling her shop would be bittersweet. There would be no way to escape this fact. She knew better. Rosemary always knew. Finola had been relieved her mother was finally selling the business. Her mother was at *retirement age* after all. Rosemary figured Finola was just relieved she wouldn't have the business forced on her.

"Just think mom," said Finola over the phone one evening. "Soon you can spend more time with Vincent and Harrison."

Rosemary thought about the two little boys. She hoped she would be a good influence on their lives. Rosemary knew that once she retired Finola would want her to babysit a lot more often. Her first order of business would be a wardrobe update for the two boys. Currently Finola dressed them in matching outfits, as if they were twins instead of brothers born two years apart. Rosemary thought they were an after-school special just waiting to happen. She hoped her grandmotherly intervention wouldn't be too late.

"Well, what do you think?" asked Rosemary.

Julia took a sip of the tasty beverage and gave her boss a thumbs up.

"This is perfect Rosemary!"

The two women carried the pitcher out to the front of the shop and set it under the counter. They sat on tall stools enjoying their drinks as they watched customers mill about the shop inspecting various flowers and plants. Rosemary had instituted a few new shop rules since her retirement was still two years away. Every Friday was now casual Friday. *Really casual Friday*, hence the pitcher of margaritas. Jimmy Buffett eased out of the shops speakers. If Rosemary couldn't make it to the beach for a couple of more years she had decided to bring the beach to The Blue Orchid.

"Ok, what about that guy?"

Rosemary looked across the shop to see who Julia was pointing out. He was a short man with messy blonde hair. He wore an immaculate navy blue pinstripe suit. Rosemary had never seen him before so the man definitely wasn't one of her habitual liars. The man shifted nervously as he stared at a display of daisy arrangements. Ah.

"He's been unfaithful," said Rosemary with firm conviction.

"What? How do you know that?"

Julia straightened up and stared at the man in the crisp suit. She looked him over and frowned.

"I don't see it. He just looks like your average business man. How do you know?"

"His body language for starters. His back is stiff as a board. He looks like he's up against a wall. Cornered. Caught.

"Now look at the way he's eyeing those arrangements. Daisies. That's a sweet and innocent flower. He probably thinks if he projects innocence that will help him buy forgiveness.

"His hair is an absolute mess. He's been running his hand through it a lot. Nerves probably. He also looks…sweaty. Sort of anxious. Yes, I'd put my money on infidelity."

"Wow." Julia let out an amazed sigh.

Julia turned her kind blue-grey eyes on Rosemary.

"I'll never be able to do that."

"Yes, you will," responded Rosemary with confidence. "We have plenty of time to practice. By then you'll be an old pro."

Rosemary glanced at Julia and saw she looked unsure. She had a flash of herself at thirty years of age and suspected this is how she must have looked when she first opened The Blue Orchid. It had taken Rosemary a while to realize her self-worth; to grow in her confidence. Those things took time. As her father would have said, 'Be not the slave of your own past'. Oh, how John Pope had loved Emerson.

Rosemary preferred, 'Finish each day and be done with it. You have done what you could'. Or maybe, just maybe, 'The reward of a thing well done is to have done it'. Yes, Rosemary thought that quote fit her perfectly. She just knew. Rosemary always knew.

~ ~ ~

Cassie brushed out Sylvia's long dark hair then gathered up the sides with her favorite pink bow clips. Sylvia sat contentedly as her mom worked on her often unruly hair. From the moment her daughter had been born with a full head of hair, Cassie knew Sylvia would be a girly-girl. Today she had dressed herself in a pink sweater, skirt and tights. The tights on the little girl were twisted and bunched up and the sight made Cassie laugh to herself.

Suddenly Joseph burst into the room, Noah on his heels.

"Mom! Noah hit his head!"

Cassie bolted up from her bench and ran over to Noah. His forehead was a little red but otherwise her youngest boy looked fine.

"Does it hurt Noah?"

Noah shook his head at his mom and let out a silly laugh. Cassie let out a relieved breath. It was hard keeping an eye on the children without Marc to help her.

"How did Noah bump his head Joe?"

Joseph squirmed then finally blurted out, "He kept trying to play with my fire truck and I didn't touch him much but he sorta hit his head on the table."

"Joe! I've told you to share your toys with Noah!"

"But mom! Sil doesn't have to!"

"She's a girl! Noah doesn't care about her toys."

Cassie's oldest son let out a frustrated sigh. Now that cold weather had finally settled in the kids couldn't go outside as often to run around and burn off their excess energy.

"Joe," said Cassie after taking a deep breath and counting to ten, "take Sil and Noah to the kitchen and have a cookie each, ok?"

"Really mom?" asked Joseph, his little face radiant with joy once more.

"Yes."

All three kids scrambled from the room while screaming in delight.

"One cookie!" yelled Cassie down the hall.

Cassie sunk back down on the bench in front of her bedroom vanity and looked at herself appraisingly in the mirror. She had purple shadows under her eyes. Noah had been sick the past few days and she had stayed up each night with him. Since he couldn't go to daycare Noah had also spent all day with Cassie at home. He had been fussy the entire time. She would be glad when the children were a little older. Of course, she never wanted to wish away her time with them. She just wanted them to sleep peacefully through the night so she could do the same.

A dark shadow loomed behind Cassie, startling her.

"Sorry Cass, I didn't mean to scare you," said Marc quietly.

Cassie stared at his reflection in the mirror. She hadn't seen him for several days. He too looked tired. Marc hadn't shaved and had a thick layer of dark stubble across his chin and cheeks.

"How was your flight?" she asked.

"It was good."

Marc leaned down and kissed the top of his wife's head. He had been away on a sales trip and Cassie had missed him greatly. She spun in her seat, stood up and wrapped her arms around his waist. She buried her face against Marc's chest. Cassie heard a low, rumbly laugh resonate from his chest.

"I missed you too," he said as he tightened his arms around her.

Cassie and Marc had spent the last few months in counseling trying to save their marriage. At first she thought it wouldn't be possible. Marc had been badly hurt by her dalliance with Ethan Carson. He had reluctantly agreed to go to counseling, but only for the sake of the children. But as the weeks had passed, Cassie and Marc began to repair the damage and see that there was a lot of love still between them.

In their sessions Cassie had finally come clean about her love for Eli. When Marc had told their counselor that he knew Cassie's love for him as her husband was nothing compared to her love for Eli it had ripped at her heart. She hadn't ever fooled him. Marc had known all this time.

"I don't want to steal that from you Cass. I know you loved Eli in a way you can never love me. He was your first love. That is always special. I *know* that. But can't you carve out a different love just for me? Something that isn't for Eli, but just for me? For us? For our family?"

In the last few weeks Cassie had done just that. For the first time since the eighth grade, when she had met Elijah Epstein, she let a part of him go. In her heart she already knew he had been long gone, but it was a truth she had never wanted to admit to herself all these years. She had thought if she kept on loving him always, even though he was no longer with her, that he would be alive even if it was just in her heart. For years that had been better than nothing.

But now she needed to save her marriage to Marc. In a way almost losing Marc, as she had lost Eli, had jolted her awake. The first time Cassie had met Marc she couldn't stop staring at him. The day he had helped her gather up her scattered papers Marc had intrigued her. Now she was determined to view him with open eyes. Cassie wanted to really *see* her husband. All these years she had viewed him with blinders on. She wanted to share a passion and love with Marc that would rival her love for Eli. She didn't know if that was possible, but for the first time she was willing to try.

Cassie had resigned her volunteer duties at Weatherwood Playhouse, but she had taken away something wonderful from the experience. A new friendship. Eve hadn't let Cassie slink away never to be heard from again.

The two women now had a standing coffee shop date each week. Cassie had never had a friend who was female. Eli had been her best friend growing up and then she had married Marc. At times it seemed strange to share her feelings with another woman, but she enjoyed her time with Eve. When Cassie spent time with Eve she wasn't a wife, mother, daughter or girlfriend. She was just a friend. This was an unexpected delight.

"Are you serious?"

"Yes!" Eve cackled in delight.

"How do you know this?"

"Because I caught them in the prop room together! I thought you'd like to know since she's your son's teacher."

"Well, well, well...Mrs. Rodriguez and Ethan Carson."

Cassie shook her head and joined in Eve's laughter.

"That should make the next parent teacher conference interesting. What do you think Cass?"

Cassie clinked her coffee mug with Eve's and the two women burst out laughing once more.

When Cassie left the coffee shop that day she noticed the leaves on the trees had fallen to the ground. Their limbs were stark and bare, but for once the sight didn't fill her with sadness. She recalled that this leafless state was only temporary. Come spring they would burst again with life. Cassie couldn't wait for that to happen. This time she would be ready for the soft green leaves, a revived life and all it had to offer. Cassie just had to be patient and wait for it to happen.

~ ~ ~

Dani shifted from her left foot to her right as she stood in line. Just moments earlier she had checked her college post office box and thought it was empty. But just as she began to shut the small metal door she saw a flash of yellow. Dani scooted down and peered further into the slot. Near the back, almost ready to fall out of the other end, was a yellow card. Dani's pulse sped up. A package!

Dani reached her slender hand into the square opening and closed her fingers around the yellow card. When she pulled the card out she examined it closely to see who had sent her a package. But the yellow card simply instructed her to go to the customer service window at the other end of the post office. Dani sighed to herself. That would mean having to deal with Mr. Herbert, the post master. He was a strange fellow who seemed a little too dedicated to his job. As she got into line she could hear him talking to the customer already at the window.

"Mr. Ackerman, this is *not* proper packaging material. Do you think this will make it through the system?"

Mr. Herbert seemed to forget that most of his customers were college students who had spent their lives banking online and corresponding electronically. Dani had friends who had never even been inside a post office. To her generation the idea of sending anything via snail mail was unthinkable. Why pay for something you could do online, faster, for free?

Mr. Ackerman, who looked more like a pimply faced student than a *Mr.*, opened his mouth to respond.

"It will not!" sniped Mr. Herbert, cutting off the young man before he could answer. "This covering is not sufficient. I suggest you take it back and try again. Next!"

And just like that the teenager was dismissed and the line surged forward. Mr. Ackerman was left standing off to the side, returned package in hand, still in shock. The package he held was wrapped in bright red and blue happy birthday paper. No wonder it had been rejected. Dani looked at the yellow card again and wondered what awaited her when she made it to the window. For the past month Dani had been following up on the clues Shelby had placed in the manila envelope. Each day she would walk across campus to the post office in the hopes that her little five by five box would hold a clue about her birth father's whereabouts.

Pat Derring had been wonderful in helping Dani decipher his late wife's sloppy handwriting. He had already had Dani over to his house for dinner several times since the night they had met. Dani could see why Shelby had fallen in love with Pat. He was kind, caring and funny. Pat had sat with Dani for hours while he took her on a tour through old photo albums. The pictorial journey of Shelby's life had been amazing. Pat was someone she could confide in and mourn with, for while Dani was discovering her birth mother, she was also grieving her death at the same time. Pat was a comfort to her.

Dani's family was coming down to visit her at college for the first time in a few days during Family Fun Weekend. She had dissuaded them from visiting her until now. While searching for her birth mother Dani had felt protective of that. Finding Shelby had to be her first priority. But now that she knew, Dani wanted her family to know about Shelby too. She also wanted them to meet Pat, who was becoming family to her. Dani had decided to tell them about her new search for her birth father. She was tired of keeping secrets. It was time for the truth to come out.

The older woman in front of Dani concluded her business at the customer service window and exited to the right. Dani stepped up to the counter. From here she could clearly see Mr. Herbert. He was still diligently stamping the envelopes from the previous customer. He shoved the items down a metal chute and turned to face Dani. She didn't say a word but merely handed over the yellow card. She hadn't really thought about it much before now, but maybe Mr. Herbert was just over-worked. Maybe that was the reason he was always so grumpy.

"Box number?"

"Excuse me?" asked Dani. Her voice shot up an octave.

"What is the box number? I can't retrieve the parcel without it. I'm not a mind reader!"

Dani swallowed and squeaked out, "303."

Mr. Herbert disappeared behind a door and retuned a moment later. He had a manila envelope in his hands. He handed it to Dani then barked, "Next!"

Dani exited to the right and walked back down the hall filled with long rows of tiny mail boxes. The manila envelope shook in her hand. This was it. Her first clue! The first piece of the puzzle that was her birth father.

Dani stared at the envelope transfixed. Suddenly a pair of strong arms wrapped around her waist from behind giving her a jolt.

"I knew I'd find you here."

Dani twisted around in the locked arms and looked up into Trace's dark green eyes. He smiled at her then quickly bent down towards her while tilting his head and claimed her lips with his own. His kiss was warm and Dani forgot all about the envelope in her hand. Trace's arms tightened around her and she snuggled in closer to his body. When he was finished greeting her he let her go and smiled down at her once again.

"How did you know I'd be here?"

Trace laughed. "It's three-thirty. All the mail had been slotted by then."

Dani let out a laugh. Trace was beginning to know her every habit. After she had discovered the truth about Shelby, Dani had decided to follow her roommate Casey's advice, even though the nerdy high school student in Dani couldn't possibly believe anyone as handsome as Trace would want to be with her. One evening about a few weeks ago they had gone to a late-night movie. A comedy of course, as Dani had an intense dislike of horror movies. Dani had left the palm of her hand open on the arm rest in between them in the theatre. Five minutes into the movie Trace had silently reached over and slid his hand into hers.

Instead of acting cool about it though, Dani had been shocked. She had quickly turned her head and looked over at him with wide eyes. In a swift movement he had reached over and leaned in for a kiss. Dani had been so rattled she hadn't even closed her eyes. But she had known instantly that this kiss was something quite different. Something wonderful. Dani thought about Reed Roth's sloppy French kiss and compared the two. Trace hadn't tried to force his tongue down her throat. He had kissed her fast but sweetly. Trace had tasted of peppermints. Now, she couldn't get enough of Trace's kisses.

"Four days and counting."

"Four days?" echoed Dani.

"Until your folks get here and they finally meet the boyfriend."

Dani laughed nervously this time. She had finally plucked up the courage to tell her mom about Trace over the phone last weekend. A horribly awkward conversation about "being careful" had cropped up then. Dani had hoped the floor would open up and swallow her at that moment. Still, Dani couldn't wait to see the look on Chelsea's face when her little sis got an eyeful of Trace. The thought made her smile.

"What's that?"

Trace pointed to the manila envelope still gripped in her right hand.

"Oh! This came today! It's from that agency…"

Dani trailed off as her thoughts left the perfection of her boyfriend and settled back on the information the envelope might contain.

"I can't believe you haven't ripped it open yet," said Trace.

"I was waiting."

"For what?"

"For you."

Trace smiled at her and Dani knew she would be taking these next steps to find her birth father with him by her side. This thought pleased her greatly. All the pieces were finally sliding into place. There were no mysteries that couldn't be solved now.

~ ~ ~

Alicia tried to lift the grey plastic tub with her arms but it wouldn't budge. Why was the container so heavy? She pried the lid off and peered inside. A partial collection of her books rested safely inside. Alicia smiled as she saw spine after spine of well-loved titles. She snapped the lid back into place and tried to figure out how to get the heavy tub to the peach bedroom at the back of the house. With a resigned sigh Alicia sat down on the wood floor, placed her back against the end of the grey tub, and using her feet as leverage pushed backwards.

The plastic tub inched across the slick floor. This wasn't the most graceful or effective way to move the tub, but it was the only way she would be able to get the books to their destination. Alicia never would have packed the container so full she couldn't lift it, so she assumed Ben had. Odessa and her son had helped her pack up her apartment several days ago in preparation for today's move. Alicia hadn't taken many items with her when she had first moved, but in the last year she had somehow managed to accumulate quite a bit of stuff. Alicia couldn't fathom how her book collection had grown in such a short amount of time.

As she continued to scoot the tub down the narrow hall her eyes took in the familiar wood floors and white walls. Alicia was finally home. A small part of her still couldn't believe she would once again inhabit the blue house. As of six pm today Alicia also no longer worked for the bank. Right after work Ben had pulled up to the curb in front of her apartment and helped load all her belongings. Alicia had been so grateful for Ben's help even though he was breaking work rules by using the brown van for personal reasons. He hadn't seemed perturbed by the situation though and said he would "handle things".

Alicia stopped pushing the tub down the hallway for a moment as she sat on the floor thinking about Ben. A slow smile crept across her face as she thought about him. He had helped her handle a lot of things in the last few months. Ben was the most incredible man she had ever met. It was rare for Alicia to trust or put her faith in anyone. But she trusted him; had an unswerving faith in him. He had earned that privilege. The morning after their first date Alicia had heard a soft thud outside her door. She had woken up panicked thinking Dwayne and his crew had found her. She had bashed in the headlight on his Jeep after all. But when Alicia had looked through her peep hole no one was standing in the hall. She had plucked up her courage and cracked the door leaving the chain in place. As she peeked out into the hallway a brilliant kaleidoscope of color near the floor caught her eye. Sitting just outside her door was a lush arrangement of flowers from Ben.

An attached note had simply stated: I wish I had given these to you last night. I hope you got some sleep and have a happier day. Ben

That had been the first time a man had ever given her flowers. Alicia could still recall how they had looked on the nightstand beside her bed. The flowers were the last thing she saw at night before falling asleep and the first thing she saw in the morning when she woke up. The scent of them had sweetened her bedroom for over a week.

Alicia's stomach suddenly gurgled bringing her back to the present. Ben had left twenty minutes ago to get them some Chinese take-out. Just the thought of egg rolls, lo mein and hunan shrimp made her mouth condense with drool. Her stomach gave another lurch. But instead of thinking about food she resumed shoving the grey tub down the remainder of the hall and into the peach bedroom.

As the lid was unsnapped once again Alicia began placing the volumes on the built-in bookshelf. She had decided to use her old bedroom as a study. Alicia would be returning to finish her associates degree in a few weeks and she would need a quiet place to study. This bit of fortune had occurred thanks to Odessa. Alicia wasn't sure what she had ever done to deserve a friend like her but she was mighty grateful.

One evening after work Alicia had brought a large cheese pizza over to Odessa's hair salon. The two friends had sat in the swivel chairs enjoying the savory treat while country music filled Nubia Hair. After they had stuffed themselves Odessa produced an envelope and handed it to Alicia.

"What's this?" she had asked.

"Just open it."

Alicia tore open the envelope and pulled out a slip of paper. It was a check for a large sum of money. She had stared at it baffled for a few moments, unsure of its purpose.

"I don't get it. What's this for 'Dessa?"

Odessa let out a cackle as usual.

"That is the Odessa Bryant ex-husband college fund."

Alicia continued to stare at Odessa with a confused expression painted on her face.

"I want you to take that money and use it to pay for the remainder of your college education. That should be enough for tuition, books and anything else you might need."

"Oh! I can't take this. This is too much!"

"No, it isn't. Look, you need some help. Let me help you."

"I can't. Besides, in another two years I'll have saved enough -"

"You keep saying that yet each time the time frame lengthens. Just let me help you with this. Besides, you've earned it."

"Earned it? How?"

"By going to counseling these last couple of months and getting the help you need. I'm very proud of you."

After Alicia's semi-disastrous first date with Ben, she had taken his words to heart. A few days later she had approached Odessa to ask her for help. Once a week Alicia attended counseling at the Community Health Center. At first Alicia hadn't thought she'd like telling a complete stranger about her problems. But talking through her concerns and burdens of the last two years had helped Alicia come out of a fog. Sometimes she felt like she was waking up from an unpleasant dream.

Alicia had sought out Odessa originally so she could fix the mess that was her hair. But Odessa had really helped fix the mess that was her life. She didn't know how she would ever repay the kindness Odessa had shown her. When she had mentioned this to Odessa her response had been, "grandbabies." Alicia's head had spun at that idea. Odessa had just laughed.

The front door slammed and Alicia walked out to the dining room. Ben had set several white boxes with metal handles down on the dining room table. Alicia's chest swelled at the thought of sitting at her grandmother's dining room table once more. Gram had bought the table when she had won the little blue house. Ben looked up at her approach and smiled.

"Hey baby," he said.

He came around the table and gathered Alicia into his arms.

"You hungry?"

"I'm starved!" she said.

Ben got a wicked glimmer in his eyes as he stared at her lips. She knew that look. Boy did she know that look! Before she knew what was happening he had leaned down and given her an appetizing kiss. Alicia forgot all about the delicious food on the table. When he finally let her go she was dazed.

As they sat down to eat Ben asked her what she had been up to while he was gone.

Alicia shook her head to clear it and said, "Just re-shelving my books."

Alicia tasted the warm lo mein noodles. It was heavenly. She chewed thoughtfully for a moment and then said, "Can you help me do something?"

"Anything you want."

Ben winked at her.

Alicia giggled. "Stop it! I'm being serious."

"So am I baby. So am I."

Alicia laughed again. Ben always made her laugh. She was so in love with him she realized with a start. She had hoped that he might be moving in with her shortly. Alicia just had to work up enough courage to ask him. Ben would never make that kind of move unless she asked. He was too gentlemanly and old fashioned in a lot of ways. She liked that about him.

"Alright, what do you need my help with?"

"I…I want to bury Vanessa's journals out back, under the big tree we used to sit under as kids. I never finished reading them. It just didn't feel right."

"Of course, anything you want," he said.

Alicia smiled. Anything she wanted? As she stared at Ben over the table she could think of lots of things she wanted from him. But she could take her time. She was *here*, after all. Right where she wanted to be. She had landed safely.

~ ~ ~

Cynthia was starting to get restless and shifted from one foot to the other every few minutes. The most graceful maid of honor she was not. Cynthia stood off to the side behind Maddie as she and Jackson said their vows to one another. Michael and Cynthia had attended several weddings together, but she couldn't recall any of those ceremonies lasting this long. Maddie and Jackson had gone all out for their wedding day and the ceremony was no exception. They were currently closing in on forty minutes of time spent at the alter.

Growing impatient Cynthia discretely turned her head and scanned the large crowd watching the ceremony. Her eyes roamed over hundreds of heads but she didn't succeed in locating her fiancé. She should have asked him where he was going to sit in the celebration hall so she could have given him a smile from the alter platform. Their time to get married was coming soon. Cynthia still had a lot of details to iron out. She didn't even have a dress yet.

As Maddie and Jackson exchanged rings Cynthia let out a sigh of relief. The ceremony was almost complete. The wedding couple finally kissed and the room full of guests burst into applause, cheers and whistles. Maddie turned towards Cynthia, retrieved her bouquet, and beamed at her best friend. The bride was absolutely radiant. As the group descended the middle of the hall Cynthia was obliged to take the best man's arm. She didn't know him as he was a co-worker of Jackson's. Cynthia scanned the hall again wondering what her fiancé thought of her arm linked with another man. The idea of him being a little jealous made Cynthia smile.

As soon as the wedding party was out of doors Mrs. Tilman, the event coordinator, hurried them over The Landing's manicured lawns towards the new gazebo. The sun was just about to set casting a warm red glow on the water near the boat slips. Cynthia couldn't wait for this part to be over with. She did not like having her picture taken as it always made her feel awkward. As the wedding party approached the gazebo Cynthia saw the peach and rose globes glowing in the dusky evening. Her stomach gave a flip as she remembered the lunch she had shared with Evan in that very gazebo. His face suddenly flooded her memories and she began to lag behind the rest of the group.

Maddie and Jackson were ushered into the gazebo for the first photos so Cynthia lingered outside near the soft light of the glass globes. Images of Evan's black hair, intense blue eyes and the rest of his beautifully sculpted face swam before her. Cynthia tried to control her breathing, but the thought of him made her pulse race. She closed her eyes and tried to shut him out.

Suddenly Cynthia felt a pair of strong arms encircle her waist from behind. She was pulled back against a warm body. Cynthia opened her eyes and looked down to see a crisp white dress shirt covering the arms that held her. One of the hands left her waist and moved up the length of her arm towards her neck. Cynthia shivered as the hand brushed back her long chestnut brown hair.

Cynthia laughed, "You are going to mess up my hair for the photos. Maddie will get mad."

"I can't help myself," said a low, soft voice. "I'll just have to apologize to Madelyn later."

Cynthia twisted in the man's arms and placed her hands around his neck. She ran one of her hands through the silky hair at the nape of his neck before looking up to see sparkling blue eyes staring down at her. Evan smiled at her then pulled her into a long, lingering kiss.

"Stop right there!"

Evan and Cynthia froze into place.

"You are getting your lipstick all messed up!"

Maddie was glaring at both of them with her hands planted firmly on her hips. Evan reluctantly let Cynthia go and Mrs. Tilman rushed over with some spare makeup to fix the smudged lipstick.

"Tell your fiancé to keep his hands off you until *after* we've taken all the group photos."

Evan gave Cynthia a quick kiss on her forehead before she was led away by her best friend. As she posed for the photos Cynthia's mind wandered back to Evan. It was hard for her to believe sometimes how much her life had changed in the past few months.

After Cynthia had visited Evan on his boat late that one night the impromptu visit had only caused her more confusion and heartache. She had hated seeing him in such an intimate setting when they were no longer a part of each other lives. The next morning Cynthia had called in to work and spent the whole day in bed thinking. She thought long and hard about everything.

As night fell one thing had become very clear to Cynthia. She had to break off her engagement to Michael. He deserved better than her. She didn't want to build a life with him and that wasn't fair. He was a good guy, but looking back Cynthia realized she hadn't ever really been in love with him. Her love for Evan all those years ago had been the real thing. She didn't feel that for Michael. It wasn't even close. Michael had merely been a distraction. A runner-up as the victor of her heart. Cynthia felt ashamed that it had taken her this long to figure it all out.

The break-up had not gone well. Michael had pleaded with her to stay and give them another chance. But Cynthia knew she couldn't allow that to happen. It tore at her heart to see him in so much pain. Michael had always been good to her. In a way, she couldn't believe that her love meant that much to him. But it had. It was one of the worst nights of Cynthia's life. By the time she had made it back to her tiny candy factory apartment she was exhausted. For the next two weeks Cynthia had wandered through the paces of her life like a zombie. Or at least someone with a wounded heart.

Then one night, walking home from work late as usual, she noticed a tall man hidden in the shadows of her building's doorway. Cynthia came to an abrupt halt and her heart started racing. Fear rooted her to the side-walk. She knew she should turn around and run the other way or yell 'fire' but she was paralyzed. That's when the man had stepped out of the shadows and into the street light. His midnight hair gleamed in the glow. Cynthia's whole body relaxed as she realized it was Evan. Then just as quickly she tensed once more. Why was he here in the city? How did he know where she lived?

Evan walked up to Cynthia slowly and cautiously, as if he were afraid he might scare her off. She was scared of Evan. She was terrified of her feelings for the man who had abandoned her years ago. He made her heart ache in a way no other man ever had. Two weeks later Michael was already fading away from her. But the man who now stood opposite her, the memory of him had never left her even though thousands of days had passed. The love she felt for Evan, and the pain he had caused her, bubbled up fresh.

"I didn't mean to startle you Cyn," he said quietly. "It's just me."

Evan had his hands shoved into the side pockets of his navy pea coat. Even on dry land he looked like a sailor. Cynthia would have smiled or laughed at this realization if her whole body wasn't frozen into place. She had the strongest impulse to reach out and touch him so she too shoved her left hand into her coat pocket while her right hand gripped her work bags tightly.

"What are you doing here?" Cynthia asked, her voice barely a whisper.

"I had to see you once more."

Evan looked away awkwardly. He kept staring down at the sidewalk, but his eyes couldn't seem to stay away from her face for long. They kept flashing up at her repeatedly.

"What do you want?" she asked.

Me. Say me. The thought had risen from somewhere deep in her core, but Cynthia shoved it away. She couldn't afford to have such thoughts.

"I know you don't want me," he said slowly, almost as if he didn't want to say the words. "I know you want to be with him. Michael."

The name 'Michael' barely made its way out of his mouth. His teeth had clenched down and the name came out unwillingly.

"I just wanted you to know that I understand. You want a life with him. I won't stand in your way. But I just had to tell you one last time that I'll always love you Cyn. I know it's much too late. And I know it's selfish of me to stand here and say these words to you.

"If I could erase all the years that have separated us, I would. I wouldn't have been so stupid and reckless and left you behind. I wouldn't leave you behind…"

Evan trailed off, blinked his eyes and looked away. Cynthia's work bags had grown heavy in her right hand so she switched them to her left hand and shoved her newly freed right hand in her other coat pocket. Her left hand gripped the bags tightly. The movement caught Evan's eyes. Suddenly his body tensed and she realized he was staring intently at her hand that was curled around the bags. His sharp eyes flashed up to meet hers.

"Where is your engagement ring?"

Cynthia didn't say anything. She was too overwhelmed by Evan's recent words to form something that made sense. She stared off into the city landscape. Fear had paralyzed her once more.

"Cyn, where is -"

"It's over!" she blurted out. "It's over…"

Neither of them said anything for a moment. Cynthia closed her eyes and waited for him to speak. Suddenly strong hands gripped her upper arms. She felt Evan's warm breath on her face. The scent of soap and salt air overwhelmed her senses. Cynthia opened her eyes and saw that Evan was only a few inches from her face. His eyes stared right into hers, as if they were reading her thoughts or unlocking all her secrets. God knew he could. He knew her better than anybody ever had. Evan leaned forward and placed his forehead against hers lightly.

"We belong together Cyn. Don't you know that? I've traveled halfway around the world and couldn't ever erase you from my mind. I told you once that no matter where I went, it would always be you. Do you remember that?"

"Yes," Cynthia whispered.

"You wanted the truth. That is the truth. I loved you then, I still love you, I'll always love you. Do you love me? After how stupid I've been? Can you love me after all this time?"

They both held their breath waiting for Cynthia to respond. Her body trembled but she didn't say anything. She already knew the answer. She had known the truth, that she loved Evan with everything she had, that night on his boat. She had been so terrified of her feelings. It was the reason she broke off her engagement to Michael. The truth was she still loved Evan. Would always love Evan. He was her perfect match.

"You said once before that you'd love me forever," she said softly.

"I *will* love you forever Cyn. I promise!"

Evan quickly moved his hands to her face and kissed her passionately. She dropped her bags on the sidewalk and wound her arms around him. In that moment Cynthia could clearly see a new map laid out before her. Her life was with Evan. They had only taken a detour from that life. But now they were back on course.

On their wedding night Cynthia presented Evan with a rolled-up piece of parchment paper tied with a black cord as they lay in bed wrapped up in each other. She had reached underneath her pillow and pulled the gift out. Inside was the route for their honeymoon sailboat trip.

Evan's engagement gift to her was a restored blue-grey Ranger sailboat. Cynthia had almost cried when she saw it rocking gently on the shore waves in the boat slip.

"What's this?" Evan asked, his blue eyes twinkling at her mischievously, as he took the roll of parchment.

"The beginning of our future," Cynthia whispered, this time knowing it was true.

ABOUT THE AUTHOR

Luona Blankenship lives in Virginia where
she received a degree in History with a
minor in Theatre from Sweet Briar College.
She has always loved writing stories
and creating new worlds.

www.ingramcontent.com/pod-product-compliance
Lightning Source LLC
Chambersburg PA
CBHW022101170626
46808CB00002B/537